MW01505058

Shadows of My Irish Dog

My Irish Dog Series, Volume 2

Douglas Solvie

Published by Douglas Solvie, 2024.

This is a work of fiction. Similarities to real people, places, or events are entirely coincidental.

SHADOWS OF MY IRISH DOG

First edition. April 15, 2024.

ISBN: 978-4991354021

Written by Douglas Solvie.

PROLOGUE

Time can heal or harm, and chance can provide freedom or misfortune. In this little village of Galbally, time and chance had almost seen the end of Spencer at one point. Time and chance had also saved him—from himself mostly. That seemed so long ago now.

In the end, he had stayed, though that had not been his intention. The real reason why, the real truth, was something known to only a few. A holiday turned to a nightmare turned to a dream come true. But stay he had.

Galbally, in the native Irish tongue, roughly translates to "town of the foreigner." Spencer had been the foreigner, and the town had been and was—well, just that—a town. Now, Spencer was almost a minor celebrity in this quaint farming community inside the eastern edge of County Limerick in the south of Ireland. Even so, the locals didn't shower him with any undue attention or treat him any differently than anyone else; they just knew him and his story—at least some of it, at least the parts that could be told.

CHAPTER ONE

The ancient monastery had taken the dog, killed her like she was nothing. The monastery had saved his life, and that was something. As they drove by, he didn't even glance at the pitiful ruins of Moor Abbey.

Spencer rolled down the window as the car traveled along the mile stretch of Route 663 between the abbey and the village called Galbally. This was the last section of road on the way from their home near Bansha, another small village in neighboring County Tipperary and about twenty minutes northeast. Spencer was sitting in the unfamiliar territory of the passenger seat. His daughter Erica had insisted that today she would work on her Irish driving skills. She needed the practice, but Spencer's nerves had him regretting the decision.

"See, Dad. I told you we should have left earlier. The runners are already headed back to town," she said, throwing her father an exasperated glance.

Spencer looked at his watch. The time was thirty minutes short of noon, and they probably should have left a bit earlier.

"We do have a business to tend to, you realize," Spencer said. "Besides, watching sweaty people run single file along a country road is about as exciting as watching paint dry. Just keep your eyes in front of you and try not to knock anybody over, will ya?"

"Ha, ha. Very funny. I'm not the one who banged up the car mirror last week."

Spencer smiled at Erica and scanned the countryside to his left. He could see just a few glimpses of the River Aherlow as it ran toward the abbey through the open field of tall grasses. He tried to listen for its sound, but the wind gushing into the car and the roar of voices cheering on the runners drowned out everything.

The air seemed unusually crisp this morning after last night's rains. Yes, the weather is beautiful, and today's going to be a good day, Spencer thought as the car rounded the last bend before entering Galbally.

Today was Saturday, and today was the Galbally Tractor Run, an annual event each August as summer gave way to fall. The fundraising event was a mix of running and cycling, a vintage car gathering, and, of course, the tractor run. Spencer had only heard stories until now, but he could hardly wait to see the mass of tractors as they made the home stretch to Galbally along this same road. He couldn't explain the reason for his excitement, but tractors in rural Ireland were like mosquitoes in the Amazon; they were omnipresent, not only in the fields but often on the roadways. And, more importantly, to Spencer's mind they helped define a way of life around here.

"Erica, we're never gonna find a place to park in town," Spencer said as the car quickly got stuck behind a pile of others making their way into the village. "Take the next left up here, and we'll park at Killian's. He said he'd hold a spot."

"Roger that," Erica said.

Ten minutes later the two of them were walking across the span of a small, arched stone bridge that led into the town proper. Soon, off to their right, was the Grafton Pub, an establishment owned and operated by Spencer's best friend in Ireland, Killian Conner. The entrance door was wide open, with patrons spilling outside and into the street. Spencer couldn't imagine what it was like on the inside. The smell of ale and stout invaded the nostrils, along with a good dose of cigarette smoke. Laughter and loud conversations filled the air. People were everywhere. The Galbally population of a few hundred had swollen to several multiples of that today.

Spencer stood and waited on the pavement outside while Erica made her way through the mass of drunk and soon-to-be-drunk revelers to sneak a peek through the open door of the pub. She popped inside before returning a few minutes later.

"I didn't see Killian. Do you wanna go into the pub anyway?" Erica said, calling Spencer away from where his eyes were set. His back was toward her.

"Dad, did you hear me?"

Spencer turned to face Erica. "Yeah, sure, I guess."

Just a short while before Spencer had noticed a strange man standing on the opposite side of the town square. The man's stare was unrelenting and fixed solely on Spencer. At least it had seemed that way.

This strange man was someone with whom Spencer was familiar. His name was Angus, and he was a well-known oddity around here. Although Spencer was sure Angus had a home somewhere, he seemed to play the part of the local vagrant, maybe the only one in the village. Over his time in Galbally, Spencer had seen Angus on numerous occasions, sometimes loitering on street corners or hauling aluminum cans and glass bottles for recycling from one location to another.

Where he saw him the most was at Killian's place, the Grafton Pub. The man generally sat at the far end of the bar counter, keeping to himself and washing down one pint after another. As destitute as he appeared, Angus always seemed to have an ample supply of money for the important things. Spencer had no idea of the man's age. He guessed somewhere in his mid-forties, maybe older. Except for Killian, no one talked to him, and Angus reciprocated in kind. Spencer didn't know Angus well; he didn't know him at all, and they had never exchanged a single word. Regardless, the man gave Spencer the willies, and today was no exception.

Spencer swiveled his head to take another look. Angus was still there, his eyes still burning into Spencer.

He gave Angus a furtive glance, noticing that even on this warm day he was in his usual attire of an old woolen trench coat that hung to the top of his thighs. Underneath was a tattered brown sweater. Rubber boots, the kind a fisherman or farmer might wear, came up to his knees. His beard was an unruly mess of gray and black whiskers on a weather-beaten face.

Everything about him was dirty and unkempt. On the ground below him stood a white mongrel of a dog that didn't look much better than Angus. The two were seemingly inseparable, except when Angus was in the pub. Then the dog stayed outside patiently until his inebriated master decided it was time to go home or to wherever.

The unnerving stare of Angus had Spencer feeling uncomfortable, and Erica soon noticed her father's unease.

"Dad, you okay?"

"I'm fine," he said, then giving her his full attention and plastering a fake smile on his face.

Erica looked hard at her father and then across the square. She could see the odd man looking in their direction.

"Who's that guy, Dad, and why does he keep staring at you?" she asked.

"Just a fella from town. Believe me, he's as weird as weird can be, so there's no telling."

"Why does he keep staring at us?" Erica repeated as she gave Angus another glance.

"Forget about him, Erica. Come on, let's go," Spencer said.

Erica shot another look at the man. She then took a wide stance, extended her right arm up high with her knuckles pointed outward, and summarily flipped Angus the bird.

"Erica! Don't do that!"

"Why not? He deserves it. Creep."

Spencer couldn't argue. He shrugged and turned around to head up the main street of this village.

"I thought you wanted to go to the pub?" Erica said.

"Nope. I won't be going in there today. Not now, at least. Not with all those people. We can catch up with Killian later."

Erica frowned but didn't say anything.

Spencer had no problem being around people, but the Grafton Pub was kind of his spot. When he imbibed there, nowadays and in the past, oftentimes it was just he alone, maybe another local or two, with Killian or his son tending the bar. Besides, Angus had him feeling unsettled, and he wanted to move on.

"Let's check out O'Dwyer's and see if it's any better," Spencer said.

Spencer took a last look, and he could see Angus walking in the opposite direction and heading along one of the roads leading out of town to the west, his dog in tow. Phew! Spencer was determined not to let the unwelcome episode ruin his day.

They dodged people one after another as they walked along the concrete pavement that fronted the main businesses. Except for the color, the architectural design of all the stucco buildings was exactly the same: two stories of the same height, an obligatory chimney, and not even a space to slide a finger between them.

Soon they were in front of the other pub in town, the signboard of which proudly proclaimed its dual function as "Pub and Undertaker." O'Dwyer's was just as crowded as the Grafton.

"Well, this isn't going to work," Spencer said. "How's a guy literally dying of thirst supposed to get a frickin' beer around here?"

"Look, Dad," Erica said as she pointed across the small square to the other side.

Spencer's eyes followed her finger, and he soon noticed the makeshift beer garden. The line of thirsty patrons was long, but at least they wouldn't be cramped inside a noisy, foul-smelling pub.

"Yes, that's what I'm talking about!" Spencer exclaimed. Spencer hardly ever drank before the official drinking time. Today was an exception, and he wasn't about to be the only one in this town without a few pints in the belly.

He and Erica made their way across, past the tiny patch of green that held the celebrated plaque of Galbally's title as "Ireland's Tidiest Town." The inscription read 1994, but Galbally remained quite tidy in Spencer's estimation. The town would definitely need some tidying after today's festivities.

"Dad, I can wait in line, so why don't you just chill while I get the beers," Erica said.

"Thanks, Erica. Remember just one or two for you today. You're the designated driver, as you so willingly volunteered. I don't want us to have to walk back to Bansha."

"Or stay the night at Killian's," Erica said.

"Or stay the night at Killian's."

Spencer took a seat on a nearby bench as Erica made her way to the end of the line. He was not at all surprised that half the people in the queue were the same runners who had just crossed the finish line a short time before. Beer is liquid, too, he thought and smiled to himself. Thoughts of Angus had already receded from his mind.

Spencer glanced over at Erica as she stood in line. *One year ago I never would have dreamed this, living in Ireland with my daughter by my side,* he thought. One person was graduating from college with no plans. The other was embarking on a new life and a new business, in dire need of help and perhaps some company. It didn't seem real to him. But it was real. Sometimes the stars align.

Erica returned with two large plastic cups filled to the brim with ale from a local brewery in nearby Limerick, and Spencer cleared his mind.

"Thanks, Erica," Spencer said as he grabbed one of the cups and took a big swig. "Man, I can't believe how many people are here. Killian said it was a big event, but I never expected this."

"Yep, quite a change from the usual quiet Galbally, that's for sure," Erica said.

They sat on the bench, people-watching, until their cups neared empty.

"Say, why don't we wander over to the store? I doubt it, but I want to see if Colin's around today," Spencer said.

As they began to rise from their seats, the sudden touch of a hand on his left shoulder startled Spencer, and he flinched.

"Mr. Spencer, how are you? I haven't seen you for ages."

He turned around.

"Oh, Mrs. Murray! Sorry. You surprised the heck out of me. It has been a long time."

"Oh my, silly me," Mrs. Murray said. "I shouldn't be sneaking up on people like that, should I now? You've come down for the big event, I see."

"Yeah, we wouldn't miss it for the world," Spencer said. "I've heard a lot of stories about fearsome tractors rumbling down the city streets."

"Yes, it will be quite the spectacle. I can assure you that much," Mrs. Murray said. She glanced at Erica.

"By the way, this is my youngest daughter, Erica," Spencer said. "She's been helping me out at the inn over the summer."

"Lovely to meet you, Erica," Mrs. Murray said as she turned and gave her full attention to the young lady. "You're as pretty as your father is handsome."

Spencer smiled inside as he watched the tinge of red take over Erica's face. She had always been uneasy with compliments, but this time she somehow managed to verbalize a thank you.

The three of them talked for the next ten minutes. Spencer told Mrs. Murray that the bed and breakfast in Bansha was doing just fine and was more work than he had ever imagined. He also explained to Erica that Mrs. Murray ran the local animal shelter and was a well-known advocate in these parts for animal rights. He didn't tell Erica everything, however, especially how and why he and Mrs. Murray first met.

The conversation finally ended, and Mrs. Murray signaled her departure. She walked a few steps and turned back in the direction of Spencer and Erica.

"By the way, Mr. Spencer, you wouldn't happen to be in the market for a new dog, would you? I've got quite a few looking for a home, and even a couple that look similar to Shandy."

"No, not really," Spencer said. "In fact, I picked up a golden retriever pup just a few months back. I know I should have looked through the shelter first, but I really wanted a golden."

"Certainly, I understand," Mrs. Murray said. "We naturally don't have any of those in stock. They go for quite a pretty penny, I'm told. At any rate, perhaps I'll see the two of you again at the tractor run. They should be on the final lap any time now."

With that, Mrs. Murray dropped into the crowd and was soon talking with another acquaintance. Spencer nudged Erica, and they began walking back across the town square in the direction of Murphy's store.

"Mrs. Murray sure seems like a nice lady," Erica said as they went. "What was that thing about a Shandy? I'm assuming that's the name of a dog?"

"Oh, she was just a stray dog I found when I first came. Couldn't find a home for her and so ended up leaving her at the shelter."

That wasn't exactly how things had unfolded, but now wasn't the time or place to explain to Erica what had occurred when he first came to Ireland and to this village in particular. Maybe there would never be a good time to explain the unexplainable.

"Boy, you sure are a man of mystery, aren't you?" Erica said and grinned at her father. "What else haven't you told me?"

"Wouldn't you like to know? If I told you everything, I'd have to kill ya."

They both laughed and were soon in front of Murphy's store. Just as they were about to enter, a voice boomed loudly over the PA system:

"Ladies and gents, attention, please. Rumor has it that the manly machines are five minutes away from the abbey. They'll be making the home stretch soon thereafter. Grab your wife, husband, child, or drunken mate and line up on the road, out of harm's way. And don't forget those donations! This is all for a good cause, mind you, so let's all do our parts according to our means."

Spencer ducked his head into Murphy's store and scanned for Colin. He wasn't there, but Spencer spotted Colin's mother behind the cash register, with a line of five people waiting to check their purchases. He gave her a quick wave.

"Not in there. Let's go find a good place to stand. I guess my second beer will have to wait until the run is over," Spencer said.

Spencer and Erica walked about a quarter of the way to the abbey and found an opening where they wouldn't have to fight others for a look at the tractors. The atmosphere around them was almost euphoric in its excitement. Spencer could never have imagined that watching a procession of tractors would affect him this way, but he felt the same as everyone else.

About fifty yards down on the same side of the roadway, Erica spotted Mr. and Mrs. Allard, a young couple from France staying at the bed and breakfast. Erica and Spencer waved at them, and the couple waved back. Spencer was happy to see them having ventured this way for the big event.

"Did you have a chance to try out your French?" Spencer asked Erica.

"A little," Erica said, "but their English is so good I felt embarrassed. That doesn't mean you can't take me to France, however. As you promised."

Spencer smiled without replying.

In no time, the first tractor, the speed of which astonished Spencer, appeared. More tractors came one after another, separated by only intervals of maybe five or ten seconds. For the most part, they looked pretty much the same: smallish, about an average man's height, a long box nose, with two small tires up front and two large ones in the back. The colors were all over the spectrum. The drivers waved as they went by, and the spectators cheered, threw up their arms, and waved back.

Occasionally, a different tractor would appear, a bigger type with an enclosed cab, proudly sporting its manufacturer on the front of the cab and a yellow warning light on top. Horns blasted, and the smell of diesel fuel saturated the air.

Spencer wondered how much one of these machines would cost. He had a lot of open land attached to the inn. He could do something with the acreage, and a tractor might come in handy down the line.

He looked over at Erica, and smiles were exchanged. He was glad to see his daughter enjoying this rare festivity. She didn't socialize much other than with guests at the inn, and perhaps this would be a move to somewhat remedy the situation. Spencer had found out long ago that part of the allure of Ireland was its people. He wanted Erica to emerge from her half-closed shell and enjoy what this land had to offer.

After ten minutes, the last tractor passed, and the crowd of adults and children of all ages let out a big hurrah in unison. The dispersion was quick, with some folks heading to parked cars, some heading in the direction of the abbey, and most heading back to the village. There was still much celebrating to be done, and Spencer figured the festivities would go on the rest of the afternoon and well into the night.

Spencer watched the backside of the last tractor as it entered town.

"Let's head back to the village, Erica. We'll have a couple of more beers and hopefully run into Killian somewhere, though I'm sure he's gonna be busier than ever."

Once back in town, the crowds at both pubs were bigger than before, and that was no surprise. Erica and Spencer made a beeline for the beer garden before the queue got any longer. They purchased another ale for Spencer, Erica satisfied to just take a few small sips from her father's cup. An assortment of people whom Spencer knew came and went, and Spencer introduced Erica to each one of them, more than pleased to show off his daughter to the locals and prove he had a life somewhere before coming to Ireland.

"Listen, let's just pop into the pub quickly and say hello and goodbye to Killian," Spencer said. "I'm getting tired, and I want to be home before today's check-in turns up. You ready to go?"

"Yep. I've had enough excitement for one day, and Buster has been strapped to that chain since Mrs. O'Donnell left. Why don't I go get the car? I'll park and wait for you on the other side of the bridge until you're done."

"Sounds like a plan," Spencer said. "I won't be long."

As Spencer began squeezing his way through the masses and was about to enter the Grafton Pub, he heard Killian's voice and saw him approaching from a few stores up.

"Spencer, there you are, finally," Killian said. "I was just out looking for you. The pub's a god-awful mess today, and this has been my first chance to sneak out. Got my boy and Jamie tending bar presently, but they'll be needing my assistance soon enough."

"Hi, Killian. We tried to go in earlier, but so many people. Anyway, we are heading out, and I wanted to say goodbye."

"Why don't you come in and have yourself a pint? On the house, of course."

"Thank you, but not today. We've got a guest checking in fairly soon."

"Well, at least tell me that you enjoyed the tractor run. I warned you it can be quite a scene to behold," Killian said.

"It was actually really great, Killian. Thanks for getting us to come out."

Killian looked out across the activity of the town and then returned to Spencer.

"Listen, Spencer, can you spare a few minutes? I've got something I'd like to share with you."

The smile had left Killian's face, and Spencer felt uneasy from the swift change of tone in Killian's voice. He could only wonder what Killian had to share. They had had enough conversations over the last year that Spencer knew the difference between casual banter and a serious discussion.

"Sure, Killian," Spencer said hesitantly. "Erica is off picking up the car from your house, so she'll be a few minutes."

Killian led Spencer around the corner and toward the backside of the pub to a small treed area by which the smallest of streams ran. A couple of drunken revelers were just finishing relieving themselves, and Killian gave them a disapproving stare as they quickly zipped up and left.

Killian waited a few seconds and then spoke: "You know, Spencer, it's been some time since you and I have talked about matters of the past. You do realize it's been almost a year now, don't you?"

"Yes, the time hasn't been lost on me," Spencer said, fully understanding the man's meaning. "Why are you bringing this subject up all of a sudden?"

"Let me cut to the quick of the matter," Killian said. "I don't know how to say this, but something happened here near the abbey over the last few days. I've a sneaking suspicion, just intuition mostly, that it somehow relates to you and Shandy and everything that went on."

"Something happened? What is that supposed to mean?"

Spencer felt the small drops of perspiration forming on his forehead.

"I'd prefer to share the details when we have more time," said Killian. "Might you make your way back here tomorrow, when things are a bit quieter?"

Spencer didn't know what to say, let alone what to think. What had happened one year back was something he would never forget, for the experience had truly changed his life, and in a good way, but getting to that point was something that had entailed more downs than ups.

"Sure, Killian, I guess. If you say it's important."

"I'm sorry to trouble you with this, but, as you Americans say, it is what it is. By the way, have you told Erica about what happened, about the real reason you ended up staying here in Ireland?"

"Oh, just bits and pieces. Certainly not the details. After all, you and I and Colin made a pact we would never share the story with others."

"I see," said Killian. "You may have to disclose more than you like with her, depending on how things go. Anyway, don't worry for now. I'll be seeing you tomorrow. Shall we say around eleven?"

"Sure, that would be fine, but what the hell are we talking about here?" Spencer asked, his irritation building.

"Tomorrow, Spencer. Tomorrow," Killian said without missing a beat. The smile from before returned to his face. "Well, I've a madhouse that requires my undivided attention. I best get in there before things get even more out of hand."

Killian placed his hand on Spencer's shoulder, and Spencer shook his head, letting his ire fade as he watched Killian go around the corner and disappear into the pub. He began walking toward the bridge, only a short distance away, and he could see Erica in the waiting car on the other side.

What the hell was that all about? And the thing with Angus? He had some thinking to do on the ride home and probably throughout the night. He'd keep this from Erica.

"How's Killian doing? I bet he's in beast mode dealing with all those people," Erica said as Spencer jumped into the car.

"Seems to be doing great. Busy, but he's gonna make some serious money today, so no complaining allowed. Let's get back and see how our Buster is doing."

The car pulled out from its parking spot on the side street and made its way toward Moor Abbey. As any inexperienced driver should, Erica kept her focus directly on the road in front of her. She didn't notice, but Spencer did. Partially hidden, Angus was standing in a thicket of trees next to the right-hand side of the road, his mutt cradled in his arms. The eyes followed as they went by.

CHAPTER TWO

F*our days earlier*
The young couple had already passed by the dilapidated monastery quite a few times over the course of their short getaway, but they hadn't stopped to check it out. They had been far too busy doing things that appealed to them both.

Today, another trek through the nearby mountain range was completed. As they approached the intersection where the monastery met the street leading back to their accommodations, the man insisted they pull over. The long day had tired them both, but Sean Kelly liked to do what he liked to do. He was a hardcore history buff and one who sometimes had to be persuaded not to stop at each heritage site he happened to come upon.

As the car came to a halt in front of the abbey, his wife Clare first resisted and finally acquiesced, the same as she had so many times before. Sean smiled. He would have done the same for her. He loved Clare, and she loved him, and small sacrifices for each other helped make their marriage work.

A few hours of daylight remained. Their break here would be short, and then they would pick up some food in the village for tonight's dinner.

Sean and Clare Kelly were the quintessential young professional couple. They were still young enough that they hadn't gotten around to the parenthood thing quite yet. Their "baby" was a brown and white terrier named Penny. Sean liked Penny for the most part, and Clare absolutely adored her. They both maintained interesting jobs that paid well and kept them busy. They had agreed that real children could wait—maybe next year, or the year after. Penny was more than enough for the time being.

Which of the two was more handsome was a difficult proposition. Sean was well over six feet tall and looked like he could have pursued a career as a professional model. His brown, wavy hair and neatly trimmed beard accentuated his green eyes and muscular build. He was a cool guy, nobody could deny. He was also a bit of a nerd. Studying history and visiting historical sites were things of which he couldn't get enough.

Clare could have been a model as well and had even dabbled in the trade when she was a teenager. Now she was a marketing executive in an unrelated field. At heart, she was a very down-to-earth woman with no pretenses. Her long blonde hair, blue eyes, and near-perfect physique turned more than a few heads.

They were a couple who had everything, and escaping for both long and short vacations was a passion they both shared.

The front doors on both sides of the car opened simultaneously. Sean stepped outside, reached over, and grabbed the handle of the rear door. Out jumped their small dog, her exhilaration at freedom off the charts, even though she had only been stuck in the car for less than twenty minutes now since coming down from the mountain trail.

She scrambled around the empty parking lot for a few moments and then immediately began heading for an enticing grassy area across the main road. Sean glanced over as Clare yelled at Penny to stop. A random car sped down the well-traveled thoroughfare and zoomed by them. This was a simple country road, more or less, but soon another car went by and then another and then one more.

"Why don't you put her on a lead?" Clare said to Sean with a worried expression. "This road's far too busy to let her roam freely."

"She'll be fine," Sean said.

He called out to Penny, and she scampered over to him, away from the road and nearer to the abbey. Penny followed her master over to the signboard next to the crumbled remains of the abbey's open entrance.

Sean's eyes fixed on today's history lesson, and he began reading, first on the initial signboard and then in more detail on the one next to it. Moor Abbey, he silently said to himself as he gobbled up the details of its past. He had never heard of this place before, but there was no reason he should have. The number of historical ruins in Ireland was limitless, and a person could spend a lifetime trying to see them all.

Clare loitered in the background behind him, a slight frown on her face and her arms crossed, not at all sharing her husband's predilection for things of long ago. Sean knew all of these things, and he understood she was also standing there to act as a barrier between the abbey and the road, just to make sure a certain dog didn't get any more wild ideas about crossing again. Clare was more than a little protective of their pint-sized mongrel, and that was fine with Sean—kept the both of them safe and out of trouble.

Satisfied he had learned enough today, Sean removed his reading glasses and stuffed them back into the front pocket of his button-down hiking shirt.

"Come on, let's go inside," he said without turning to his wife. "I promise, only a few minutes, and then we'll be on our way. This place has quite a past, it does."

Sean imagined Clare was likely shrugging her shoulders behind him, but he was glad she didn't object. She caught up with him at the entrance of stacked stones, and together they stepped in. Penny had already made her way halfway through the structure, bouncing from one wall to the next and smelling anything in between that caught her fancy.

"Penny, you be good now," Clare called out to the dog as it continued to dance around the hollow interior.

Sean paused at essentially the only inside piece that remained in this abbey, a stone tower still standing straight in the center. Its rocky structure reached high into the late afternoon sky, the entire way covered in green vines that obscured the dark recesses of windows that were once used to scan the open countryside. He thought about the friars who had lived and were murdered here. He thought about what their lives must have been like those hundreds of years before.

"Let's get out of here; this place is giving me the creeps," Clare said after only a few moments of standing there.

"Okay, just another minute or two," Sean said, not understanding what on earth made the place creepy.

He pulled out a camera from his backpack and began snapping a few pictures, just like he always did.

By now, Penny was busy at the rear of the abbey. Next to her was a small ledge that ran the distance from one side of the building to the other. The abbreviated wall was only slightly higher than Penny when on all fours, and above it the remainder had disappeared long before. The dog rose on her hind legs, her front paws resting on the ledge, taking in the view of the intriguing world outside. She squatted down and, in one quick motion, launched herself over the ledge to the other side. Sean watched the whole episode, thinking nothing of it.

"Penny, don't you go out there!" Clare said as she too watched Penny's abrupt departure from the abbey.

Sean gave up on a final photograph as he caught Clare sprinting to the back of the abbey. He watched as she stepped through the opening and began scanning the building's wooden fence perimeter and the green field of grass just beyond.

"Penny, Penny, where are you?" Clare said.

Slightly worried himself at this point, Sean ran out of this enclosure of stacked rocks and soon joined Clare. With their eyes searching every piece of countryside within view, together they screamed and shouted and called for their dog. Penny was nowhere to be seen.

"She's gotta be around here somewhere," Sean said. "How the hell could she have disappeared so quickly?"

He really couldn't imagine how Penny could have been there one second and gone the next. He glanced over at Clare.

"Listen, I'll go down to the road and look," he said, pointing to his right at a narrow one-lane road that ran alongside the abbey and paralleled a smallish river that flowed below it. "You start in the opposite direction, and we'll meet up a ways down."

"Clare, did you hear me?"

"Yes, Sean," she said. "Let's hurry. We've got to find her."

Without another word from her, Sean watched as Clare trotted away in the direction he had indicated, her head swinging from side to side as she went, desperate to locate her dog.

Inside, Sean was beginning to feel as frantic as his wife looked and sounded. Penny liked to roam and discover as much as the next dog, but she was a bit of a scaredy-cat as well and would generally never venture too far on her own.

Sean soon arrived at the small paved road and first followed it up to where it ended at a stop sign that stood just left of the abbey, adjacent to its entrance. He stood at the intersection and looked across the larger main road. He looked at his parked car on this side of the road, thinking she might have gone there. He looked everywhere in between and beyond. No Penny.

He headed in the opposite direction, jumping off the road to check along the river and around the greenery on its banks. He stayed on this side of the stream, but his eyes went to both sides, just in case. He called out Penny's name over and over again as he went.

Fifteen minutes in, and when he thought he had gone far enough, he climbed up and over the riverbank, crossed the road, and scoured the opposite side back toward the abbey. Along the way he caught sight of two dogs, residents of a large house above him. His dog was not with them. They barked incessantly as he walked by, but he hardly noticed.

He made his way back to where he had started and cut across the open field to where Clare was now standing. Her head was pointed toward the ground.

"Anything?" he asked.

"No, nothing," Clare said as she raised her head and looked at Sean. The tears slowly streamed down her cheeks, and she soon was gulping for air as the uncontrolled crying commenced.

"My Penny, my precious Penny," she said. Sean gently clasped her forearm as she tried to catch her breath. "Sean, what are we going to do?"

"Don't you worry. We're gonna find her, we are," Sean said. He hoped his voice sounded more convincing than he felt inside. Doubts of finding Penny were already entering his mind.

He wrapped Clare in his arms and held her tightly as she continued to sob. He could feel the wetness of her tears as they began to soak into his shirt. Sean looked around as he embraced his wife, hoping Penny would appear and this would all be over. He couldn't fathom what could have happened to their pet.

Just then, a dog's yelp, off in the distance, penetrated their ears. The sound was quick and sharp and only once. It seemed to have come from somewhere near a large oak tree that was standing firmly in an open area on a small hillside above. Sean was certain it had been Penny; he knew her voice like he knew the back of his hand.

Their eyes went immediately to the oak. In the air above blackbirds flew in and out of the tree and circled around and around its top. Sean looked up at the birds. He almost felt dizzy as they cawed and screamed and made a commotion that filled the air uncontrollably.

Not knowing exactly where to go, the couple sprinted in the direction of the tree, Sean in the lead and Clare close behind, both calling Penny's name the entire way. When they reached the base of the tree, the blackbirds dispersed and flew off in the direction of the abbey. Some continued flapping to destinations unknown, and some landed on the abbey's tower and hopped into the empty recesses, their voices persistent and annoying.

Sean and Clare walked around the tree and for hundreds of yards from its radius. They knew the cry they had heard had been hers, but Penny was not to be found, and there was not a single trace of where she could have gone. As they came back and stood there next to the tree, lost as to what to do next, a bone-chilling blast of cold air smothered their bodies. It then disappeared as quickly as it had come.

CHAPTER THREE

Sean and Clare Kelly spent the rest of the afternoon and evening, until the light of day was no longer their friend, searching for Penny. They wandered up and down each road in the vicinity and visited each rural house that offered a sign of hope. No one had seen the dog, and there were no clues to follow and no explanation for the animal's sudden disappearance.

Sean could see Clare was at the end of her wits, and he did his best to comfort her. When they returned to their self-catering lodge in the small village of Galbally that night, neither had an appetite. Sean forced Clare to eat some fruit and leftover salad from the previous day. He hoped there was still hope. They would have an entire day to search again tomorrow. But the dog's crying out, a sound they had both heard so clearly and so distinctly, was a bad sign. Sean could only guess what it meant.

The next day, however, was more of the same—searching and searching from the early morning hours and finding no trace of poor Penny. They traipsed wherever they could: through empty fields, through the interspersed forests, and up and down the River Aherlow for a mile or two in each direction.

As morning transitioned to afternoon, Sean and Clare decided to focus their attention on Galbally, which wasn't but a few minutes' drive from the abbey and the area where Penny had disappeared. They were not expecting to find the dog in the village, but they hoped to meet someone who might have seen her.

They found an open spot right after entering town and parked the car. Sean got out. His eyes ran down the small central road that held the majority of the open stores in Galbally: two small grocers, a couple of pubs, a takeout restaurant, and a few others that didn't announce their business, if any. Sean and Clare divvied up the establishments equally and inquired within each, showing a picture of Penny at each stop. In fifteen minutes they were done, meeting at the end of the street. No one had seen Penny.

Sean scanned across the town square and the roads that came from several directions to converge on this spot. On the other side, brightly colored stucco buildings similar to those on this side were present, but only two, a butcher and a small coffee shop, seemed to hold any promise. Clare headed toward the butcher and Sean the coffeehouse. On his way, on the far right of the square, in an enclosed space surrounded by a short concrete wall, Sean couldn't help but notice a tall metal pole holding an Irish flag that swayed in the slight afternoon breeze. Next to it was a large gray marble and concrete memorial statue to local heroes who had perished in the Irish War of Independence from Great Britain. He stopped briefly and read their story on the plaque at the base of the statue. Even with the plight of the lost Penny occupying his mind, Sean couldn't help himself when a chance to learn something new presented itself.

The coffee shop and butcher rendered the same result as the other places, and Sean and Clare met back in the middle of the square, next to another steel pole attached with long arrow-shaped signs indicating the distances and directions to nearby villages and towns. Sean studied the arrows intently, hoping to find some meaning, some clue that might lead them to Penny. But he knew nothing of meaning would be found in the pieces of shaped metal. He looked down from the pole and shook his head, hoping to break loose the mental cobwebs that were beginning to obscure his judgment.

They discussed what to do next and where to go. The various roads that ran into and out of Galbally were generally sided by places of residence. Desperation was knocking for the couple, and they weren't beyond a little knocking themselves. Again, they split duties, with Sean taking north and west of the square and Clare south and east. They couldn't possibly cover every available home, but they would do what they could for the next two hours.

Clare had been fairly composed throughout the morning and early afternoon, seemingly full of belief and prayers, but Sean could sense her dejection as the day extended. It took a bit of cajoling to convince Clare of the importance of this one last attempt. As he watched her head down the nearest street of her designated route, he could taste her misery. He, too, knew that their efforts were becoming futile.

Around 4 p.m. exhaustion had gotten the better of the both of them, and they met back in the square as planned. The only place they hadn't yet visited was the first of the two pubs in town. Sean had purposely saved it for last, knowing they were going to end up there when the day was over. They needed a break in the worst way, and Sean needed a whiskey. He realized the chances of finding their runaway dog grew slimmer with each passing hour. Daylight remained, however, and tomorrow might somehow bring a different outcome. For now, they required some time to gather their senses and rest their bodies.

Sean and Clare walked through the entrance of the dimly lit bar and took their pick from all of the empty seats that beckoned them. A lone grubby-looking man, likely a village local based on his appearance, was the only other customer. He sat at the end of the bar, nursing a half-full pint. They sat down at a table close to the counter, and their drinks soon arrived. Sean sipped on his first glass and quickly decided he was going to be needing more than one of these.

He was glad for the distraction of the pub owner engaging them in casual conversation, asking where they were from, how long they were around for, and the usual exchange between a barkeep and his customers. The small talk with a stranger offered a welcome respite from the weary and stressful day.

After a few drinks the conversation led to where it was intended. Sean and Clare shared the story of the disappeared Penny with the man working the bar. His name was Killian, they soon learned, and he seemed to take a genuine interest in their probable tragedy. But he could not offer any advice beyond what Sean and Clare had already attempted. Killian did tell them, however, that more than once he had witnessed a lost dog turn up again when it never should have. The small comment seemed to brighten Clare's mood somewhat, and the alcohol did the same for Sean.

"You know, if a dog runs away, you're best to just let it be. No good will come from trying to find her, I imagine."

Sean threw his attention to the local at the end of the bar, the one who had been there when they first entered. Until this moment the man hadn't whispered a word and had been so quiet that Sean had almost forgotten he was even present.

"For God's sake, what are you on about, Angus?" Killian said, his tone sharp and uncharitable. "I don't recall inviting you to this conversation."

The man sat on his stool without replying, his head pointed down at his pint of ale, as if he were contemplating its contents. He rotated the glass around in a circle over and over again. Sean studied him briefly, wondering what he had meant by the strange remark.

"Don't be paying him no mind," Killian said quietly to Sean and Clare. "He's well into his third pint and generally doesn't make much sense even when he's sober. Anyway, let me get you another round, this one on me."

Sean watched as Killian went behind the bar and soon came back with another whiskey and a glass of white wine. Killian brought an ale for himself, and the three of them spent the next fifteen minutes talking about things not related to wayward dogs. When the drinks were dry, Sean and Clare departed the pub that evening, filled with a small sense of renewed hope and determination that tomorrow they would find Penny.

As they left they noticed a small dog of some mixed breed lying right next to the entrance of the pub. The white, matted coat was so dirty it could have been confused for another color. Clare, as was her habit, reached down to pet the animal. Before her hand got there, and without raising its head, the dog let out a low-pitched growl, a warning it wasn't in the mood for unsolicited attention. Sean grabbed Clare's hand, and they began the short walk back to their accommodations.

The next morning Sean again stopped the car at the north end of the parking area of Moor Abbey, and he and Clare headed out in different directions. They each reenacted parts of previous searches. Sean again took the river and Clare the roads and open fields. After two hours of scouring both sides of the stream, Sean pulled his phone from his pants pocket and called his wife. He would meet her back at the abbey. They would eat an early lunch, and then Sean had one last idea of where to look for Penny.

If the efforts still didn't produce, they'd hustle to the town of Tipperary in the afternoon and have some lost-dog posters made up. They were both due back at work in the morning, but that wasn't going to happen. The stay at the inn had already been extended, with a checkout for tomorrow, Friday. They would extend longer if need be. Sean knew Clare wouldn't leave here until Penny was reunited with them or until it was painfully obvious she wouldn't be.

As they ate their lunch, Sean could hardly get Clare to say a single word. She was as distraught as he had ever seen her. She picked at her food, taking only small bites and placing the remainder back into the plastic container. Her gloomy demeanor soon had Sean feeling the same, but he had to be strong for his wife. If Penny weren't found, however, he was truly afraid of what would become of Clare.

Clare loved Penny with all her heart, more than Sean thought possible for a person to love an animal. Though they had talked about getting a pet several times throughout their marriage, Penny had come into their lives rather unexpectedly. A friend of a friend knew someone who was making a move overseas. Taking a pet became more of a hassle than it was worth, and soon the owners were looking for a new home for their dog. Introductions were made, and Sean and Clare were soon paying a visit to Penny's home. Clare took one look at her potential new pet, and that was all it took.

Sean had resisted at first, arguing that owning a dog would hinder their frequent travel plans. But Clare wouldn't be dissuaded, and Penny was soon theirs. The dog had been about one year old when she entered the Kelly household, and her second birthday was coming up shortly. Clare was even planning a doggy party of sorts, with decorations, gifts, and treats for humans and canines alike. Sean feared the party would never happen. They had to find Penny.

As Sean finished off the sandwich that he had hardly tasted, he shared the idea in his head with Clare. The plan was a long shot at best, but he had to try something; he had to give his wife a sense there was still a chance.

Northwest of the abbey and of the river, just half a mile or so away, there was a small mountain—if it could be called that—covered in a deep canopy of coniferous forest. A commonly used hiking trail, one of a few that ran the distance of this valley, paralleled the mountain at its base. Sean knew they needed to search any area they had not visited yet, and this was one of them.

Because there was no visible road leading to their destination and nothing showed on the phone's GPS, they left the car in the abbey parking area and set out on foot. In due time they reached the green hillside and began walking the main trail for a few hundred yards in the direction back toward the village. They proceeded slowly, yelling out Penny's name as they went, stopping and waiting to hear something in return.

Each time they were greeted back by nothing but silence. The silence was so intense that to Sean it seemed almost unnatural. He listened for the chirp of a bird or any other familiar sound of nature. He heard nothing but their own voices and the soft noise of their feet on the brown soil of the path. Why? He kept his thoughts to himself.

Finally, they were able to find a smaller footpath that veered to the right and made its way up the small mountain and through the forest. Sean looked ahead. The path forward did not look inviting, but he knew they had to go. He wondered again why everything was so quiet.

As the two of them made their way up the trail that was equally rocky as it was muddy, day almost seemed to turn to night. The towering Sitka spruce trees, each one standing as straight as an arrow and only a few feet apart from the one next to it, obscured any brightness that tried to seep through. Underneath the suffocating canopy, no vegetation grew on the ground between the trees except a continuous bed of lichen and heavy green moss that covered the forest floor.

The trail itself offered both a degree of light and a small open space between them and the wall of trees that resided on both sides. They slowly climbed up the hillside, careful in trying to avoid the occasional small running streams of water that seemed to seep out randomly from the green vegetation next to the path. As they walked Sean studied the forest beside them. The darkness within seemed never-ending.

"Sean, this place is creepier than the abbey. Let's go back now. We're never gonna find Penny in here," Clare said. She seemed more dejected than ever. Sean watched as she reached down and with her index finger scraped the soft, dark mud already accumulating on the sides of her off-white sneakers.

He realized she was probably right, and he was beginning to feel the same about the disquieting nature of this place. But he wasn't about to be detoured by the imaginary spooks of a forest. And he wasn't about to leave any stone unturned in their search for Penny. Besides, it was becoming obvious that, in this short time, they were already nearing the top.

"Just hang on a bit longer," he said. "Let's don't give up just yet. We're getting close to the top, and then we'll decide what to do."

He wondered whether they would follow the trail down the other side, if there were still a trail to follow at that point.

As they trudged along the final stretch to the top, they took turns calling out Penny's name as they went. Each time the sound bounced back as if the forest were impenetrable.

Then he heard it, and Sean stopped dead in his tracks. Clare followed suit. He turned around and looked at his wife, who was looking at him.

"What? What did you hear?" she said.

Sean raised his index finger to his pursed lips and held it there.

It came again, indiscernible mostly, but whatever it was held the faint tinge of a dog's whimpering. Whatever he was hearing, it was directly to the right of the trail, how far in difficult to tell.

Clare needed no convincing as to what was going to happen next. Before Sean could speak he watched as his wife took off and began a sprint between trees and into the darkness beside them.

"Penny, Penny, we're here," she yelled, tearing through the woods toward her supposed target.

"Clare, slow down. Slow down, damn it!" said Sean as he began chasing after her.

The soft texture of the moss-laden ground underneath felt almost as if he were running on cushions. But the going wasn't easy. Small mounds of the mossy surface erupted every few steps, kind of like a miniature mountain range on the forest floor. Almost immediately, Sean's foot caught on one of the protrusions, and he stumbled, sending him face-first into the ground.

He hoisted himself back up and quickly continued. As he ran he caught a brief glimpse of Clare. She rounded one tree, dashed between two more, and disappeared from his sight once again. But he could see where she was headed. Out in front a small dome of light penetrated the dark forest. Sean was perplexed and couldn't imagine what it was or from where the light originated. Still, he knew he had to go there.

"Clare, where are you?" he said again and again as he chased after her. "Clare, Clare!"

Sean halted. He had lost track of Clare's whereabouts, and the glow that had been shining so bright had vanished. Except for the soft squishiness under his feet when he took a small step, only quiet pervaded the woods around him.

"Clare, where did you go? Stop and wait for me!"

He waited for her response. Nothing was received. Then, at a forty-five-degree angle from where he stood, the light reappeared no more than twenty-five yards ahead, radiating from above. He ran forward and pulled up. Clare was standing directly in front of him, directly underneath the shining illumination.

She turned in a complete circle, as if she were admiring the setting around her. She stopped her motion and looked in Sean's direction, a calmness present and a huge smile beaming from her face. Sean stared at his wife and then checked everything else within his vision, wondering why the air had suddenly become so chilled, just like two days before near the abbey.

"Sean, I think I found Penny," Clare said. "She was here just a second ago under this light. I'm certain we can find her again. She told me she wants us to find her."

Sean knew Clare well, all her quirks, all her facial expressions, everything that a man should know about his wife. The person in front of him was not the woman he knew and loved. She seemed oddly serene in a situation that was exactly the opposite.

"Come on now, Sean, help me look for her before she goes again," she said.

The illumination surrounding her grew much brighter and more intense. Sean was reminded of a sci-fi movie and an alien ship beaming a light down on the unwitting and mesmerized humans below.

And then, over her left shoulder, he saw the angry beast. If Sean had been asked how to describe what he was seeing, he wouldn't have been able. A wisp of wind and a fog-like haze with no tangible form except for two large dark spots, almost like eyes, danced around within it.

Sean looked at Clare again. There was no terror on her face, almost as if she were unaware of what was happening. Her lips moved as if she were praying, but this time no sound came from them.

"Clare, come over to me now," Sean calmly said, trying to dislodge his wife from whatever had stepped into her soul. "Let's go back."

Clare's mouth began to move again, but the words were unclear. Sean dashed forward, determined to free her before it was too late. As he stood next to her, without the slightest warning, the overcast skies that had been present all day unleashed a deluge of rain. Sean wiped the moisture from his face and grabbed Clare's hand and pulled. She wouldn't budge, not even an inch. He tried again, but she stood her ground with a power that wasn't humanly possible.

"Damn it, Clare, what are you doing? We've gotta get out of here," he said, shouting the words. He yanked her arm once more, but the result was the same.

"No, I won't go with you, Sean," she said, still as calm as could be.

She was drenched now, her long hair hanging flat and in strands against her head, and her mascara running parallel streaks down her face.

"I'm going to stay here and look for Penny," Clare said. "She needs me. Can't you understand?"

"Clare, please come with me. Please."

Sean gave one last pull. An ear-piercing shriek filled the air behind his wife and resonated forward. Sean watched as Clare turned around and finally recognized her true predicament, somehow broken out of her trance. She turned back to him. In her eyes were tears. They broke from their barrier and streamed down her face, only to be lost in all the rain.

Certain she would now come with him, Sean tried again. As he pulled, his hand ripped free from hers, and his body was thrown ten yards backward by some ungodly force. His rear end smacked the ground behind him as he landed hard on a small mound of green. He scrambled to his feet and looked ahead again at Clare. The terror on her face was real. He sprinted forward, and then something made him stop.

In an instant Clare was sucked upward into the air and into the glare. Her body levitated vertically, maybe five yards up, completely static and almost lifeless, as if she couldn't move her limbs or her head. Sean cried out as he forced himself to watch the unspeakable scene. How could he help her? He didn't know what to do. Sean concentrated on Clare's face. She looked down at him, such horror in those wide-open eyes. The eyes pleaded softly with Sean to save her.

Before Sean could yell out her name again, Clare was thrown backward so fast and with such violence that it was incomprehensible. In another instant she was gone. She was completely gone. The light remained. The dark eyes continued to dance around inside.

Sean stood in complete shock for a few seconds, trying to comprehend what had just happened. He hesitated as to what to do next. The rain stung his eyes as he looked at where Clare had been but where she was no more. He was afraid beyond belief, but the adrenaline flowing through his veins told him not to give up.

He moved a few steps forward and yelled out Clare's name. He retreated as the light intensified, almost as if it were angry. The dancing eyes stopped their motion. Sean could feel their focus. The chaos above him began filling with gloom, like a building thunderstorm cloud as it grows from inside and eventually envelops all in its path.

Sean thought about running. Clare was gone. There was nothing he could do for her now. But maybe he could. Then the light, and the darkness within, grew larger and expanded until Sean was standing directly below. There he was, in the midst of it, so alive and alone. He couldn't move. He looked into the light; he looked into the sky. The relentless rain pounded and chilled him, but he didn't notice. He looked where Clare should have been. He looked back down at the ground and into the forest outside the light, searching for an answer. Everything went black.

CHAPTER FOUR

Spencer threw back the sheets as the sun peeked through the half-open blinds of his bedroom window. He glanced over at the small clock on his nightstand: 7 a.m. already, an hour past his normal wake-up time. Yesterday had been a good day for the most part, except for the episode with Angus and then the conversation with Killian. *Damn him!* Their brief talk had weighed on Spencer throughout dinner and into the rest of the evening. Two hours or more of tossing and turning had finally brought sleep, but not sound and not enough. He was feeling the effects this morning. He wondered what to expect when he met Killian in Galbally.

He reached down and tousled the hair on Buster's soft head, and the dog reciprocated with a lick across the back of Spencer's hand.

"Good morning, Buster. Did you sleep well? Better than I did, I bet."

Buster was resting on the same white rug where the dog named Shandy had lain one night just this past spring. By all measures the dog that had visited Spencer that day had been a real one, but time had told him otherwise.

Spencer watched as Buster jumped to all fours, his tail wagging as he made his way across the expansive room. He sneaked through the slightly open bedroom door. This was a set routine. Buster would wait until Spencer woke up and then make his way downstairs to be let outside by Erica or Mrs. O'Donnell, whoever he met first. Once done, he would come back inside, fully expecting his morning food to be waiting in his dish in the kitchen. He wasn't the only one who was being trained around this house.

Ten minutes later Spencer got out of the shower and exchanged the damp towel for jeans and a beaten-up beige polo shirt that Erica had been threatening to throw out for some time. He stood in front of the full-length mirror and checked his look. His handsome face, taller-than-average height, and reasonably toned body would be the envy of most men his age. Still, Spencer struggled with the aging process. He had never thought about it much until he reached his fifties. Now halfway through the decade, his short-cropped hair was more salt than pepper, especially on the sides, and the lines on his face seemed to increase in number each time he bothered to examine in detail.

He smoothed his hand over his upper lip and chin, thinking the whiskers were too long and needed trimming, but he'd worry about that later. A meeting with Killian, after all, didn't require him to look his best. He was much more concerned with words than appearances on this day.

Spencer made his way down the carpeted stairs, making a mental note to pull the ancient fabric this winter and see what resided underneath. The list of off-season maintenance projects seemed to grow with each passing day.

In the kitchen Mrs. O'Donnell, the morning chef at this bed and breakfast, was well into her usual morning routine. She was donning her red and white cooking apron and standing tall over the stove, fussing over breakfast for the inn's guests. Today there were only the French couple and a lone man from London. Breakfast was served each morning between six-thirty and nine. Guests were asked to designate a preferred time at the beginning of their stay or on the night before, and Mrs. O'Donnell was never amused if someone didn't keep their promise. She could be quite temperamental at times.

Occasionally, Spencer would receive some negative comments about the woman's demeanor as he went through the online reviews of the inn, but the majority of the remarks were effusive in their compliments. Her cooking skill was in a category by itself, and Spencer knew she added a certain character to the place. He felt very fortunate to have her in his employ, and he would keep her on for as long as she wished or when things got to the point where his own cooking was up to the task. That was a thought for another time.

"Good morning to ya, Mr. Spencer," Mrs. O'Donnell said without a smile as Spencer entered the kitchen. "What'll you be having this morning?"

Spencer had long succumbed to the habit of someone cooking breakfast for him each morning, and Mrs. O'Donnell's morning fare was just too good to refuse. And she readily obliged, as if she were his mother and expected him to begin each day with a hearty meal. Not today. His appetite was pretty much nonexistent.

"Morning," said Spencer. "I think I'll pass on breakfast today, or maybe just grab a bagel and cream cheese later on. But I could use a cup of coffee."

He wondered whether he looked as tired as he felt.

"Oh, come on now. You'll never grow up to be a big boy without eating a proper breakfast," she said.

Spencer looked on as Mrs. O'Donnell set the utensils down and used a hand to reinsert a loose strand that had just barely escaped from the tight bun of hair that rested on the top of her head. He had never seen her with a different style and often wondered how long her thick gray hair would be when let down. She poured a cupful of coffee and handed the steaming mug to him.

What Mrs. O'Donnell lacked in decorum, she made up for with a biting wit, a trait she had undoubtedly refined over her seventy-plus years. At times, Spencer had to stifle himself from laughing out loud at some of her quips, but he did his best to keep their relationship professional. They were never the types to become friends with one another anyway, and Spencer preferred it that way. He also knew that the day she called him Spencer rather than Mr. Spencer would never come.

Spencer was his surname, but anyone close to him and anyone who knew him well simply called him Spencer. This custom had been in force for years, but convincing people in Ireland to follow the same protocol wasn't always an easy task.

Spencer held the cup below his face and let the aroma of the coffee fill his nostrils. He took his first sip. Perfect, as always. He wasn't in the mood for chitchat, and small talk was generally a lost cause with Mrs. O'Donnell. He needed to head to the patio on the east side of the house, where the thoughts always became clearer with the combination of solitude and piping hot coffee (and sometimes a glass full of alcohol).

"Where's Erica?" he asked.

"Out with Buster, I do believe," she said. "You know you need to get that animal neutered one of these days before he begins making courtesy calls on the female dogs in the neighborhood. He'll be having yearnings soon enough, just like all you men do."

Spencer stifled a chuckle, glad to find a bit of humor this Sunday morning.

Mrs. O'Donnell generally showed a pretense of not caring much for Buster, but Spencer could see through her. More than once he caught her secretly sneaking morning leftovers to the dog when she thought no one was around.

Spencer studied the black contents of his mug as Mrs. O'Donnell scooped up the perfectly cooked sausage and vegetable omelets from the oversized fry pan and placed them on the two white plates already adorned with an assortment of fresh berries from the garden out back.

"Yeah, I know," Spencer finally said, as Mrs. O'Donnell turned her body slightly sideways, pushed open the swinging kitchen door with her shoulder, and walked into the dining room to serve this morning's guests.

Spencer stepped outside and could see Erica and Buster a short distance away on a hill overlooking the river. The hill was just beyond the wooden fence that enclosed the property's yard and was covered in knee-deep grass and a plethora of wildflowers that beckoned to be viewed. He gave a wave, and Erica waved back. He turned around and just stood for a few moments, admiring his home, his eyes flowing from one side to the other and then up and down. He had poured his heart and soul into the Square One Bed & Breakfast, for the simple reason that this place was his. When he purchased the inn early last winter, he knew he had lucked into something special. He hadn't looked back since.

This inn, this house of his, meant more to Spencer than he could have ever imagined. Physically, the place was nothing special. The white two-story structure started right where the road leading to it ended. The mass of the surrounding grounds was impressive, with the cut green grass on all sides and carefully positioned patches of brightly colored flowers here and there.

Trees of all kinds and all sizes had been previously planted and scattered around with no obvious thought given to aesthetics or a master plan. Spencer thought the trees lacked symmetry and order. He wanted to remove a few, maybe plant some new ones, but that could wait until time was more available.

From the outside the large house was fairly nondescript, though Spencer especially liked the partial brick facade on the lower level at the main entrance. The second floor showed two large windows from the front. Spencer's bedroom and that of Erica resided behind those windows. On the opposite side of the house, on the same floor, were two guestrooms, and there was another guest bedroom on the first floor. The only other exterior feature of note was the brown chimney stack that protruded from the far side of the roof. The fireplace to which it belonged was situated in Spencer's den on the ground floor.

The Square One still required a fair amount of work in Spencer's estimation, but it was fine for the time being. In comparison to six months ago, it seemed like a palace. The hours and days and weeks of fixing, painting, and remodeling had paid dividends. Still, big plans routinely flowed through Spencer's mind. But he had time, lots of time. His intention was to spend the rest of his days here.

Spencer returned his attention to Erica and Buster. Erica picked up the discolored and punctured tennis ball Buster had placed at her feet and gave the sphere a good toss into the tall grass twenty-five yards away. The dog took after it, zigzagging the entire way and scrambling around in circles until he again found what he was looking for. Within thirty seconds Buster and the ball returned to Erica.

Spencer stood in silence and looked at his daughter. He was surprised at how much she looked like her mother now, with long and straight black hair that naturally parted to the left. Her beauty was also natural, and most days she went without makeup. Large dark eyes complemented her fair complexion and were the first physical feature a stranger might notice upon meeting her for the first time. She was taller than and not as petite as her mother had been, and her strong facial features, including a sharp nose, were similar to his.

"Erica, throw me the ball once," Spencer said. She complied, and Spencer gave the ball a heave with all of his might. Soon, Buster's tail disappeared into the high grass on a slope down toward the river.

"See, that's how a real man throws a ball," Spencer proudly stated.

"Well, when I become a real man, I'll certainly let you know," Erica said as she traipsed off after Buster.

Spencer chuckled.

"Erica."

She turned around. "Yes, Dad."

"I'm going to head to the river this morning, and then I've got to go back into Galbally to see Killian."

"Again?"

"Yeah, just a small thing I've got to take care of."

"Okay, I'll see you when you get back."

Spencer moved to the patio and soon finished the first mug of coffee. Within a few minutes Mrs. O'Donnell brought out a refill. Though he tried his mind was racing too much to think clearly, and Spencer decided he'd head for Galbally early. Maybe he'd stop by Moor Abbey, which he hadn't done since all of his adventures there so many months back. He didn't care for the abbey much, but at the same time the setting was special to him. The monastery was the very first place he had stopped when he came to this area as a visitor.

When he walked back into the kitchen, Mrs. O'Donnell was nowhere to be seen, and the adjoining dining room was quiet, the guests already having finished their meals and likely getting ready for a day of playing tourist. Spencer placed his empty coffee cup in the sink. He went to the back porch, put on his fishing gear, and began walking the trail above and parallel to the River Aya.

Spencer took his time as he made his way, enjoying the natural beauty around him. His affection for this land continued to grow with each passing day. The nearby village of Bansha and its people had welcomed him with open arms, and he felt he was gradually becoming one of them. After all, he was the crazy American who had purchased a somewhat beaten-down bed and breakfast that had failed miserably in its prior life. This act alone had earned him a certain level of respect.

The River Aya provided him with peace of mind on the days he needed solace, and today was one of those days. And the river had given up its share of brown trout that Spencer only acquainted himself with briefly before always returning them to the water in which they belonged.

In only half an hour, Spencer had accomplished what he had set out to do. He took a last glance at his prize, bidding adieu to the monster brown trout he had just released from the barbless hook at the end of his fishing line. Fish this size weren't caught every day, and this one had taken Spencer a good ten minutes to land, forcing him into a waist-high hole of water under a mess of overgrown brush before he could wrestle the creature into his net.

Nice, he thought as he watched the trout slowly disappear into the dark shadows of the cold water. *I nailed your butt, old fella, and I'll do it again next time.* He began wading through the water toward the riverbank. Now it was time to face Killian.

Spencer steered the Subaru 4WD to the right at the intersection on the outskirts of Bansha and began the short drive to Galbally. The road led southwest and meandered through the Glen of Aherlow, a beautiful, scenic valley abutted on the far side by Ireland's highest inland mountain range, the Galtees.

The route was one he had taken many times in the past, including the first time he came to Ireland, but he hadn't been to Galbally in more than a month until yesterday. His new occupation had kept him far too busy over the summer to allow for a social visit to Killian's pub.

He sipped more from the silver metal cup of the old-fashioned coffee thermos he had brought along. He recalled the first time on this roadway, that particular day meant as nothing more than a final attempt to locate decent fishing waters before the vacation in Ireland ended. That day had brought much more than he had bargained for and was the beginning of something he could never have imagined.

As Spencer left the valley, the car rose over a small bridge that spanned the River Aherlow. This water was a place he had fished as well. As with most of the other rivers and streams Spencer had fished during his initial arrival in Ireland, back then this river too had produced nothing more than a cold tramp through flowing water.

At the end of the bridge, right before Route 663 takes a ninety-degree turn on its way to Galbally, Moor Abbey rested silently on the opposite side. This abbey is where Spencer had stumbled upon the stray dog named Shandy. Of course, he hadn't known her name just then, but the name was revealed with time, as was much more.

On that day Shandy was wearing no collar, and Spencer had no way to identify who she was or from where she had come. He also had no way of knowing Shandy was suffering from cancer and had only a short time left on this earth. That, too, would be revealed as the days went by. And the knowledge would become the defining element of Spencer's eventual quest to save a little dog.

The chance meeting with Shandy had foreshadowed events that seemed only a dream these days. Shandy became his dog in a way, but in reality he had never really known her. Spencer had only held the small brown and white terrier mix in his arms on a total of three occasions.

The first was when he had first found her, and the second when she had taken her dying breath. In the interim he had spent a couple of weeks irrationally trying to find her, for reasons that were obscure at best. He could explain the reasons now, maybe, but at the time he had begun questioning his sanity.

The last time Spencer had seen Shandy was several months later, when some manifestation of her came for a final visit after he had moved into the Square One. The Shandy who visited that day had seemed and felt completely real, but Spencer knew now that she had been but a ghost or spirit. She had only stayed briefly before disappearing and leaving his life forever.

Spencer pulled over in the parking lot of the abbey and found himself alone on this quiet morning. Of course, the abbey looked the same as it always did. The beaten-up relic was literally hundreds and hundreds of years old, and no one would ever notice a change from one day or even one year to another.

He exited the car and felt the gravel move under his feet as he began moving to his right toward the entrance of the structure. He raised his head and surveyed the abbey, as he had numerous times in the past. All remaining these days were the outer walls, level on the sides and tapering into a spire shape at the front and back, and a tower, situated in the middle of the structure and rising high into today's overcast sky. Domed entrances or windows of various proportions were present on both sides. Here and there assorted recesses hid within the walls. A black cast-iron gate, perhaps leading to a now-defunct staircase, guarded one of the recesses.

Outside, near the entrance, was a plaque with a brief description of the abbey's history, written in both English and Gaelic. The monastery was founded by the O'Brien clan in the thirteenth century, and the structure went through its ups and downs in the ensuing years. Ultimately, the friars inhabiting this residence a couple of hundred years later were massacred for reasons not accurately known.

Spencer crossed the road and took a quick stroll down to the nearby river. He threw a couple of small rocks into the water and watched the small splashes. Like the Aya, the River Aherlow by now had also surrendered a few fish to Spencer's fly rod, but he didn't come here often. There were too many other, more productive rivers in these parts where time was better spent. He climbed back up the bank and wandered over to the lone picnic table, still set as before in a small section of cut grass directly across the main road from the abbey. Right next to this table is where he had spied Shandy for the first time, and the road in front is where her life had tragically ended a few weeks later. She had been the victim of a car driven too fast, but her death was much more and a death that was inevitable and one meant to happen.

Spencer wiped his bare palm across a small section of the brown picnic table and cleared away the thin accumulation of dust and yellowish pollen, watching the particles float through the air as he clapped his hands together. He climbed on the bench and sat down on the top of the table. His sorrow for Shandy had run its course for the most part, but this place still brought back many memories, some good and most bad. He wondered whether things of the past would now continue in one form or another. Killian had said something related to Shandy had happened, but what could it possibly be? The dog was long gone. Spencer gently rubbed his midsection with his right hand, jumped down to the green grass, and crossed the road to the other side.

As he pulled his car out of the parking area, a dark blue sedan with two men in dark suits left the road and came to a stop in front of the abbey. Through his rearview mirror Spencer observed the pair as they opened the doors of the car. He thought nothing of it.

The drive into Galbally was a short one from the abbey. In no time Spencer rounded the last bend of the two-lane road and pulled into town. He found an open parking spot in front of Murphy's store and stared up at the bright green awning.

If Colin wasn't here yesterday, he won't be here today, Spencer thought. Colin, along with Killian, was one of the first persons Spencer had met after coming this way. Colin's family owned Murphy's store, and Spencer had met the young man there the same day he had happened upon Shandy. As the days went by, Colin would eventually become Spencer's willing cohort as he searched for Shandy. They had been through a lot together.

Nowadays, the young man had left his job at the family store and moved on to bigger and better things. He lived near Clonmel, about an hour's drive due east. Colin's nascent dream of becoming an Irish fly-fishing guide, a dream inspired partly by Spencer's recommendation to simply take up the hobby, had come to fruition. Spencer made a mental note to call Colin and see how he was doing.

Spencer stepped out of the car and immediately was recognized by an older gentleman strolling down the other side of the street, broom and dustpan in hand. The man's name was Ted, and the other villagers referred to him as Tidy Ted. He was a fixture in the community and had earned his moniker because he could be seen, almost on a daily basis, out doing his volunteer work. One day he would be sweeping the sides of the streets. The next day he might be seen picking up loose litter. The next would find him applying a fresh coat of paint to the trestle of a small bridge.

"Mr. Spencer, how ya? Come down for a day of Galbally sightseeing, have you now?" the man said jokingly.

"Yeah, something like that, Ted," Spencer yelled back. "Any day is a day worth visiting Galbally."

"You'd be right about that. And were ya down yesterday for the glorious Tractor Run?" Ted asked.

"You know I was, Ted. We bumped into each other briefly," Spencer said and watched the man succumb to a quick bout of thinking.

"Oh, lordy, you're right, Mr. Spencer. Me mind must have been thinking about the mess being made."

Spencer glanced around and noticed the town was in almost spotless condition already. No doubt all had pitched in, and Ted would tolerate no other way.

"No worries, Ted. The village looks as beautiful as ever."

Tidy Ted grinned, gave a quick wave, and kept walking.

Spencer walked down the pavement alongside the tightly connected buildings. The Grafton Pub was only three places down from Murphy's store. The time was just short of eleven. Without knocking Spencer pushed open the door and stepped inside an establishment that he knew all too well.

Killian stood behind the bar, pulling freshly washed and rinsed pint glasses from the sink and placing them gently on the drying rack.

"Good morning, Spencer," Killian said. "You're right on time. Just cleaning up a bit from yesterday and last night. It was a late one, to be sure. Had to chase the last ones out with a broom. To top it off I was obliged to take the wife to the early church service this morning.

"These big events are becoming too much for a decrepit old man like me. In fact, I'm not even opening the pub today—I need a good dose of rest and quiet."

"Morning, Killian," Spencer said from across the room, forcing a half-hearted smile he didn't feel.

He walked over to the bar, pulled out a stool from under the counter, and sat down in front of Killian.

"Can I get you anything?" Killian said.

"A pint of stout is what I need, but I think I'll take a pass on that. I'd take some coffee if you have any made."

Killian turned to the coffee pot behind him and poured a mug full of the hot liquid.

"Black as usual, I assume?" Killian said as he set the cup down in front of Spencer.

Spencer nodded in agreement, wrapped both hands around the mug, and felt the warmth penetrate his body. He brought the coffee to his lips and took a small mouthful, his eyes on Killian, who was placing the final rinsed glasses on the rack. Spencer studied Killian as the man silently continued his cleanup work. The two were comfortable enough with each other by now that moments of silence were nothing uncommon.

Spencer had admired Killian's appearance from the first time he met him. Physically, he was nothing special: average height and weight, kind blue eyes, an earnest smile that was always at the ready, and a full head of well-kept gray hair. He was ten years older than Spencer, give or take a year or two.

What impressed Spencer the most was Killian's way with people. His demeanor was calm and slow, with an air of intelligence that was natural and never showy. Within minutes of meeting anyone people felt at ease in his presence. Spencer envied Killian in that regard, but he knew he could never be like him.

"So, Killian, why am I here this morning?" Spencer finally asked. He wasn't feeling the need or inclination for casual conversation.

Killian finished wiping down the sink area with a damp cloth before looking up.

"The reality is that it may turn out to be nothing, but I do feel otherwise," Killian said.

Spencer watched the man as he turned around and poured himself some coffee. He faced Spencer again.

"Let me start at the start," Killian said. "A few days back—Wednesday, in fact—a younger couple, in their early thirties I would imagine, came into the pub late in the afternoon and ordered a couple of drinks. Said they were from the Galway area and just down here for some trekking in the Galtees. Nothing out of the ordinary, to be sure, but I could tell something was amiss. You know how I am.

"We chatted for a bit and eventually they confided their dog had gone missing. We conversed some more, and it turned out they had stopped by Moor Abbey late the day before. You know, just the usual, checking out the abbey as people often do.

"They were inside the abbey, with the dog not on a lead. Then apparently the dog snuck out the backside and disappeared. After a bit of searching they finally heard a bark off in the distance. Of course, they ran directly to where they had heard the sound, but the animal was nowhere to be seen. They said they spent the rest of the afternoon and evening scouring the area until it became too dark."

"That's all?" said Spencer. "You called me down here to tell me that? Dogs disappear all the time."

"Patience now, Spencer. There's more to be said."

Spencer tapped his fingers up and down on the wooden countertop, anxiety getting the better of him.

"That was four days ago when the couple was in the pub here," Killian continued telling the story. "They had spent most of that entire day searching for the dog. And their plan was naturally to go out again the next day. Funny thing is they haven't been seen since Thursday morning."

"Well, they must have just given up and gone home," Spencer said, hoping to put an end to this conversation but knowing it wasn't likely.

"That would be the practical conclusion, but they would have taken their car with them, wouldn't they have now? Strangely enough, the car hasn't moved from the abbey parking since," Killian said. "You drove by the abbey on your way here; you may have noticed it. A tan SUV, I do believe."

Spencer didn't feel like telling Killian he had stopped at the abbey. He thought back and recalled there had been a vehicle at the far end of the parking area. But he hadn't seen a single other person while he was there, except for the two men who had shown up as he was leaving.

"Yeah, I guess I did notice a car or two when I passed by," said Spencer. "I didn't pay much attention. How do you know all of this?"

"The two of them were staying at Mrs. Kennedy's inn, just like you when you first came this way," Killian said. "When they didn't turn up at the reception to check out on Friday, she naturally became alarmed. Checked their room, and all the belongings were there. Anyway, she didn't know what to do and rang me up straight away. I made a call to the guards shortly after, and they sent a patrol out."

Living in a new country requires a certain amount of adaptation, and Spencer still hadn't become accustomed to referring to the police as the guards or Garda, as they were called in Ireland.

Killian continued: "Spencer, I've a feeling you're not going to like what I'm going to tell you next."

Spencer felt the acid percolating in his stomach, and he braced himself. He impatiently watched as Killian filled some more coffee into his cup and set it down on the counter.

"Well?" said Spencer. "What is it? Spit it out."

"The guards found the couple's dog, dead as can be, about two hundred yards from the abbey down next to the river. The dog's body was hidden in a space among some thickets, but it really wasn't hidden much. Fairly easy for them to find, I'm told," Killian said.

"Do they know how it died?" Spencer asked.

"No, that part is still a mystery, but they kindly convinced Dr. Mahir at the veterinary clinic to have a go at it today," Killian said. "I imagine they'll have a conclusion by the end of the day. It won't be something I'll be privy to, not right away at least."

Spencer thought about what Killian had just said. The whole situation seemed unfortunate and sad, but he wasn't quite yet buying what Killian was selling, that there was some relevance to Shandy.

"So what, Killian," Spencer said. "That doesn't mean anything. A dog got lost and died. It doesn't mean anything."

"Would you like to hear the most interesting part?" Killian asked.

"Okay."

"The dog looked eerily similar to your dog—I mean Shandy, not Buster. She was a wee thing and a terrier of some sort. Even a similar color to Shandy."

Now things were hitting closer to home, but Spencer remained dubious. At the same time Killian had seldom led Spencer astray. Even if only Killian's intuition, the subject had to be taken seriously.

Spencer had known Killian for almost a year, and the two had developed a deep friendship. In fact, if it hadn't been for Killian, Spencer never would have stayed in this country, instead returning to his lonely life as a hotel executive in Singapore or perhaps retiring and settling back in the U.S. Even taking ownership of the Square One Bed & Breakfast would never have happened without Killian. Business licenses, visas, bank loans, you name it—none of it could have happened without Killian's assistance.

When Spencer first came to this village, his mental state was in a bad place. But, Killian, a mere stranger, had taken the time to know him and then, over the course of a few weeks, the time to help him see his life more clearly. Killian was a sage in a way, and he understood the nature of the frail human condition more than most, at least in Spencer's estimation. Yes, Killian, along with Shandy, had provided the impetus for Spencer to change who he was and who he would become.

Spencer tried to discount all he had just been told. He wrapped his hands tightly around the coffee cup, lost in thought and trying to discern whether Killian was on to something.

"Spencer, are you hearing me?" Killian said after letting some time pass.

"Yes, Killian, I heard you. I'm sure that's not the end of what's going on, so tell me the rest."

"Well, actually, that is the end of the story, at least for now," Killian said. "The young couple is still missing, of course, so this is all much more than a case of a deceased dog. The guards from Bruff have given way to a detective team from Limerick. I have on good authority they are in town presently and probably already out at the abbey as we speak.

"Things are being kept on the hush-hush for the time being. You know, no sense in getting people alarmed. But it won't be a secret for long. I imagine they'll be cordoning off the abbey before long. They probably would have done so yesterday, but with the Tractor Run happening I suppose they decided to hold off."

Spencer thought back to the car that had pulled into the abbey parking lot as he was departing. Killian was right. Those had to have been the detectives.

When Killian had finished relaying all the information he had, Spencer had nothing to cheer about, but he wasn't particularly alarmed either. He had found happiness in this land, and he meant to keep it. The past was the past, and that past when he first came to Galbally had been as warped as could be. He knew a repeat of the experience was next to impossible.

In the weeks spent a year back chasing a lost and dying dog, Spencer had gone through a lot of trials. On a few occasions he had more or less entered into a parallel universe that revealed things from this world and things that were not of this world.

More than once he had come face-to-face with a menacing entity that had been quite clear in its intention of bringing death to Shandy. The reason was not transparent, but the correlation had undoubtedly been the dog's cancer. In the normal world the Grim Reaper was only something of ghost tales, but Spencer had discovered, quite by accident, the thin overlap between reality and what lies beyond. The force was nothing he ever saw in a physical form, but of its presence there had been no mistake.

If Spencer had been alone each time, he would have chalked up the unnatural experiences to hallucinations or imagination, to visions brought on by the anxiety and the mental duress he had been under at the time. But Colin had been there, at least for parts, and they had experienced the unnatural together. The first time had been within the confines of Moor Abbey, and the last time in his car when Shandy passed away on the seat next to him. He would never forget the chilling air just after Shandy had taken her last breath.

Killian wrapped up telling all that he knew, and it was enough for Spencer.

"So, where do we go from here?" Spencer asked.

"If I knew that, I'd be a bit of a soothsayer, I would," Killian said, barely laughing at his tongue-in-cheek comment and trying his best to lighten the mood.

Spencer frowned. He was feeling restless and was ready to head home. He rose from his seat and walked over to the case that held the trophy brown trout. He had admired this fish since the very first day he had walked into the Grafton Pub. The case had been covered in dust that day, but today the glass surrounding it was spotless. Fifteen pounds and two ounces had made the trout the biggest ever taken from the nearby Suir River, but that was 1962, and Spencer was quite certain the record had been broken since then. He rubbed his hand over the case as he waited for Killian to finish what he had to tell.

"Honestly, I don't know," Killian continued. "We'll see what Dr. Mahir says first, and I'll try to keep apprised of anything the boys from Limerick come up with. They certainly won't be telling me anything directly, mind you, but you know I have my ways. For now, just go home and carry on as usual. There's nothing more we can do without additional information."

Spencer frowned again, his open palms sliding backward over the top of his head, as was his habit when he wasn't feeling quite right. He returned to the barstool and picked up his coffee cup, then set it back down without drinking the remaining contents. Spencer stared at the blank wall-mounted television set above Killian's head and sat quietly for several moments, as if contemplating the dark inanimate screen.

"Why don't you give me that Guinness after all," he said.

S pencer made his way out of the pub and was soon walking down the short distance of pavement toward his car. He looked up at the sky and felt the wetness of a weak rain that had just begun to fall. How appropriate, he thought. He immediately ran into an older couple he knew and exchanged pleasantries for a short time before getting back into the car.

He flipped a sharp U-turn and headed out of town in the same direction he had come. The rain picked up force, pelting the car's windshield, as he headed down the road toward Moor Abbey.

When he arrived near the monastery, he could see long lengths of blue and white tape fluttering in the breeze. One tape went from the far end of the parking lot to the other side, held in place in the middle by a metal pole that disappeared into a small mound of portable concrete squarely set on the ground. The entrance of the abbey showed another piece of tape strapped from one wall to the next. Around and behind the structure were the same.

The two men were there, dressed in black suits and with umbrellas poised above their heads. They intermingled with several uniformed officers dressed in raincoats, all of them taking turns talking to one person and another and pointing here and there. One patrol car and a white Garda van joined the blue sedan, which was now parked off to the right on a narrow road that paralleled the river and ran behind the abbey.

Where the police vehicles were stopped was the very road where Spencer, driving his car, had first seen Shandy as she sat across the way next to the picnic table. He had spotted her after an hour or two of unsuccessful fishing on the River Aherlow. She had been alone and undeniably lost or abandoned. He had noticed her by chance through the glass of his windshield after pulling up to a stop sign, and with her imploring eyes she had beckoned him to help her.

Against the odds and after hours of effort, Spencer had succeeded in finding a temporary home for her that day, at a farmhouse just outside the village, with a young woman and her two children. As he departed the house with the confirmation that the family would either keep the dog or find her a worthy home, Spencer was feeling good about himself, pleased to have acted the Good Samaritan. The dog had been cute and a good companion for a couple of hours, but he hadn't known her. He hadn't even cared about her that much. Besides, there had been fishing to be done, and the damn animal had interrupted his plans enough for one day.

Then something very peculiar happened. Spencer had gone back to Galbally, to the store where Colin was working, to wash up before getting on with the rest of his day. After he left the village, the road took him directly by the farmhouse where he had just left the dog twenty minutes earlier. And there she was, standing at the end of the gravel driveway, staring him down and burning her eyes into his as he drove past. She continued to watch him—and he her—until Spencer had driven out of sight. Her new, albeit temporary, owners were nowhere to be seen. Spencer had thought about stopping, thinking she might need help again, but he didn't want to take the chance of once again being burdened. Besides, she would be just fine.

Sure, it was likely just a coincidence that she had appeared in the driveway just as he was passing, but Spencer couldn't shake the image from his mind. He had thought about it endlessly throughout the rest of the day and into the next. What did it matter? He would never see that dog again anyway. But he would.

Two days later Spencer returned to the house, for reasons he couldn't truly comprehend or begin to explain. Peculiar became strange. The very same lady, the one with whom he had entrusted the care of the lost mongrel, opened the front door and greeted Spencer like she would any visitor. That's when the first real shock hit. Within thirty seconds of conversation, the young woman indicated, quite forcefully, that she had never met Spencer before and that certainly no dog resided in her home. Spencer was taken aback, really taken aback, and the words he needed to refute her claims wouldn't come. After all, he had no real evidence to prove anything from two days earlier. With the woman on the verge of calling her husband, or perhaps even the police, to get rid of this unsolicited stranger, Spencer had slunk away without putting up a fight.

And then peculiar became outrageous. A day or two later Spencer returned to the home, in a covert fashion and initially from a distance. He didn't know what he was going to do there, but he had to know what the hell was going on, why the woman had denied all that had occurred. He viewed the house for a good ten minutes from inside the safety of his parked car. When it seemed apparent that no one was home, he moved in for a closer look. With a quiet trepidation he performed a slow surveillance around the perimeter of the house, going window to window and everywhere in between. What he found was nothing, literally nothing. The house was completely empty: no curtains, no furniture, no trace of the place being inhabited. Cobwebs and dust covered all of the outside windowsills. The lawn surrounding the house hadn't been cut in weeks. The postal slot of the front door was stuffed and overflowing with flyers and other junk mail. The family had disappeared, as if they had never been there at all, and Shandy had disappeared with them.

Spencer had thought it plausible, even probable, that a family move-out had simply occurred the day before. However, a subsequent conversation later that day with the young Colin, who had done some investigative research of his own, had told him otherwise. The house was a rental, and no one had occupied it for the past six months.

There was no alternative but to suggest that Spencer had possibly and quite suddenly lost his mind. What other explanation could there be? He had been feeling mentally unwell for some time, for years and years and maybe longer. Perhaps he had finally succumbed to the rabbit hole he had known he would venture down one day.

He had gone to sleep that night convinced he was mad. When he awoke the next morning, however, for some unexplainable reason, he knew that wasn't the case. Something else was going on here. Hell, Colin could more or less verify everything that had happened between Spencer and the dog; he had that proof at least. Yes, something else was going on.

Spencer had never been a believer in the paranormal; he had never even given the subject much thought. But he became certain that he had now stumbled onto something not of this natural world. He wouldn't have called it an opportunity. He had no idea what it was. But he was certain that this little dog, which had appeared to him so quickly and so unexpectedly, came into this life for a reason. From that moment forward he determined that he would, one way or another, find the answer. And that is when the real adventure with Shandy had begun.

Spencer pulled the car into an open space across the main road that ran in front of the abbey, hoping to remain discreet and unnoticed. He rolled down the partially steamed-up window and stared at the vehicle of the disappeared couple. Spencer wasn't a devout man and had no interest in religion, but he had previously experienced a small dose of divine intervention on this very spot. Although he was fairly certain they would show up eventually, he said a silent prayer for the man and woman, just in case, just to be safe.

He studied the scene in front of him for a good fifteen minutes. As he did so he wondered again about the story Killian had just told him. Something bad had happened here, again, at this abbey. But he seriously doubted it had anything to do with him or Shandy.

Suddenly, an image of Angus flashed across his mind. Was there any chance the peculiar episode of yesterday had anything to do with this? Not likely, he surmised, but he should have mentioned the matter to Killian anyway. He'd do so later.

The rain let up briefly, just as he was about to leave and head back to Bansha. He stared up at the dark overcast sky, and within moments the birds appeared. Off in the distance behind the abbey, he could see the blackbirds departing from their nests hidden in the large deciduous trees. They filled the air, flying back and forth between the trees and the tower of the abbey. They perched high up in the tower's empty, dark windows, going in and flapping back out again, and then flying back to the trees. The scene was unsettling and one Spencer had seen before.

He rolled the car window up, pulled onto the road, and headed home. The rain began to unleash as he went.

CHAPTER FIVE

After Spencer left the Grafton, Killian stood behind the bar for several minutes, trying to make sense of things. His head was reeling, his mind racing. Over the years he learned to expect the unexpected. Maybe he was wrong this time. He hadn't convinced Spencer that trouble might wait ahead, but he had a feeling. He always trusted his feelings.

He refilled his coffee cup an inch or so from the top. From under the counter he grabbed his personal bottle of whiskey and gently topped off the cup until the liquid reached the brim. He sauntered around the end of the bar, walked half its length, and sat on the stool Spencer had been using. He sipped the contents of his drink and felt the warmth enter his system. He had some thinking to do and at least one phone call to make.

Killian had owned the Grafton Pub for thirty-one years, seven months, two weeks, and four days. He could likely even remember the number of hours if pressed. He had moved here to Galbally from Dublin to embark on a quieter existence, his own kind of premature mid-life crisis. He had brought his wife, young son, and daughter. That daughter was now married and had returned to Dublin, and that son was now a grown man, also married, and part owner of this establishment, although Killian still seemed to do the bulk of the work.

Galbally had been good to all of them, especially to Killian, who ranked as an unofficial elder in this community. He was well respected and the go-to man here when someone had a problem that needed fixing. In Ireland, not being a native of a particular small town or village can lead to a degree of non-acceptance for the newcomer. Killian had experienced the same here for a few years, but that was no longer true. He had proven his worth over and over again, and it didn't hurt that he had grown up in a village just a couple of counties away.

Running a pub naturally had helped Killian to find his place in Galbally. For some in this village, without Killian, they'd have no one else to listen to and provide potential solutions to their problems.

This life fit Killian to a tee. He thanked his lucky stars daily. His previous existence as a tax accountant in Dublin, something his domineering father had pushed him to pursue, had been nothing but misery. The professional interactions were infrequent, and the work was excruciatingly boring. Killian had spent most of his long mundane days stuck in a small, one-windowed office, pushing numbers from one section of a form to another.

During those years in Dublin, Killian had never felt as if he were making any contribution to society. And he hadn't been helping anyone, except his highbrowed corporate clients who cared about nothing, except saving—and making—money and scamming the government out of any tax revenue possible.

Killian was a people person, and he was most certainly not a pencil pusher. He knew back then that, at some point, he would have to make a change. He had always felt that his calling was in performing a service to others, something real, something that helped ordinary people. Many would have argued that owning and running a pub in a small village didn't fit the bill, but Killian knew otherwise. From the first day he saw the Grafton Pub, before he had purchased it, Killian knew this was where he belonged.

His family, especially his wife, had resisted at first, not wanting to give up the comfortable city life. But attitudes change over time. They all knew, then and now, that it had been the best decision for all of them. Once in Galbally, Killian transformed from a slightly grumpy, totally uninspired man to someone who affected, in a positive way, every life he touched.

Killian possessed a wide range of mental skills, and one of the most fascinating abilities, something known to few and never shown to anyone but the select-yet-random strangers who entered this pub and his life, was an uncanny sense, a sixth sense in a way, related to dogs. This competence wasn't something he had ever trained for or something he even knew he possessed until he became a bar owner. Over the years he had shared life with a fair number of his own dogs, but his canine-related stories never involved any of them. Rather, they involved peculiar occurrences originating from people, and their dogs, he did not know until they made themselves present to him.

The people he met were holidaymakers mostly, some foreigners, but the majority Irish. They brought with them tales and troubles and sometimes great personal anguish. All were searching for something; all were searching for answers. In common were this village, a dog, and a troubled soul or two. It was almost as if Galbally and the Grafton Pub—and Killian in particular—had some magical pull, something that drew people this way. He had never understood the reason why, and he couldn't explain it or even attempt to try.

Some of those who came had been helped by Killian, and some hadn't, at least while they were here. What happened after they left, Killian generally didn't know. But Spencer, Spencer—he had been different. His otherworld experience with the dog named Shandy provided something Killian had never seen or experienced before. The first time Spencer had entered his pub, Killian could tell the man wasn't right. Yes, he was personable, courteous, and even self-assured to a point. Still, the cloud of gloom that hung over his head was telling, and Killian knew a lot about gloom.

Most might not have seen the hidden emotion in Spencer, but to Killian it was obvious. He knew then Spencer was a man in need of guidance, although the story didn't unfold right away or in a manner Killian had expected.

Only after several meetings did Spencer reveal his true self to Killian. Over the course of conversations, it became clear Spencer was one mentally distraught, depressed, and anxious man. No one would have called him crazy because he didn't readily show or give any clues to what he was feeling inside. And he wasn't crazy at all but rather simply lost and alone. Spencer was someone who had gone through life surviving but never living. The litany of reasons was a long list, most of which Spencer shared with Killian over time: a messed-up childhood, a personality disorder or two, lack of purpose in life, a deceased wife, poor relations with his children, and most importantly an existence not well performed. At the end of the day, he was just a desperate man living a life of quiet desperation.

Before Killian had learned most of the details of Spencer's unhappy life, the narrative with Shandy had already begun to unfold. The beginning was not much, the innocent occurrence of a stranger in a strange land picking up a stray dog and rescuing her. That, in turn, had become a vanished dog that would reappear again and again, but only to Spencer (and to young Colin when he was with him). The episodes had grown in intensity each time and soon included a spirit—or something akin to a spirit—that had aspirations that soon became all too clear.

Killian had never met a man so determined and intent as Spencer. Chasing a dog with which he had no real relationship did make Spencer seem a bit on the crazy side, but Killian had known there was a reason. His relationship with the dog Shandy soon had Spencer hoping—more than realizing—that Shandy had come into his life with a purpose, and there was no stopping the lengths he would go to find out why, even with the clarity that his own life was possibly in peril. Deep despair can be funny that way. Why stop when the alternative is a return to normalcy, a normalcy that offered little and that was meant for those who give up too easily?

As Spencer had chased Shandy other events also began to take hold, seemingly unrelated but all part of the master plan meant for the man. Killian could sense the connection soon enough, but Spencer had taken until the very end to understand.

First off, Spencer had become the target of suspicious locals, mistakenly convinced he had designs on young Colin in a way a grown man should not. At the same time a one-night accommodation in Dublin before Spencer had come this way turned into an unwanted association with criminal elements who were determined in their own right. The two unbelievably culminated on the same dark night, just after Spencer had given up hope of finding Shandy and just before he intended to leave this place for good. He was subjected to not one but two physical altercations that rightly could have and perhaps should have killed him. A stay in the hospital and several days and then weeks of recovery had been his reward for surviving.

But dying that October evening had not been Spencer's destiny. The night had been one more piece of the puzzle that had finally led Spencer to find what he had been seeking. And, later on, the realization of what was meant for him came only moments before he was, once again, preparing to leave this village forever. The hard knocks suffered here produced a blissful ending and a new life for Spencer. Not so much for the pitiful Shandy, but she had performed her duty just as she was supposed to, saving a lost man from a life unlivable.

Killian took another deep gulp from his whiskey-laced coffee and set the cup on the countertop. Immediately, the cell phone next to him vibrated. He picked it up, his heart racing with anticipation.

"Hello, Kevin," Killian spoke into the phone with slight trepidation. "Sorry you're having to work on a Sunday. Have you finished up already?"

"Good day, Killian," the vet said. "Yes, the guards were quite persuasive about me getting this done today. I made a point of getting in early this morning and finished an hour ago. There's not much to tell you, unfortunately."

"What do you mean?" Killian asked.

"I spent more time than I generally would on this one. Thought I should, you know, with the guards being involved and all. Covered her from top to bottom and everywhere in between. I can't find a damn thing wrong with the dog."

"Then how'd she die?"

"No idea," Dr. Mahir responded. "I suppose I would classify it as natural causes. That's certainly what I'll write in my report."

Killian was surprised, but he wasn't. Now he was certain something truly was amiss.

"Okay, Kevin, I understand, although I don't. How can a perfectly healthy dog just up and die all of a sudden? There must be more."

"As I said, I don't know, Killian. If I had more to tell you, I would. You know that. And by the way, are you gonna tell me why you've taken such a grand interest in this dog? Things are happening around here, with the Garda being in town, and you seem to know more of the details than I do."

Killian stared silently at the phone before speaking again.

"It's a long story. One I'd rather not discuss right at this moment. Maybe some other time. Maybe over a drink here at the pub. But I do appreciate your letting me know. If anything changes, you'll be sure to give me a call, please."

"Sure thing," the vet said. "Killian, make sure you keep this to yourself and only yourself. I could be in a fair bit of trouble if the guards got wind of our discussion. I'll be giving them a ring as soon as I'm off the line with you."

"Of course," Killian said. "Mum's the word. I'm much obliged, Kevin."

Killian pushed the screen to disconnect the call, and he set the phone on the counter and stared at the device for a few moments. He grabbed the whiskey bottle, screwed off the cap, and poured a small amount more into his cup.

He hesitated to call Spencer with the news. The man had truly been through so much here, and now there was the possibility—maybe even the probability—that more was destined to come.

In the meantime some things needed doing. Killian called his wife and told her he wouldn't be having lunch at home. He grabbed his jacket and an umbrella and began the fifteen-minute walk to Moor Abbey.

CHAPTER SIX

The vehicle slowly motored up the short distance of gravel road that acted as the entrance to the Square One B&B. The gravel and dirt transitioned to asphalt pavement in front of the house, and Spencer headed for his usual parking space along the west side. Mrs. O'Donnell had just backed up her car and was heading in the opposite direction, her morning duties likely done for the day. Spencer threw up his hand to wave as she passed by and got the slightest hint of a smile in return—it was always difficult to read the woman's emotions and facial expressions.

Spencer got out of the car and hit the door-lock button on the key fob. There was no reason for locking the vehicle because this was one of the safest places he had ever lived. Old habits die slowly. He quietly slid through the front door of the house and began climbing the stairs in the direction of his bedroom. Before he was halfway up, paws and claws could be heard scrambling for traction on the wooden floor below. Spencer turned around, and within seconds his golden retriever was bulleting up the stairs toward him.

Buster always seemed to brighten his mood, regardless of the circumstances, and today was no different. Buster had already been several months old when Spencer purchased him from a breeder who lived nearby. Now that the dog was almost a year old, he was close to reaching his full adult height. He was still rather lean though and mentally he maintained much of his puppy attitude.

Choosing Buster's name had been easy for Spencer. When he was still quite a young boy and into his college years, his family had raised a total of three dogs named Buster. The first was a black lab, the middle a golden retriever, and the last a border collie.

The middle Buster had always been Spencer's favorite, a dog he had loved with all of his heart. When the time came for Spencer to decide on his latest dog, the breed and the name were a no-brainer. He couldn't be happier with his choice.

"Hey, buddy. Yes, I see you," Spencer said as he scooped Buster's face into his hands. "Stay down now. We really got to teach you not to jump up on people."

Spencer took a seat on one of the carpeted steps and let Buster show his affections. The dog settled down after a few seconds and nestled his face into Spencer's chest and held it there while Spencer gently rubbed Buster's head with his right hand.

His nose soon let him know something wasn't right, and Spencer performed a couple of quick confirmation sniffs of his hands and shirt. *My God, what a stink!* Buster unburied his head and gave Spencer a quick lick across the chin before scrambling down the stairs and in the direction from where he had come.

"Erica, you down there?"

"Yes, Dad," a voice echoed from down the first-floor hallway.

She rounded the corner of the stairwell and stood in front of Spencer, Buster at her side.

"I didn't hear you come in," Erica said, looking up at her father. "How was your meeting with Killian? Anything interesting to report?"

"No, it was nothing really," Spencer said. "He just needs some help with a small project he's working on. Nothing that important."

He knew his little white lie was likely unconvincing, but he didn't care at this moment.

"Buster smells like he's been to a maggot fest inside a dead cow," Spencer said. "He needs a bath in the worst way."

"That's a bit of an exaggeration, but I haven't lost my sense of smell, Dad. He must have been out rolling in something. I'll take him outside as soon as I'm finished with the laundry. And once the rain has completely stopped."

Spencer looked at the dog and playfully admonished him. "Buster, quit rolling in shit, you mangy mutt!"

Buster cocked his head sideways, giving Spencer that inquisitive look dogs often do.

"But I still love you," Spencer said, patting the dog on the head. He focused again on Erica.

"You know, I'm beginning to think Buster likes you more than me."

"I suppose we do get along pretty well," Erica said sheepishly, "but you'll always be his number one. You know that. He sure is smart though. I'm amazed how quickly he picks things up when we're out in the morning."

"Yep, he's a keeper, for sure. What's on the docket this afternoon?"

"Just finished servicing the two rooms, and the laundry's halfway done," Erica said. "No one else arriving until tomorrow, so we can take it easy the rest of the day. Why don't you get out fishing again?"

Spencer liked the idea and thought the solace might provide the right environment to get his head straight.

"Yeah, maybe I will," he said. "I've got a few things to take care of first."

"The rain's supposed to be done soon, so you should go," Erica said. "Anyway, I'll make us a late lunch in a half hour or so, if you haven't eaten already."

"No, I haven't, and that sounds great. Just give me a holler. I'll be up in my room."

Spencer climbed the remainder of the stairs to his room. Once there, he sat on the foot of the queen-size bed. His shoes flew off, and he lay back, his feet dangling over the edge and just barely touching the floor. The palms of his hands rubbed back and forth over his closed eyes for a few moments. He stared at the white plaster of the ceiling above him.

Maybe Killian was right—maybe he should tell Erica about all that had happened to him here in Ireland when he first came. Except for the occasional fond remembrances of Shandy, he had essentially put it all behind him and hardly gave those particular matters a thought anymore. Things were better that way.

Killian hadn't said it directly this morning, but the insinuation was clear to Spencer. In Killian's mind the dead dog and the missing couple were, in some way, connected to Shandy. If they were, in fact, related to Shandy, then the possibilities ran deep, deep enough to consider that something evil from the past could be making an encore presentation. Not likely, Spencer told himself once again. Not likely, but possible. After all, he had been there. He had seen it all. It was possible.

But if there were even the slightest chance he would have to resurrect the experiences of the past, at least at some level, he knew it would interfere with his life, and Erica's. He wondered how much longer she would stay here. They had only casually discussed the subject. As far as he was concerned, she could stay as long as she wanted.

Erica's showing up in Ireland three months earlier had been unanticipated. She had remained the most distant from Spencer after her mother's death from cancer two years before. She had been a college student at the time. After the funeral she never visited Spencer in Singapore again. Instead, she had spent all of her time in Ann Arbor, studying, working odd jobs, and essentially fending for herself.

Even before her mother's death, Erica had always been the most distant child. She was considerably younger than her siblings and quite unlike them, at least back then. While her sister and brother were both gregarious and outgoing, Erica had been demure and borderline anti-social. They were into sports and clubs, while Erica had been into books and studying. Her personality had been obstinate and generally rebellious. That attitude had extended to her family, her teachers, and even her friends, of whom there hadn't been many.

She hadn't gotten along with anyone in the family except for her mother. Being the youngest sometimes lends itself to that advantage, and Erica had taken full advantage. Spencer's wife, Naomi, had doted on Erica like nobody's business. She could do no wrong and had always been the winner in any squabble with her sister or brother, or even with Spencer.

Spencer recalled an incident when Erica was only six or seven and the family was living in Canada. He had chastised her for not completing a household chore. Erica became so upset that she threatened to run away. Her mother was absent for the day, so Spencer decided a lesson needed to be taught. After she stated for the third time that she was indeed running away, Spencer obliged her. He even packed her a lunch and snacks for the road, and he stuffed the contents into her pink backpack. He opened the front door and told her it was time to leave, that she would be happier in a world out there where everyone understood her.

Erica's defiance got the better of her, and out the door she went, her backpack over her shoulders and an expression of "you'll be sorry" on her angry little face. She headed down the street, went a couple of blocks, and stopped at a city park. There, below the shade of a tall cottonwood tree, she broke out her lunch. When she was done she took out her favorite Harry Potter book and read for the next two hours while sipping on a container of fruit juice. Spencer and the other two children took turns watching her from a distance, making certain they were out of sight and that she was all right.

When Erica grew weary of her new life on the road, she threw her book back into her backpack and soon walked through the front door of the house as if nothing had happened. When her mother came home that evening, the tears and sobbing wasted no time in coming as Erica informed Mom of how Spencer had thrown her out of the house and that she had only returned because she knew her mother couldn't live without her. Spencer, of course, ended up catching hell from his wife.

But Erica had matured now, and the change was evident. Though still strong-willed and opinionated, she was no longer the rebel she once was. She was definitely not a people person, but she could hold her own in a social context when and if she had to. To Spencer, none of that mattered. He was simply happy to have her back after all of these years of uncomfortable silence and contrived interaction between the two of them. And she had become a blessing when it came to the Square One B&B.

Although Spencer had always been a businessman, running a bed and breakfast was something outside his bailiwick. Sure, Mrs. O'Donnell's cooking skills filled a need in that department, but he couldn't count on her to assist with all the other work that needed to be done. He also couldn't do everything on his own, and that's where Erica came in. She had graduated from university last spring and had been somewhat disinclined to begin looking for a full-time job.

An idea presented itself, and, with some cajoling and persuasion, Spencer finally convinced Erica that a summer in Ireland might be something beneficial to the both of them.

Yes, the fact was Spencer didn't want Erica to leave. Her being here had become his crowning achievement so far, one of many steps, some accomplished and some not, in reconnecting with his children, and Spencer didn't want to do anything to upset the delicate balance.

Spencer made up his mind. Although he thought the dead dog and missing couple were likely nothing and would blow over soon, there was a chance things could progress. He should tell Erica of his past here in Ireland, about the story with Shandy. The father-and-daughter relationship had become quite strong, and he didn't want to keep secrets.

Spencer sat at the small table in the kitchen and watched while Erica stirred a long wooden spoon in the pot, steam rising to the vent above. She portioned the soup into a bowl for each of them, reached over to the frying pan, and flipped the sandwiches one more time.

She was making an old family lunch favorite: tomato soup and cream crackers with grilled cheese sandwiches. He hadn't eaten this particular meal in what seemed forever, and the scene brought back memories of Erica's mother and his family. This had been one meal they could all agree on—no vegetables really or other contrarian ingredients one of the kids would complain about.

"Wow, I haven't had this for so long," Spencer said as Erica set the bowls and plates on the table.

"It's very simple, but I thought you might like it," Erica said. "There are a lot of things Mom used to make I remember. I even have some of her old recipes that I keep in a folder and take with me everywhere."

"Your mother was an excellent cook," Spencer said and went silent for a few moments.

Erica sat down across from her father, and they conversed about this and that until their bowls and plates were empty. Spencer sneaked Buster, who had been patiently lying and waiting on the floor below, a large piece of crust as he finished his meal. Spencer smiled as Buster's tongue wrapped around his mouth and nose, making certain not a crumb had been missed. The dog rose to his feet, seeing whether his master had any additional offerings.

Buster's unpleasant essence made another attack on Spencer's nostrils. He looked through the kitchen's four-pane window to see the rain had ceased. *Good, bath time.*

"Thanks, Erica," Spencer said, lifting a napkin to wipe the corners of his mouth. "Just as good as I remember. Listen, there's something I'd like to discuss with you if the rest of the laundry—and Buster's bath—can wait for a while."

"Sure, Dad. What is it?"

Spencer started at the start and ended at the end. He told Erica of his chance encounter with a small stray dog and the adventure that ensued. He told her of the involvement of Killian and Colin. He told her of the local thugs who had beaten him up. He told her about the other man named Owen, not a local but a thug nevertheless, and how he most likely would have killed Spencer if not for Shandy appearing out of nowhere and forcing the man away.

When he told Erica of Shandy's death, Spencer struggled to keep his composure, stretching his face every ten seconds or so to make certain the tears didn't release. He hadn't talked about the tragic ending for quite some time, if ever.

On that day, after weeks of trying and never quite being able to get his hands on the dog, Spencer had essentially given up. He was to leave Galbally the next day and return to Singapore, where his self-described pathetic life would resume in full force. He had taken his car to Moor Abbey for a final trip down memory lane. Though it hadn't been his intention, he fell asleep in the car soon after finishing his lunch. He dreamed of things that could have been and a dog that had become his.

When Spencer awoke from his slumber, to his utter amazement, Shandy appeared across the road in front of the abbey. He had no idea how long she had been there. She was playing with some schoolchildren in the picnic area, dodging them as they chased after her. Soon she was sitting quietly and staring directly at Spencer from the other side. The word *coincidence* was no longer part of Spencer's vocabulary, and he realized that she was there for him. The reason, of course, was not known. Maybe a final goodbye before Spencer left Ireland forever? He wondered how she could have possibly known, but then again she had always seemed to be a step or two ahead of him.

A few moments later Shandy did act out her final goodbye, but the farewell was not a kind one. Before Spencer could stop her, Shandy ran to him, across the road and directly into the screeching tires of a passing sports car. The accident was an accident, at least to the eyes of those who saw the scene, but Spencer knew differently. Shandy's time had come, and the Grim Reaper had performed its duty as required.

Finally, and most importantly, Spencer told Erica of a spirit or ghost—likely the same Grim Reaper that had taken Shandy—that had come along for the ride and had shown its displeasure, more than once, in Spencer's interference with the runaway dog. The instances were not that many, but they had been enough. Spencer had wandered into a world where he didn't belong. But that was long ago now, and Shandy was long gone as well. Spencer couldn't begin to fathom, regardless of Killian's suspicions, why the ghost, or any ghost, would be making a return visit.

When he was done, he breathed a sigh of relief. He felt mentally and emotionally exhausted, for he hadn't thought about the entirety of this story in a long time, and he had never relayed the tale to another person.

"Dad, that's frickin' unbelievable!" Erica said. "Why haven't you told me anything about this before?"

"Honestly, in a way I guess I've been trying to forget about it all," Spencer said. "Besides, Colin, Killian, and I promised it would forever remain a secret among the three of us. I'm sorry, Erica, maybe I should have told you earlier."

"I have so many questions," Erica said. She seemed so excited in this tale of mystery and suspense. "Maybe the first is what really happened to Shandy? You said she visited you one last time, but then what?"

"I have no idea. I'm not even certain she was here," Spencer said. "Maybe it was simply my imagination or a hallucination. I don't know. I mean, I saw her die with my own eyes months before; I held her in my arms after she died. What came back to visit me that last time was just a fantasy or it was Shandy's ghost or I don't know what. It was such a strange thing, but maybe I accepted it for what it was. I was just happy to see her again."

"Do you believe what I have told you?" Spencer continued.

"I guess so," said Erica. "It's a pretty wild story, but it's not like something you could make up. Does all of this relate to your meeting with Killian this morning?"

"Yes, it might be related in a way," Spencer said.

He went on to explain what Killian had shared with him earlier this day. He also made it clear he wasn't entirely convinced about Killian's concerns.

"What exactly does Killian think might happen?" Erica asked.

"I don't know. We never really got that far in our discussion. I guess that maybe the ghost will or has returned."

"Oh, Dad, that's ridiculous!" she said, rolling her eyes just enough Spencer couldn't miss the reaction. "Do you really think some spirit would just show up out of the blue again? What for?"

"I don't know why, Erica," Spencer said. "But I can tell you what I went through before wasn't a whole lot of fun."

"So you believe in ghosts," Erica said, "that just come and go as they please?"

"I don't know what I believe. I'm just telling you what happened. Do you...believe in ghosts?"

"No, Dad, I don't," she said, but Spencer didn't miss the hesitancy before she answered.

Spencer was beginning to regret having told her anything at all. The adventure he had experienced with Shandy was implausible at best and utterly ridiculous at its worst. His tale was not one anybody would share lightly, unless that person wanted to be classified as mentally unstable or worse.

"Listen, Erica, I know this is all pretty hard to take in, but it is what it is for now. I think Killian's concerns are way overblown and that this will turn out to be nothing at all."

Spencer hesitated for a moment. He was reluctant, but he had to throw out the option and at least give her a choice.

"If things get bad for one reason or another, maybe we should consider heading back to the States, you at least."

"You know that's not going to happen," Erica said calmly yet defiantly. "We have no idea if there's anything going on, so why would I leave? Besides, I like it here, and there's no place for me to go anymore."

That last part was true. After Erica's mother passed away, Spencer moved into a smaller apartment in Singapore. The small abode had become non-essential when Spencer hung his future and fortune on this new life in Ireland. This was the only home Erica had.

"Okay," Spencer said reluctantly. "Just promise me you'll agree to leave if things get out of hand."

"Yes, I'll leave once I'm in mortal danger and some ghost starts chasing me around," Erica said with just the right touch of sarcasm.

Spencer let the comment pass and helped his daughter put things back in the refrigerator. He began filling the sink with hot water and dish soap, walked to the table, and began removing the plates and bowls.

"Let me do the dishes, and then I think I'll take your advice and do a little fishing this afternoon," Spencer said.

"That's a good idea, Dad. I'd say you need it."

Spencer didn't know if the last quip was another dose of veiled sarcasm, and he didn't care much. She might find out soon enough. Then again, maybe not. Maybe he was overthinking things. The dead dog in itself didn't necessarily mean much, and the couple was simply missing at this point. Hopefully, they'd turn up soon. Then this could all be put to rest.

He gave Erica a peck on the forehead and watched as she and Buster walked down the hall to the laundry room.

Thirty minutes later from the window of her bedroom on the second story of the house, Erica peered through the dirty frame of glass as her father headed down the well-worn trail on his way to the River Ara. He was decked out in his angling gear, with his fishing rod resting on his right shoulder as he walked. She had finished the laundry, and now she required a little time to think.

Buster's bath would have to wait until later because, in a first, Spencer was allowing the dog to accompany him on a fishing excursion. Erica wondered why. As she watched, the dog veered off the path constantly, dashing in and out of the grass on each side in search of any movement, sound, or smell that would delight the senses.

Buster was still young, and both Erica and Spencer knew keeping him out of the water when the fishing started was likely foolhardy. But Erica sensed her father wasn't overly interested in catching fish this afternoon. More likely, he just needed to get out of the house and into nature. She had learned that when Spencer was troubled, he either sat on the porch with a beer or a cup of coffee or he headed to the river or to the mountains.

Erica was still trying to wrap her head around the tales Spencer had shared a short while before. The whole thing seemed pretty outrageous, and she questioned how much of the story was factual and how much was her father's imagination or perhaps his misinterpretation of reality.

Over the last weeks Spencer had begun sharing a lot with her. One item of discussion was a confession of his terrible mental state at the time he had first come to Ireland. He told her of his protracted depression and his inability to come to terms with or make sense of his life. He told her how he had felt so lost and unable to conquer any of his demons. But until today he had never told her about Shandy and the dog's role in this new life.

How much of today's conversation was accurate, and how much was related to a psychological condition that perhaps wasn't fully resolved yet? Spencer had just admitted some of his experiences with Shandy might have been his imagination. What other parts of the story had he imagined?

She decided to give credence to both. If there were more to all of this, more to come, she would believe when her eyes convinced her. She promised herself that one day soon she would talk to Killian, check his side of the story. She hated to doubt her father, but she needed to know more.

She considered things further. Spencer was certainly not the type of guy to make things up or even embellish anything. She knew that much, at least. He had a lot of faults—or he did have—but lack of honesty just wasn't one of them. This all seemed so difficult to reconcile.

Yes, this story of Shandy was out of this world by anyone's standards, but Erica was intrigued. Although she generally kept the subject to herself, she had always had a casual fascination with the supernatural, parallel universes, alien life, and anything else not part of this static world that seemed so mundane at times. After all, she had been an avid reader her entire life, with ghost and horror tales being a favorite genre. She glanced at the collection of Edgar Allen Poe short stories that rested on her nightstand and gently touched the book with her fingertips. She turned back to the window to watch her father and Buster round a corner and disappear.

Maybe her dad was okay, and maybe he wasn't. Regardless, her coming here was one of the best decisions she had ever made. The last few months with her father in Ireland had begun filling a void in her life that had been eating her up inside since her mother had passed away. Growing up, her father had been present, but in her opinion, and that of her sister and brother, he had never been what he should have been. He seemed to take only a passing interest in family life, always finding an excuse to put his job or something else first. He had provided well, and, in some ways, she and her siblings had a childhood that most can only dream about. But theirs had not been a family in the true sense. Wasted years perhaps, but time was still available to all of them, except to her mother.

As the summer began to wane, with autumn just around the corner, Erica had grown much closer to Spencer. Their late-night discussions had been eye-opening and something she, and he, had needed. They conversed about life and dreams and things of the past.

And one of those topics was something very close to Erica's heart. She had always known, even with all of his shortcomings, that Spencer had loved her mother. Perhaps he hadn't always shown that love like he should have, but Erica knew it had been real. She just didn't realize how strong it had truly been and how strong it still was. Their conversations had slowly revealed a man she hadn't known, a man who was as devastated by losing his wife as she and her siblings were in losing their mother.

What had she done when all of that had been happening? She had more or less completely blown Spencer off, paying no heed to the fact that he might have been suffering as much as she had. Her older sister and her older brother had done the same. She realized they had all left their father alone, alone to deal with his emotions and sorrows by himself. She was determined to make amends.

She could see that her father was a changed man, a man who had mostly and finally found himself. And Ireland was responsible, and Killian and Colin, and perhaps a small dog named Shandy.

She would wait and see about their discussion of earlier today. She would give Spencer the benefit of the doubt regarding the Shandy story, some of it, but she felt quite assured the idea of an evil spirit returning was unfounded. Things like that don't happen in the real world or in real life. She liked reading about other worlds, but her interest began and ended there.

Regardless of what happens, she would stay here with Spencer until all was well and good, and she might not leave at all.

As expected, the first fishing expedition with Buster had not turned out well, but it hadn't been a total failure either. Sure, the dog had had a lot of fun, but busting through the water before Spencer even had a chance to cast his line had not been conducive to catching fish. After an hour or so and a few sharp reprimands, however, Buster began to settle down and allowed Spencer to approach the last few deep pools without any hindrance.

The fish, however, weren't biting today and the water not clear as a result of the earlier rains. The big brown trout Spencer had taken this morning was nowhere to be seen. After a final unproductive cast Spencer waded back through the knee-level depth of the river to where Buster was patiently waiting on the bank. He tousled the dog's head, and Buster took that as a cue he was free once again to roam where he pleased.

Spencer watched as Buster jumped into the water once, came back out, and then shook himself partially dry. The dog quickly began an ascent up the hill. Spencer followed up the steep bank, reached the top, and began disassembling his four-piece fishing rod. When he had completed the task he called out to Buster, who had already disappeared into a grove of deciduous trees, and together they began walking down the trail toward home.

Being out here on the river had calmed Spencer's anxiety somewhat, but what was on his mind was still on his mind. He thought back to his conversation with Killian and wondered again where this was all headed. He tried to recall everything about his brief encounters with the spirit that had haunted him during his chase of Shandy. The element he remembered the most was how the air had always chilled whenever the spirit was near, or when he assumed it was near. The cold air had never lasted long, never more than a few seconds, but the ungodly presence of something sinister was never in doubt.

Spencer and Buster rounded a bend in the trail, its path still next to the river and sitting above a length of conifers that ran parallel. Between them and the trees ran a fence line that belonged to a nearby farmer. Spencer had long since made friends with all of his neighbors, and he was free to wander where he liked when out on his fishing excursions.

There was always a fence to cross here and there, and many were single strands of electric fence that were easy enough to lift a leg to get over. Buster, of course, went under them and had learned, through the course of a few unpleasant shocks, to proceed with caution. The fence today, however, was a more traditional one, with four strands of barbed wire running horizontally and connected to solid wooden posts every ten yards or so.

Since he had been fishing the River Ara and since living in this area, Spencer had come across an occasional squirrel, especially in places where deciduous trees predominated. Today, however, as he and Buster walked next to the fence line, was a sight Spencer had never come across in his life, not here, not anywhere.

About twenty yards ahead Spencer could see something hanging from the top wire strand of the fence. He couldn't make it out at first. As he drew near he realized he was looking at a gray squirrel. His eyes fixated on the target ahead, and he walked forward. What he was now seeing was one of the strangest things he had ever encountered: The animal was there all right, but it was no longer among the land of the living. Spencer grabbed a small stick from the ground, and with the end of it he gently poked at the hanging and still squirrel.

What had happened was evident. A barb from the wire was squarely and securely lodged in the loose belly skin of the squirrel. A smattering of crimson red darkened the off-white fur where the knife-like protrusion had made its mark. The animal had probably been tight-roping the wire when one misstep caused a small slip and then a sharp grabbing poke in the abdomen that left the squirrel hanging upside down with no way back up and no way to dislodge itself from the small piece of iron that had secured its fate.

Spencer looked at the squirrel's eyes, one a normal dark color and the other already glossed over. He examined the squirrel's paws and could see the small traces of blood that stained them. The body was still fresh, and Spencer could only surmise that the unfortunate incident had happened earlier today or during the previous night at the latest.

Buster could see the subject of his master's attention. He began jumping up, trying to get at the deceased animal, and Spencer gave him a sharp smack on the head. This squirrel had likely suffered enough, and now it hardly deserved to be unceremoniously eaten by a curious canine. Buster whined and agitated, but he knew enough by now of Spencer's various demeanors to stay down when he was told.

Spencer examined the squirrel further, considering what a terrible ending it must have had, squirming and trying so hard to right itself before things were too late, its tiny paws clawing at the exposed underbelly in a desperate attempt to get free. Spencer wondered what had killed the animal. Maybe it had hung upside down too long and the blood rushing to its head caused something along the lines of aneurysm? Maybe from exhaustion? Maybe from fright? He had no idea. All he could think about was how pathetic the death must have been.

"Jeepers-creepers, Buster, this isn't something you see every day," Spencer said. The dog's gaze alternated quickly between Spencer and the hanging squirrel.

But why see this today of all days? Why see something today that I've never seen before? Spencer considered these questions briefly. He had no answers.

He pulled out and put on a pair of thin gloves he carried in his backpack and gingerly removed the squirrel from the barb. He gently placed the animal on the ground. Buster whined in the background, but one focused stare from Spencer kept the dog at a distance.

Spencer picked up a bigger, sturdier stick and began digging a hole in the soft, rain-soaked ground next to the fence. When it was deep enough, he placed the squirrel's body in the hollow space, lightly touched the small varmint on its head, and covered the hole with the same soil he had dug up. He stood and stamped the dark earth with his shoe. He stared at the fresh dirt for several minutes.

Spencer did a quick look around in all directions and headed down the trail with Buster at his side.

CHAPTER SEVEN

After leaving the pub Killian arrived by foot at Moor Abbey and observed what he imagined Spencer must have seen a short while before: long lengths of blue and white tape fluttering and a half dozen police officers milling about the perimeter of the monastery. Killian's mind was set, and this was his village. He was determined to find out what was going on with the dead dog and the missing couple.

Galbally had no police force of its own and was under the jurisdiction of the nearby and larger town of Bruff. The guards from Bruff visited Galbally once or twice a week, or when they had to, and Killian was well acquainted with a couple of the regular officers. He could talk with them if nothing else.

The heavier rain from just minutes earlier was barely discernible now, coming down in only the slightest of sprinkles. Killian closed his umbrella and casually strolled over to the two fellas he knew. The usual pleasantries were exchanged, a quick conversation ensued, and Killian exited with little more information than he had going in. Undeterred, he decided to focus his attention on the detectives from Limerick.

Killian had a knack for getting people to reveal details they normally wouldn't, and he still held out hope that today would be no exception. He glanced over at the two suited men. One was on his mobile phone. The other stood in front of the abbey, scribbling into a small pocket notebook. Killian picked his target and walked over to the second man.

"Good afternoon to ya," Killian said to the man while reaching out his hand. "My name's Killian, and I run the Grafton Pub down in the village."

The detective reluctantly took Killian's hand and gave it a cursory shake.

"You know, you shouldn't be here. This area is cordoned off for a reason," the man said with a slight tinge of annoyance in his voice.

"Yes, I'm sorry," Killian said, "but I'm as close as we've got in this village to a guard, and I thought I should see what's going on here."

"That may be," the detective said gruffly. "Still, this is official Garda business, and you shouldn't be here. And you're certainly not a guard."

Ouch! Killian knew he had to play his cards right or he would end up leaving here with nothing at all. He sized up the young detective momentarily, admiring his clean-cut image of stylish dress, short-cut dark hair, and a slender but solid build. The air of confidence the man projected could not be denied, and Killian was certain he would be a tough nut to crack.

"Listen, this is a small village, and people are wondering what's going on," Killian said. "I mean, you can't set up a crime scene, or whatever this is, and not expect that rumors won't be a flying. Besides, I have some details that might be of interest to you."

"And what might that be, Mr....?" the detective said. "What did you say your surname was?"

"I didn't, but it's Conner, Killian Conner."

"So, Mr. Conner, just what is it you think you have to share with me?"

"For one thing I know there's been a dead dog, and I know there's a missing couple. The fact is that the two of them were in my pub a day or two before they disappeared. I may have been the last person to see them."

Immediately, Killian realized he might have just made himself a suspect of some sort, assuming the guards were looking for one.

"And may I ask how you know there's a dead dog and a missing couple, assuming that's the case?" the man said, now considerably more interested in talking to Killian.

"As I said, it's a small village here," Killian said.

As the detective again began to speak, a distant voice, someone yelling in their direction, could be heard off to their right and up ahead in the vicinity of the river. The detective turned and walked away from Killian while dislodging a black walkie-talkie from a leather holder attached to his belt.

Killian could only pick up bits and pieces from the discussion, but clearly something had been discovered down by the river.

The detective finished his conversation and immediately took off in the direction of the River Aherlow. After a few steps he suddenly turned back to Killian.

"You stay right here, Mr. Conner. I'll need to talk to you some more when I return."

"Why? What's all the fuss about?" Killian asked.

"Again, this is not of your concern. And on second thought, you need to vacate the area. Just leave your name and number with the officer over there," the detective said, pointing to one of the men Killian knew. "We'll be needing to talk to you at some point."

Killian watched as the man headed in the direction of the stream. He was soon followed by most of the others. Killian waited for them all to clear and walked over to his acquaintance, the lone remaining officer.

"Jimmy, I'm to give you my name and number, according to the detective, but you know how to get a hold of me. Must be something going on seeing how everyone cleared out of here in such a hurry. What's happening?"

"Wish I knew, but I'm left in the cold as usual," Jimmy said. "I suppose that's the price for being the rookie on the team. They said, 'Someone's got to guard the fort,' as if anything's going to happen at this miserable old abbey. We've already checked every nook and cranny of this place."

"What are you really doing down here anyway, Killian?" Jimmy continued.

"It's like I told you earlier," Killian said. "Just heard the guards had set up shop and was wondering what's going on. I know about the dead dog, but the guards don't send detectives to investigate dog murders, if that's what it was. What else is going on, Jimmy?"

"Killian, you know I'm not at liberty to discuss such things," Jimmy said. "Let's just say it's much more than a dead dog, all right."

"What's that supposed to mean?" Killian asked. He felt he might be getting somewhere.

"Your charm is not going to work on me today," Jimmy said. "I haven't told you much, but probably more than I should have. Leave it at that would ya, please."

Killian frowned inside, but he kept his usual composure.

Other than to Spencer and to the detective a few minutes before, Killian hadn't told anyone that the missing couple had been in his pub the evening before they had disappeared. He had thought he had the upper hand, but it was apparent Jimmy wouldn't be giving up anything today. No worries, Killian thought. There are other ways.

"I see," said Killian. "And I understand. No sense in getting yourself into hot water on my account. Think I'll head back to the pub and clean up a bit. I imagine I'll be getting a call from your detective friend in a day or two. I never did get his name—not the friendliest type, he isn't."

"His name is Detective Walsh. He's all right once you get to know him. We helped him out with another case earlier this year.

Anyway, nice to see you again, Killian. I'd give you a lift back to the village, but got to 'guard the fort' you understand."

Killian said his goodbye, crossed the intersection, and began walking back to the village. After a minute or so he cut across the road until he was beside a small stand of large trees. He glanced back in the direction of the abbey. When he was sure he couldn't be seen, he used the trees for cover until he was down next to the river.

Skulking around in broad daylight seemed foolish and undignified, but Killian had a feeling, and that feeling was going to lead him to where Detective Walsh and the rest of the guards had gone. The guard who had yelled out earlier had been in the vicinity of the river; that much was clear. If Killian wasn't mistaken it was probably near where they had found the dog. He had a sneaking suspicion they had found something else.

Killian walked alongside the river as he headed back in the direction from where he had come. The moisture-laden vegetation already had his pants legs soaked and clinging to his skin. He wished he had come better prepared. Still, the ground was soft and flat, making the going easy. The plant-covered banks were high enough that there was no worry about being seen, not even by the landowner, a person he knew well and who would have been more than a little surprised to see Killian taking a leisurely stroll next to the River Aherlow.

After proceeding for a couple of hundred yards, Killian could hear voices nearby and not too far in front of where he was now standing. He had been correct: They were right where the dog had been found or very close to it. He felt a little unwell, with a feeling of dread of what else might have been discovered.

He climbed the riverbank and sneaked across the narrow one-lane road. He then climbed up a small hill until he had a view of the area below. All of the guards were gathered in a semicircle and staring down at the ground, except for Detective Walsh, who was pacing back and forth a few feet behind while speaking emphatically on his phone.

Killian maneuvered himself slightly to the right, hoping to get a better field of vision. Finally, he could make things out, and what he saw shook him to his core. On the ground, stretched out before the guards, were two still bodies lying on their sides. The larger one, obviously a man, was precisely positioned next to the other, which Killian figured to be a woman, although he couldn't observe her features. The knees of both bodies were bent at a forty-five-degree angle, with the kneecaps of the man resting between the backs of the knees of the woman. His groin area met her backside, and his arms were tightly wrapped around her shoulders. The scene would have been touching if it hadn't been so morose. It was almost as if the man had been trying to protect his partner until they were no more and no longer ones with this earth.

Killian knew who they were, and he was pretty certain he knew what this meant. A feeling of nausea came suddenly, and before he knew it the coffee and whiskey of this morning, along with his breakfast, spewed forth on the ground in front of him. He stayed bent over until the contents of his stomach was completely out, the last remnants dribbling and hanging from the corners of his mouth. When he was done he sat down on a downed tree to collect himself. He pulled out a handkerchief from his back pocket and wiped his mouth and the perspiration on his forehead.

Killian thought about these two particular people lying dead on the other side of the road. Is this truly related to Spencer and Shandy? Or was it just a random murder of an innocent man and woman, and their dog, by God knows who? Maybe they hadn't been murdered at all.

If it were connected to Spencer, why? Why these two people? Were they simply in the wrong place at the wrong time? Was it because of their dog? Was it because of this location?

He had nothing to go on at this point. A thorough police investigation would have to be completed before he, or anybody else, would know anything for certain. Such an investigation could take weeks, if not longer, and even then he was dubious about how much information would be shared. A killer on the loose would shake this village. A ghost murderer—now that was something on a completely different level.

Killian stayed at that spot for a good ten minutes, and he didn't even bother taking another peek at the scene below; there was nothing more he needed to see.

He finally stood up, silently crossed the road, and dropped back to the river bottom. He began making his way back to Galbally. His bottle of comfort was waiting for him at the pub, and he needed a change of clothes. Then he'd decide whether to call Spencer or not.

Some things need to be discussed in person, not over the phone. Killian had waited until the following morning, and now he gingerly pushed himself to the front door of Spencer's house. On the drive over he had contemplated what he should or should not say. But he knew Spencer needed to hear everything. Together, perhaps they could draw some kind of conclusion as to what was going on.

He used the brass knocker to announce his presence. He was still feeling quite unnerved after yesterday's discovery near the abbey. Some antacid had settled his stomach, but not his mind.

The door opened, and Erica's smiling face greeted him. Killian wasn't much in the mood for small talk.

"Hello, Erica. Is your father about this morning?"

"Hi, Killian. Nice to see you as well," Erica said with the slightest tone of mockery. "Yes, he's around. Up in his room. Come on in, and I'll go get him."

"Thank you," Killian said. "I think I'll just wait for him outside here, if you don't mind."

"Sure, suit yourself," Erica said. "Can I get you some coffee or tea? I made some killer cinnamon rolls this morning. Well, Mrs. O'Donnell and I did. You should try one."

"No thank you, Erica," Killian said. "I just finished my breakfast a short time ago, and I'm quite full to the brim."

"No worries, Killian. I'll go get my dad."

Killian watched as Erica turned and headed up the stairs, leaving the wooden door open as she went. He could sense already that perhaps Spencer had shared their discussion of yesterday with Erica, and maybe even more.

Five green bottles sitting way up high, sitting way up high until they fall. As he waited for Spencer, Killian reflected again on last night's dream. He could remember it vividly, like he always did. The bottles were all tall and narrow, like a wine bottle with no cork or cap, and they were lined up parallel on a small ledge fixed to a white wall. This particular dream had been a short one, but it had ended with the first bottle, the one sitting on the far left side of the ledge, crashing to the floor below and shattering into what seemed like a million pieces of green.

Unlike most people, when he awoke each morning, Killian could remember every dream in great detail. Many mornings there were no dreams to remember, and Killian was thankful they weren't a nightly occurrence. When he was young, he had told his parents of this unique ability. His father couldn't have cared less, but his religious mother told him that it was a blessing from God. Killian didn't know what to think back then, and he still didn't, but he realized a long time ago that he bordered on the edge of being clairvoyant.

Perhaps he was truly clairvoyant because his ability extended beyond dreams. Killian could often see things that were destined to happen. He could infer meanings that no one else could. His visions, and his dreams, were not always accurate, but he maintained a pretty good batting percentage. A gift or a curse, Killian could never come to a conclusion. Besides his now-deceased parents, his wife was the only one who knew. Killian had decided long before to keep things quiet and to never outwardly react to things he saw or to what people said. He didn't want others, especially other children when he was young, to consider him some kind of a freak or to think he had demons inside him and not God.

Last night, one of the five green bottles fell from the ledge. Yesterday, a young couple was found dead near Moor Abbey. The connection was clear to Killian, and he wondered when the other four bottles would drop.

The sound of Spencer's footsteps coming down the stairway shook Killian back to the present, and he waited until his friend was standing in front of him. Spencer wouldn't be privy to the dreams of an old man, not today.

"Good morning, Spencer."

"Morning, Killian."

"Mind if we take a short stroll?" Killian said.

He turned and began heading in the direction of the river. He heard the door close behind him and soon Spencer was at his side.

"I'm assuming this isn't a social visit. Something happen? Did you get more information on the dog?" Spencer said.

"I'm sorry I didn't answer your call last night. We were at the wife's sister's place for dinner, and I had forgotten my phone. But yes, I do have some additional information," Killian said, as he turned to Spencer and forced a small grin. "It's certainly not the best news to begin a day with."

Killian waited for Spencer to say something or react, but nothing came.

As they walked along through the tall grass, Killian continued: "The conversation with the vet about the dead dog is irrelevant now, so I'll get straight to the heart of the matter. I assume you saw what was happening at the abbey yesterday?"

"Yes, of course. How could I miss it?"

Killian glanced over at Spencer as they reached the top of the hill above the river and began heading down the trail to the southwest. Killian stopped after twenty-five yards or so.

"Why don't we take a seat over there?" Killian said, pointing at a large fallen tree a few yards off to their left.

After they sat, Killian spent the next fifteen minutes relaying to Spencer all that had transpired at the abbey, and he threw in the important parts of his conversation with the vet. Spencer asked a few questions here and there, but he mostly remained quiet until the end.

"Well, I don't know whether I'm surprised or what," Spencer said. "Still, we don't know anything at this point. The couple's dead, but you don't know a thing beyond that. Isn't that accurate?"

"Yes, you're right, Spencer. I don't know anything beyond that. Honestly, I don't know anything at all, other than what I feel inside. This is way outside my comfort zone, it is. What happened with you before, and with me, was extraordinary to say the least, but we may be at an entirely different level here."

Killian looked on as Spencer stared out into the distance beyond, seemingly lost in a world of his own. Killian let him be until Spencer was ready to talk again, and after several minutes he finally did.

"You're telling me you truly believe the ghost, or whatever it is, has returned?"

"Yes."

"If that's the case, why? What would bring it back after all this time? Why would it harm two people we don't even know, people I've never even met?"

Killian watched as Spencer's hands smoothed backward over the top of his head.

"Your guess is as good as mine, Spencer," Killian said. "I thought about those very questions for some time yesterday and today. There could be a million answers."

"Such as?"

"Retribution perhaps."

"Retribution for what? That doesn't make a bit of sense."

Spencer picked up a small stone from the ground and flung it hard at a nearby tree. Killian could feel the man's irritation beginning to build.

"Listen, it doesn't make much sense to me either, but we know what happened when you were trying to save Shandy," Killian said. "My guess is you interfered with the natural order of things somehow. The damn thing showed its displeasure more than once. It didn't like you getting in the way. You're well aware of that."

"So, I try my best to simply save a little dog, and this monster gets all pissed off, after all this time, and kills somebody, somebodies. I'm not buying it."

"I don't know, Spencer. You're also aware of the history of the abbey and the dogs that lived there centuries ago."

What Killian was referencing was literally ancient history. In 1569, the friars inhabiting the abbey were murdered during a period of upheaval known as the Desmond Rebellions. The reasons are not clear. Most were put to death by the sword, spear, or some other medieval weapon, but those still surviving were trapped within the abbey. They succumbed to the most hideous of deaths when flames were set to the structure.

The friars had kept a kennel of dogs, pets perhaps, or used for some other purpose. The story goes that the anguished cries of the friars and the howls and whimpering of the dogs could be heard for miles around as they were all consumed by the raging flames and burned alive. Even a few poems had been written about the horrible event.

Spencer frowned, and Killian watched him throw another rock, this one not even coming close to its mark.

"Are you saying that what happened with me and Shandy and what happened to those friars' dogs is somehow related?"

"Again, Spencer, this is simply speculation and supposition on my part. I don't pretend to know the true answer. All I feel, and all I think I know, is that your ghost has returned."

"Geez, Killian, really? My ghost?"

"Well, he's a fair bit more your ghost than mine, that's for certain."

They both managed a small chuckle.

"You can have him or it or whatever, as far as I'm concerned," Spencer said.

"No thanks to that," Killian said.

They laughed again, but there was no joy in their voices.

"Seriously though, why take the lives of people I don't even know, assuming that's what this is all about?" Spencer asked.

"I thought about that as well," Killian said. "I doubt it was random. They were at the abbey and had a dog similar to Shandy. That's the logical conclusion, to make you understand it's related to the past. Still, none of it makes any sense."

They both sat silently for a few moments. Spencer reached into the front pocket of his shirt and pulled out a pack of cigarettes. He placed one between his lips and flicked the lighter. He watched the plume as it drifted above his head. Another habit that dies hard. Killian was well aware of Spencer's closet smoking. Erica was never to know, but Spencer had a feeling she already did.

"I take it you have filled in Erica about the past?" Killian asked.

"Yes, I took your advice and told her yesterday," Spencer said, as he blew out a puff of smoke in the direction opposite Killian. "She seemed to believe, at least some of it, I guess. At the same time I think she's suspicious and certainly isn't convinced that some ghost may have returned.

"I even told her we, or maybe just her, might have to leave if things got bad, but she's not having it and I can't force her. I couldn't bear to see her go, anyway."

Killian was well aware Spencer would be going nowhere, unless to protect Erica. And maybe Spencer was right; maybe the dead man and woman had nothing to do with the past. Maybe Killian's advanced years were taking a toll, and maybe his intuition was beginning to fail him. Time would tell, but Killian hardly ever let Killian down.

Spencer began to rise from his seat and then slowly sat back down again.

"Killian, let me ask you something. Should we be feeling guilty about all of this? I mean, assuming what you think is correct, are we—or me, I should say—responsible for this dead couple?"

Killian leaned back slightly and hesitated before he spoke.

"Spencer, you did nothing more than trying to rescue a lost dog—and yourself. That's the bottom line. Sometimes things happen in life we have no control over and for which there is no answer. "

"Yeah, things happen, like a dead squirrel hanging from a barbed wire fence," Spencer said under his breath as he looked at the ground below him.

"What? What did you say?" a puzzled Killian asked.

"Oh, it's nothing, but I guess you're right," Spencer said, bringing his head back up.

Killian watched as Spencer stood up and brushed the seat of his pants with his hand. Killian followed his lead, and they slowly began walking back in the direction of the house. They remained quiet. When they reached the front of the house, Spencer quickly turned to Killian.

"Damn! I'm glad I remembered! Killian, how well do you know Angus? I mean, really know him?"

"Angus? Why are you asking me that?"

"Just answer me, please."

"I know Angus as well as any man could know him, I suppose, but he's not someone anybody would really know. He's lived all his life in Galbally. He's about as taciturn as they get. No family, no real friends. That I know of at least. He's quite an odd man, as you know. Again, why do you ask?"

"Two days ago, at the run, he was standing across the square in town and just kept staring at Erica and me," Spencer said. "It was so direct. I was pretty uncomfortable. And then he showed up again just as we were leaving town."

"Well, nothing you could say about Angus would surprise me. He's a real oddity. Are ya thinking maybe there's some connection?"

"I don't know, Killian. It was just strange. Maybe it's nothing."

Killian hesitated for a moment. A light bulb blew up inside his head.

"Jaysus, Spencer! I had completely forgotten! Angus was there the day the couple was in my pub. He was the only other person and he said the strangest thing, something like 'You shouldn't go searching for a dog that's run away.' Something along those lines. I gave him a piece of my mind, I did, because he wasn't part of our conversation. I truly had forgotten all about his strange quip."

Maybe I am getting old...

"Well, then maybe therein lies our murderer, and we don't have to worry about no ghost," Spencer said.

Killian looked at Spencer and could see a man grasping at the straw that might solve his current dilemma.

"Don't get in front of yourself there, Spencer. Angus isn't the killing type. Of that, I'm certain. He wouldn't hurt a flea jumping from Buster's coat. No, he's not your man."

"Maybe, maybe not," Spencer said. Killian could tell his friend was in no way convinced.

"Anyway, let's not worry about Angus right now," Killian said. "And by the way, tonight we're having a bit of a celebration for an old friend at the pub. Promises to be a great craic. Why don't you and Erica journey over and have a night out? It'll get our minds on other things."

"Sure, Killian, thank you. A night out might be good for us. Can I let you know later, after I've talked to Erica? I'll need to talk with her about this latest news as well. Not sure how she'll take it."

"Sure, Spencer, sure. Just come if you like. No RSVP necessary. You're welcome to stay at my place if you're worried about driving."

Killian gave Spencer a pat on the back. He got into his car, turned on the engine, and sat there before he pulled out. He watched his friend turn the knob and enter the front door. Erica was waiting for him just inside.

CHAPTER EIGHT

Spencer felt the need for a distraction and decided to accept Killian's invitation. That evening, around six, Spencer's SUV pulled into Galbally. Open parking in front of the pub was in short supply, so Erica stopped just briefly, allowing Spencer a quick exit from the vehicle. He couldn't convince Erica to join him tonight, but it worked out just fine. She had delivered him where he needed to go, and she agreed to fetch him when he was done.

On the drive over Spencer had told her about the recent turn of events. He had tried to mask his feelings, if even a little, but whatever was happening here had now gone in the wrong direction. A ghost, Angus, whatever—it didn't matter. People had died, and this was serious business, whether murders had been committed or not.

Before getting in the car with Erica, Spencer had more or less determined that it was best they all leave, for a while at least. But Erica, as she had done a lot this summer, acted as the voice of reason. Leaving would be irrational, she told him. The couple, and their dog, was gone, yes, but there was nothing to suggest foul play at this point. A logical explanation might be forthcoming. And Spencer and Erica were in no personal danger themselves, so why would they leave? Besides, she reminded her father that he was not the kind to run away from problems. Spencer wasn't exactly sure of the last point; he felt he had been running from problems his entire life. But Erica's logic had won out. They would stay until they knew more.

"Thanks, Erica," Spencer said. "Two or three hours should be enough for me. Please drive carefully."

"No problem," Erica said. "Just give me a buzz thirty minutes before you're ready to go."

The car door shut, and Erica took off, following the short distance of circular road that wrapped around the town square and led out of the village.

Spencer opened the pub door and stepped in. The door shut behind him.

"Spencer! Spencer! Mr. Spencer! Spencer! Mr. Spencer!" The voices called out as soon as he was noticed. At least some of them were learning to drop the "Mr." part.

The whole scene reminded him of the 1980s-90s sitcom Cheers, when the character Norm would walk into the Boston-set bar of the same name.

"Spencer, you best get over and grab a seat while there's still one left to grab," yelled Killian's son Michael from behind the bar.

Large portions of the pub were relatively quiet, with only a few scattered people here and there. Off to the right of the main room opened an ancillary room for customer overflow or for people who wanted to be away from the noise and commotion of the busy bar area. A large sofa set of maroon color ran along three walls, and above it hung historical pictures of Galbally.

The bar counter was a different story. As Michael had pointed out, there was only one empty stool remaining at the wooden countertop that began at the back wall and ran forward toward the pub's entrance, taking a ninety-degree turn and then running left until it ended at another wall.

Behind each stool people were standing two or three deep. All were quite animated, and the party had clearly been in full force for a while already. Most were likely guests here for the gathering for Killian's friend, Spencer decided. He was acquainted with a great many of them. He headed to the bar, exchanging greetings with those he knew on the way. He pulled out the stool and sat down, getting pats on the shoulder from some of those nearby.

To his right sat Brian. Spencer had known Brian essentially since the get-go, from his very first week in Galbally. Brian was a bald, heavyset man who ran a local solar energy business. He had become a wealth of knowledge to Spencer, and the two had become fairly good friends once Spencer decided to make this part of Ireland his home. And more than a few nights had been spent together right here at the Grafton.

"Evening, Spencer," Brian said. "Glad you could make it down. Haven't seen you for quite a spell. No Erica today?"

"Hey, Brian," Spencer said and shook the man's hand. "We've got some guests who need a bit of TLC, so Erica stayed at the inn."

There were no guests staying tonight, but there was no point in sharing that Erica would have been more than a little uncomfortable in this confined space with people she generally didn't know. He couldn't blame her, however. Events like this were even a bit much for him at times.

"Say, have you heard about the guards being in town?" Brian asked. "Even a couple of detectives, I'm told."

I was supposed to come here to get my mind on other things, Spencer thought. He realized the goings-on at the abbey would be a major topic of conversation at a gathering like this. He could hear bits and pieces of the story being discussed as he sat there.

"Yes, Killian mentioned it to me," Spencer said. "Not really sure what it's all about, however. What do you know?"

Michael appeared in front of Spencer and set down a freshly drawn Guinness.

"Drink up, Spencer. You've a late start and some catching up to do."

"Thanks, Michael. Where's your father?"

"He just stepped out for a bit. Should be back soon enough."

Spencer picked up his pint glass, and it met Brian's.

"Slainte!"

"Slainte!"

"All I've heard is something about a dead dog and its owners perhaps having disappeared," Brian said, continuing their earlier conversation. "I'm sure it's a fair bit more than that, though. An ambulance was seen at the abbey yesterday, and the whole area is still off-limits. Something's afoot."

"Sounds like a crime scene to me," Spencer said, wondering how much people truly knew. He had, of course, seen the taped-off abbey on his way over, but the police were no longer in the vicinity, at least not when he and Erica had passed by.

"No doubt, no doubt. Something's going on, but nobody knows for certain. The guards are keeping a tight lip, it seems. Even our local sage Killian says he doesn't know anything."

Just then, the front door opened, and Killian walked through. He was cradling five or six bottles of assorted spirits in his arms, undoubtedly confiscated from O'Dwyer's up the street.

Spencer watched as Killian went around the end of the bar and behind it. He unloaded his baggage and went up and down the counter, greeting people and taking drink orders. After five minutes he wandered over to where Spencer and Brian were sitting.

"Evening, gents," he said. "Spencer, I'm glad you made it."

"Evening, Killian."

"Do you need a bed for the night?"

"No, Erica will pick me up later, so I'm good. Thanks, anyway."

"I see," Killian said. "Spencer, if you can break away from Brian for a few moments, come with me to the other end of the bar, will ya? I'd like you to meet my old pal, the one whose return we're celebrating tonight."

Spencer grabbed his glass and said a quick word to Brian, and he and Killian walked parallel on opposite sides until they were near the end of the counter.

"Spencer, this is Tommy Cleary," Killian said, addressing them both. "He's a native of these parts, but he snuck away a couple of years back. Living up north of Westport these days, for reasons known only to a choice few. Wouldn't that be right, Tommy?"

"Ply me with a few more pints, and I'll tell you why I really left," Tommy said, laughing at what was obviously an inside joke between him and Killian.

"It's grand to meet you, Spencer," Tommy continued. "Now, would Spencer be your first name or your surname?"

Spencer was accustomed to being asked that question, and he had the answer down pat.

"It's my family name, but people just call me Spencer regardless. Patrick is my first name, but it's kind of boring, so I prefer Spencer."

"All right, then, Spencer it is!" Tommy exclaimed. "Killian tells me you're a wee bit famous here in Galbally."

"Oh, I wouldn't say famous; infamous might be more appropriate."

The three of them laughed, and Tommy and Spencer ended up talking for the next fifteen minutes, while Killian resumed the duties of making certain no one in the pub was left thirsty. Tommy knew most of Spencer's story already, at least the parts that could be told. He seemed to revel in the tale of an American who was assaulted, twice in one night, right here in Galbally and then decides he's going to make a new life in this very same place. Spencer's staying here had been much more than that, of course, but that wasn't a subject to be discussed with Tommy.

Killian appeared again with another pint for both Spencer and Tommy. They shared a couple of gulps each, and Spencer decided the time had come to let Tommy be so the man could mingle with his true friends.

As Spencer began making his way across the pub, he noticed Angus, sitting at the very end of the bar in his usual spot. His face was pointed in the direction of his full glass of ale. As usual, he spoke to no one, and no one spoke to him. Spencer hadn't even been aware of his presence until this moment.

What the hell is he doing here? Spencer thought. *Stalking me?* He knew that wasn't true, and even though this was a private party, it wasn't. The pub was open to anyone who felt inclined to enter.

Angus had suddenly put a damper on this pleasant evening. *No matter. I'll just ignore him.* Spencer made it back to Brian and took a seat. He never took another peek in the direction of Angus.

Another pint, and he and Brian moved over to a spot where a couple of other fellas they knew were sitting. The circular table was just large enough for four people, built around and encompassing a wooden support beam reaching to the ceiling. Both of these men of weathered faces were wearing their soiled work clothes and baseball caps sporting the insignias of local farm equipment dealers. A gathering in Galbally generally had no required dress code.

After talking for a while, Spencer excused himself. The pints were moving their way through his system. He wandered through the back area of the pub and entered the men's room. As he stood there relieving himself, he stared up at a framed jersey, likely belonging to some local sports hero who had done the village proud with his athletic prowess. For not the first time Spencer wondered how good of an athlete someone would have to be to move out of the loo and into the main part of the pub. He snickered, washed his hands, and opened the door of the bathroom.

As he exited the door he almost fell over backward upon the shock of seeing Angus standing—and maybe waiting—directly on the other side. Spencer, shaken slightly, said a brisk "excuse me" and brushed by Angus as he made his way through the opening. As he cleared the space between them, the words came from behind.

"Ah, Mr. Spencer, you think you're pretty clever, don't ya now?"

"Pardon me," Spencer turned back and said.

"You don't fool me one bit. I know all about your past, you and that little feck of a dog called Shandy."

"Angus, you don't know a thing about me! And I'd appreciate your leaving me be."

"Oh, I'll leave you be, Mr. Spencer. You've got bigger problems coming your way than little 'ol me, that's for sure."

"Whatever, Angus. Are we finished here?"

"Where's that pretty little daughter of yours today? Sure wouldn't have minded another peek at that lovely thing," Angus said, obviously intending to get Spencer roiled.

And he did.

Spencer's eyes went narrow, and soon his hands were grabbing just below the collar of Angus's dirty button-down shirt. He pushed the man hard against the wall behind them, making a loud bang in the process and causing a picture to fall from its perch and its glass to shatter. His face was not even inches away from the face of Angus. His anger would have been obvious to anyone watching the scene, but no one was. His voice remained calm as he spoke.

"Angus, you can say whatever you want to me, or about me. I don't really care, I suppose. But don't you ever mention my daughter again. Ever!"

Angus didn't say a word in return. He simply met Spencer's eyes and said nothing. His face seemed completely void of emotion of any kind.

As Spencer held Angus against the wall, he knew already he had gone too far. Voices neared. He released his grip and began walking away, looking back at Angus one last time. The ruckus, however, had already caught the attention of others. Soon several people had gathered around, including Killian.

"What's going on here now?" Killian said. "What's gotten into you two?"

"Oh, it's nothing. Just Angus and me having a friendly conversation," Spencer said. "Isn't that right, Angus?"

Angus did nothing but glare back at Spencer.

"Well, I don't know what's happening, but the "friendly" conversation has ended," Killian said. "Angus, why don't you be on your way home? This is supposed to be a happy occasion, and I don't need this kind of headache, not from either one of you."

Spencer received an indignant stare from Killian. He wasn't in the mood to care much.

Angus made his way to the exit and out the door in no time, without saying so much as a single word. Spencer gathered himself and returned to the bar. He sat down on the nearest empty stool, and everyone left him alone. Michael placed a fresh pint in front of him, and Spencer grabbed the phone from his back pocket. Soon, Erica would be on her way to pick him up.

CHAPTER NINE

The next two days passed uneventfully. Spencer held out hope things would continue in the same manner. The incident at the pub the other night was unfortunate, but Spencer didn't feel a bit sorry about roughing up Angus. It was well deserved in his view. And Killian agreed after Spencer explained to him what Angus had said.

Spencer's mind constantly alternated back and forth between Angus and the dead couple named Kelly. He had been keeping busy around the inn since yesterday morning, helping Erica clean rooms and launder bed sheets, dealing with a clogged drainage pipe, and mowing the fairly massive lawn that surrounded the premises. He even ventured into nearby Tipperary for breakfast and other supplies, though he didn't purchase too much; the busy season would be coming to an end soon. All of these activities kept his body occupied, but his mind was more than competing.

As he sat on the back porch late this morning trying to make sense of things, he decided he would not let the recent happenings get the better of him. Sure, he was feeling a good dose of despair, mostly for the two people who had died. But he knew Killian was correct. The dead couple's dreadful outcome wasn't his doing and wasn't his fault. Sometimes things just happen.

A year back Spencer had been a weak man, lost in so many ways. The depression and anxiety were long gone now, and he meant to keep it that way. He had a thriving business and a good life. He had not only reconnected with his daughter, but their relationship was a solid one. He felt stronger than before, maybe stronger than he had ever felt. His strength would not be compromised by Angus or by some menacing ghost, assuming there was a ghost. Certainly, no evidence existed to prove there was. Still, the words spoken by Angus bothered Spencer. They were not just some unintelligible ramblings of a demented man. They had to mean something.

Killian had been keeping Spencer informed of all new developments. Detective Walsh had followed up with Killian as promised. Their one and only meeting was short and sweet and of no consequence. Killian just happened to be one of the last people to see the couple alive. Killian's brief acquaintance with Sean and Clare Kelly provided nothing to go on and certainly didn't render Killian a suspect in the deaths of the man and woman.

The bodies of the deceased couple were brought to a mortuary in Limerick, and an autopsy was performed. As usual, Killian knew someone who knew someone, and the information he needed was soon his. As with the dog, no cause of death could be determined. There was no blunt trauma, no sign of injury, and no indication of a struggle. To top matters off, the two were in excellent health, except for being dead, of course. The guards were working hard on the case and would be for some time. The abbey would be closed to visitors for the foreseeable future.

In the village of Galbally, the well-kept secret of the discovery of two bodies nearby was not a well-kept secret for long. Someone always spoke who shouldn't, and soon the news spread like wildfire through the town, the county, and beyond. The crime scene around Moor Abbey had been a dead giveaway anyway, but the tale of what had transpired grew taller and more vivid each time it passed from one mouth to another.

The detective team from Limerick had given a public statement at the town square just yesterday. Likely, rumors needed to be squashed, inaccurate media stories nipped in the bud. Yes, a young couple had been found dead at the abbey, but there was no sign of foul play, and the evidence pointed to a dual suicide, although the exact cause of death was still being investigated.

Spencer thought about all of this. There was likely more to their conclusion, but he figured the guards had decided to share just enough to settle the public fears. The last thing the police needed was the possibility of a potential killer being present in the area.

Spencer couldn't make heads or tails of what was going on. If Angus were the murderer, he must be extremely good at his craft. How else could there have been no physical harm to the couple, assuming that was the case? All information was secondhand at this point. What else did the police know? If the culprit were a ghost, well, there was no explaining that either.

Spencer took a swig of coffee, and, as if on cue, Mrs. O'Donnell stepped out and refilled his mug. She bid him goodbye, her duties over for the day. Once she was back in the house and out of sight, Spencer pulled a cigarette from the pack in his pants pocket and lit it. A couple of quick puffs, and he stamped it out with his foot. He looked over his shoulder briefly to make certain he hadn't been seen. *Ridiculous,* he thought. *I really gotta stop this.*

He lifted his phone from the table in front of him and auto-dialed Killian. He needed to talk more about the incident with Angus.

"Good morning, Killian," he said when the connection was made. "How ya doing this morning?"

"I'm just fine, Spencer. Sitting at home going over some long-delayed paperwork. Accomplishing all your work over there?"

"Yeah, I hit it pretty hard yesterday, and this morning as well."

Spencer sat up straight in his chair, his elbows resting on his knees as he talked.

"Listen, Killian, this thing with Angus is really puzzling me. He has to know something."

"Yes, I've given the subject quite some thought myself," Killian said. "The remark about Shandy was strange, but I'm not certain it contains any deeper meaning. After all, there are others in town who knew about Shandy besides you, Colin, and me."

"I'm aware of that, Killian, and I even wrote down a list: Colin's parents, Mrs. Murray, the vet. Owen, but he's as dead as a doornail. I can't think of anyone else."

"Well, someone could have let something out at some point. It's difficult to say."

"Even so," Spencer said, "no one knew any real details of what transpired. Take Mrs. Murray, for example. Yes, I went to the animal shelter hoping to find Shandy, but we only met that once, and I never spoke to her again until well after everything was over."

"What are you getting at, Spencer?"

"Just I sense Angus knows more. He said as much, about the past. And what about the comment of bigger troubles coming my way?"

"Yes, it was all strange, but listen to yourself. Even if Angus does know more, that doesn't make him a murderer. I'll admit he's been a little off, but he's just acting the maggot, being a bit of a nuisance. I don't know why, but I refuse to believe he had anything to do with Mr. and Mrs. Kelly."

"Do you believe the police statement?"

"No, not necessarily. You are well aware of what I think, Spencer. And I will tell you again that I think you and Erica should leave here."

"Right, the ghost... Okay, I'm not saying you're wrong, but I think someone should mention Angus to the police."

"I already have. Not because I wanted to or because I believe he is guilty. As you know, I did talk to Detective Walsh. You also know Angus was in the pub that day. I had no choice but to share the information."

"What did the detective say?"

"He said they would speak with him, which I'm sure they already have. Angus wasn't in the pub yesterday, so I have no idea after that."

Spencer hesitated a few moments.

"Okay, Killian, I guess you're right. If Angus is involved in this, the police will find out."

"Put Angus out of your mind. As I told you before, he wouldn't hurt a fly."

The two of them talked for a few more minutes, and Spencer set down the phone. *No, Killian, I won't put Angus out of my mind.* Spencer couldn't understand Killian's solicitous attitude toward the man.

He went into the kitchen and made himself a sandwich. Then he looked for and found Buster out back with Erica.

As he and Buster finished an afternoon trek in the nearby Galtee Mountains, Spencer thought about this morning's discussion and about Killian's uncanny ability to gather information. He wondered how long the guards could maintain their facade before admitting the couple had died for reasons that couldn't be explained. He wondered again how Angus figured into all of this.

Back in the car Spencer decided to head toward Galbally instead of returning directly to Bansha. He felt like having a beer with Killian and hoped the Grafton was open. *Why can't I be more like Killian?* he thought as he traveled down the curvy roads that led through the valley toward the village. But Spencer knew he was who he was. And at least that was a person much more comfortable with himself than he had been all of those years before coming to Ireland. He wasn't and never would be Killian, but he was a good Spencer now, and that was enough.

As the car crossed the small bridge that crossed the narrow width of the River Aherlow, Moor Abbey showed itself just off to the right. The crime scene tapes were still there, and he noticed a couple of uniformed policemen.

At the last second, right before the left turnoff to Galbally, Spencer kept going straight. He wasn't sure why; something told him he and Buster still had some walking to do. He couldn't use the abbey parking lot, so he drove until he found a public turnout point. He stopped the car. Next to here was one of the walking trails that meandered through this valley. Most of the trails around here were on private land, but people could use them freely with the granted easements.

Buster, residing in the passenger seat of the car, tilted his head toward his master, showing the inquisitiveness of a dog that yearns to know what's going on.

"Relax, Buster, we're just gonna take one more short walk."

Spencer frowned as Buster whined and moved back and forth in the small space of his seat. The dog looked out the open window, almost threatening to jump through.

"I'll let you out in a second, buddy."

Spencer opened his door, got out, and stood next to the car. He gave Buster the approval, and the dog scrambled across the driver's seat to the outside. Once Buster was out Spencer thought better of it and immediately put the dog on a lead. They started down the path and followed the trail as it skirted a small, forest-covered hill. The trail then worked its way down in a southern direction until intersecting with another that ran closer to the backside of the abbey. Off to the left was a dirt road that Spencer knew well.

The distance up the dirt road ended soon, with a four-strand wire gate with vertical posts blocking their way. Spencer also knew this gate well. Up the road and beyond was the path he and Colin had taken very late one night in a chase of Shandy. She had led them this way for reasons unknown, and they had obliged her. They had found her eventually, but only as some evil and mysterious force had been busy with a similar chase of its own. What happened had frightened Spencer and Colin out of their wits, so much so it became the last time Colin would help Spencer look for Shandy. But they had made a successful getaway, and Shandy had done the same as far as they knew.

That experience had been the first time Spencer had recognized he was dealing with something not of this world and something that presented a real danger. That night's venture into the darkness had culminated in a scene Spencer would never forget.

Though it was bound today with a thick iron chain and a heavy padlock, that night the gate in front of him now had not been secured. He and Colin had passed through in Spencer's car and used the road to follow Shandy until they were forced to go on foot. When they had returned from their pursuit, up a small mountain and back down, this wire gate, which they had left on the ground on their way in, was standing.

Only an hour or so had passed since going through the gate and coming back. The possibility the gate had been put back up by the farmer who owned the land, or by any other person for that matter, was next to zero. Yes, that's when Spencer had finally understood Shandy was in real trouble and that if he wasn't careful he might be as well.

Today, all seemed normal, as it should be. Spencer wrapped his hand around the top of one of the wooden posts of the gate and gave it a shake back and forth.

"Come on, Buster, let's get out of here. I'm dying for a beer," Spencer said.

As Spencer turned to head in the opposite direction and back to the car, Buster let out a loud bark and gave a sharp tug on the lead that Spencer held in his hand. Spencer pivoted back around. Buster stood at the gate, looking down the road in front of them, and he let out a couple of more barks.

"What is it, buddy? What do you see?"

Buster moved his head in Spencer's direction, whining and trying to pull him forward. The dog's excitement was real, and Spencer could only guess at what Buster was sensing.

Spencer hesitated to follow this particular road once again. But he also knew a dog's intuition was much stronger than his own. Today was a Buster he had never seen before, and that alone meant something that couldn't be ignored. Spencer pondered what to do.

"Okay, Buster, we'll go up just a little ways, and then we're coming right back," Spencer said.

Spencer knew they might end up going farther than a short distance. He'd rather not; on the other hand, there was something that had been bothering him for a long time, something he had always wanted to know. Today might be his one chance to find out.

When he and Colin had followed the road until it ended at a small stream at the base of the forested hill above, they had crossed the water on foot and followed a path that crawled up the hillside. The sky had been pitch dark that night once they entered the trees, the trail only illuminated by the flashlight Colin had brought along. Other than the circumstances that had brought them there, however, all else seemed normal, and the trail was a typical mountain pathway through a forest of birch trees.

Upon reaching the halfway point to the top of the hill, however, they were met with the strangest of occurrences. Gradually but suddenly the birch forest had turned into a forest of bamboo. Colin had been too scared to care, but the unnatural phenomenon had bothered Spencer at the time, and it bothered him now. He often wondered whether the forest he had seen was just his imagination or whether it was something that naturally occurs when a person steps into a parallel universe. He had never bothered to go back and check, trying to put his past experiences behind him and also afraid of what he might find. Today, if Buster led him that far, he would go, and he would know.

After making certain their intended short walk would not be seen by the outside world, Spencer lifted one leg and then the other over the top wire of the fence, just barely getting over without snagging his pants. Buster ducked down and scampered under the bottom wire. They headed down the dirt road, Buster pulling on the lead as they went and Spencer hurrying behind. Buster clearly had a destination in mind.

Within ten minutes they were at the end of the road, and in front was the stream that Spencer and Colin had crossed previously. Buster was determined to head downstream to a place unknown, but Spencer resisted, for now. He forced Buster with him up the winding path of the hill above. Unlike before, today there was light from the sun, and the path and the forest surrounding it could be easily seen.

The image of the bamboo forest was as fresh in Spencer's mind as it had been when he actually saw it, and he knew exactly where to look. They walked for five or ten minutes, and then he veered right directly at the ninety-degree turn he remembered. He looked ahead into the area around and above them. The birch trees showed no end as far as he could see. He looked around in all directions. Nothing but birches entered his field of vision. Still unconvinced, he forced another five minutes of tramping up the hill. Not a single bamboo tree was discovered.

On that night with Colin, they had gone through the bamboo forest and up the hill through a path of rocky crags. When they reached the top, Shandy was waiting for them, as if the whole episode had been planned on her part. But she didn't stay long. She had felt the ominous presence at the same time they had. Before Spencer had even the slightest chance of reconnecting with her, the dog was gone, and he and Colin were left alone. Scared out of their minds, they had hustled down the path and off the mountain, only to have a standing gate waiting for them, obviously a warning from someone or something to back off.

He wondered what else he might have imagined during those weeks of trying to save a lost dog. Maybe the gate incident had been an illusion as well, but, then again, Colin had been there. He wondered whether he had gone to a place where humans don't venture. I guess it doesn't matter anymore, he thought as he looked down and turned his attention to Buster. His dog looked back at him with imploring eyes, signaling the time had come for Spencer to follow.

"All right, all right, we can go where you wanna go now, Buster," Spencer said, questioning whether that was such a good idea.

The dog took his cue and immediately headed back down the trail with Spencer in tow. More than once Spencer had to rein Buster in just to keep up. They soon reached the bottom. Spencer stepped carefully on some half-submerged rocks to cross the stream, and Buster patiently waited on his master. Once Spencer was across they headed down alongside the slow-moving water. Buster kept quiet, but his intentions were clear to Spencer. After about five minutes the stream left the canopy of forest and headed out into an open meadow. As they rounded a last bend, what Buster had been looking for appeared in front of them.

Cemeteries were seemingly everywhere in Ireland; after all, there were centuries piled upon centuries of people who had physically come and gone from this island. But this one seemed a bit out of the ordinary, tucked back here on farmland that would be inaccessible to anyone who wanted to pay respects. The reason became clear, however, as Spencer studied things. Thick vines and other vegetation obscured almost all of the tombstones as well as the ground in between them. The majority of the stones no longer stood erect, most tilted at various angles and some completely flat on the ground.

This plot of land was a cemetery of forgotten souls and one seldom if ever visited.

They passed through the sorry remnants of an old and rusted iron gate. Spencer let Buster off the lead, and the dog began energetically moving from one place to another, smelling each grave before going to the next. Spencer could only guess at what the dog was doing. After a few minutes Buster suddenly stopped at one and sat down in front of it. He fidgeted as he sat and began to whine. Finally, he let out a deep-throated bark and looked up at Spencer.

"What is it, boy? What did you find?"

Spencer knelt and rubbed Buster's head, letting him know he had done a good job. Buster, crying again, looked dolefully at his master and back at the still-erect tombstone.

Intrigued, Spencer moved over to the grave. It was covered in an accumulation of moss and lichen, red and yellow and green and everything in between. He pulled his car key from his pocket and began scraping the stubborn growth from the face of the tombstone. Buster no doubt had a reason for leading him to this marker, and Spencer needed to know why. After some time spent scraping and brushing with the palm of his hand, the stone's engraving gradually began to reveal itself. First one letter and then another and then another. A final brush and a name appeared, just clear enough to read: Michael J. O'Donnell.

He went down five inches and began rubbing and scraping again, hoping to find dates or an inscribed message from loved ones. After he had worked his way completely through the lichen and moss, Spencer could tell dates had been there once, but they were no longer visible, almost as if they had been scraped away by something harder than the limestone of the grave. He was perplexed, but he couldn't make the dates magically reappear, and it wasn't as if it mattered so much.

Spencer stood up and examined what he had done. So what? It's just an old grave. Sure, the name is O'Donnell, and I have an employee of the same name, but what are the chances? O'Donnell was more than a little common as a surname in the land of Ireland.

Buster whined once more and moved to the empty space beside the grave. He sat down and looked up intently at Spencer, his wet eyes pleading for Spencer to understand.

"Buster, I have no idea what you're on about. What do you want to tell me?"

Spencer sat down on his haunches and softly petted his dog on the head. What are you trying to tell me? Is this related to our Mrs. O'Donnell? What if it is? What am I supposed to do then?

He inadvertently glanced down at a patch of bare ground below his legs. A slender red wasp had a petite iridescent grasshopper in its clutches. The grasshopper was still alive, but the insect was only putting up a small fight to get free, likely pretty much dispatched already from the wasp's venomous stinger. Spencer watched as the insect dragged its innocent victim a couple of inches forward and quickly stuffed it down the smallest of open holes. Within a minute the wasp reappeared and then flew off, returning a few moments later and crawling back down the hole. Out it came again and buzzed away once more.

This time Spencer, even more interested, positioned a very small round pebble so it partially covered the opening. The wasp returned and landed, seemed to do a quick assessment of the new situation, and placed itself directly in front of the small rock. It began kicking dirt backward with its lithe hind legs, opening the hole little by little as it went. Soon enough space was allowed, and the wasp was back inside. Spencer wanted to kill the wasp if it came back out again, hoping the grasshopper might then escape. He wouldn't do so today. He would let nature take its course.

He stood up and took a last look at the tombstone in front of him. He gave a final glance around this pitiful excuse for a cemetery. He shrugged and attached the lead again to Buster's collar. A slight tug, and Buster gave up his spot.

"I don't know what you meant to show me, Buster, but I'm sure not getting it. Not right now. Let's head on home, buddy."

The time was getting late, and Spencer was hungry. Maybe he'd ask Mrs. O'Donnell later whether a relation of hers was buried here, but that would be a strange question to ask someone. Besides, she wasn't the type to share personal information, and Spencer realized he knew very little about her.

They headed back to the car as dusk began to settle on the Glen of Aherlow. A visit to the Grafton Pub could wait for another day.

CHAPTER TEN

Limerick detective Danny Walsh and his partner showed up at the Square One early that Friday morning. Two days had gone by since Spencer and Buster's seemingly innocent visit to the neglected cemetery on the outskirts of Galbally. Spencer had received the awful news yesterday afternoon, but he couldn't imagine the reason for a visit from the police, especially of the detective type.

A knock on the front door penetrated the house, and from his bedroom above Spencer could overhear the conversation as Erica greeted the two men and listened to their explanation for being there. Spencer had naturally told Erica about yesterday's phone call from Mrs. O'Donnell's son, and she was as distraught as he was from the terrible announcement.

Spencer picked up his mobile phone and pulled Killian's number from the contact list. He had called him last night and explained what had happened, and Killian had insisted he would drive out to the Square One this morning. Spencer wanted to check whether his friend was on his way, tell him about this unexpected visit from the detectives.

Erica's voice on the other side of the door interrupted him, and he set the phone down on the dresser before the call even started. Erica told him about the men's arrival, and Spencer closed the door behind her after she left. He looked at his phone and then into the mirror. He pushed his index finger into the inside corners of his eyes, removing the last remnants of sleep from last night. He felt as though he had hardly slept a wink, and his pounding head was proof. He ran his fingers through his hair and put on his favorite baseball cap.

He had no idea where the conversation downstairs would go, but he would simply tell what he knew, and that wasn't much. Mrs. O'Donnell was gone, for reasons not clear, and he wondered whether her tragic death was a coincidence that wasn't. He would listen and answer, and then he would talk to Killian.

Spencer pushed open the kitchen door and walked out onto the patio, where the detectives were seated. He watched as the two men rose from their chairs. Spencer shook the hand of the first man and then that of the second as introductions were exchanged. They all sat down. Erica had already brought a pot of hot coffee for the guests, and both men wrapped their hands around the brown mugs, gathering heat in an attempt to ward off the brisk coolness of the morning.

"Would you prefer to talk inside? It's quite chilly out here this morning," Spencer said. He hoped he didn't look as nervous as he felt.

He zipped up his jacket and wiped his sweaty palms on the front of his jeans.

"No, I think it's best we stay out here, Mr. Spencer," Detective Walsh said, with no explanation given.

Spencer could tell already there was an official, or perhaps unofficial, hierarchy between the two men. The other detective, a Mr. Dunn, was clearly following Danny Walsh's lead and seemed content to sit quietly and scribble into his leather-bound notebook.

Also existent was a hierarchy of sorts in the appearances of the two. While Detective Walsh looked like he could be a fill-in for James Bond, Detective Dunn was much the opposite. He was on the short side and a bit chunky. His dark suit needed a good pressing and his face a cleaner shave. Spencer could detect a natural kindness in the man's blue eyes, but they didn't seem that way at this moment. His occasional expressionless stares were making Spencer feel quite uneasy.

"Mr. Spencer, I'm sure you know why we are here this morning," Detective Walsh said.

Spencer wasn't sure, but he would find out soon enough.

"Yes, Mrs. O'Donnell's son called me late yesterday afternoon," Spencer said. "I really can't believe it. She was just here yesterday morning, doing her usual thing."

"And what is it exactly that Mrs. O'Donnell did for you?" the detective asked.

"She is—was—our breakfast cook," Spencer said. "My daughter Erica had to take over the cooking duties this morning. We've got a couple of guests staying presently. I don't know what I'll do from this point forward. I really can't believe this has happened."

Spencer realized he was already rambling. Just listen and answer, damn it! He told himself to settle down. After all, he had done nothing wrong. Spencer pushed his body against the back of his chair and willed himself to be still. He cringed inwardly as the detective looked at him silently for a moment, one eyebrow raised.

"I see," Detective Walsh said, looking over at his partner briefly and back at Spencer. "Did she seem to be acting oddly at all the last few days, or perhaps even before that?"

"No, not especially," Spencer said, knowing that wasn't exactly true.

There, he had just told his first lie, something he tried never to do unless absolutely necessary. He didn't know why he did it. He questioned whether not being straightforward was such a good idea.

In reality, Mrs. O'Donnell had been acting strangely. She had not been one skilled in social graces, but she had been noticeably aloof, especially yesterday, the day following the visit to the cemetery. Spencer hadn't given the matter much thought until this moment, though he should have.

When Spencer spoke to her yesterday, though their conversations were always short, some of the things she said made no sense. Spencer remembered her comment about the house being so cold and damp, when the opposite had been true. The day before, unlike today, had been mostly sunny and unseasonably warm. If the temperature had been truly cool inside, he and Erica would have noticed the same.

And then there was the snide remark about Buster, how he wasn't well-behaved and how he was always in her way in the morning. She had always easily tolerated Buster. Yesterday had been different. Buster, too, was not himself yesterday, at least around Mrs. O'Donnell. Spencer noticed the dog had spent a great deal of the morning in the kitchen, following Mrs. O'Donnell from place to place. Spencer had been aware of these things, but he hadn't. After the experience at the graveyard, perhaps he should have put two and two together.

And although he hadn't mentioned Mrs. O'Donnell's unusual behavior to Erica, she too must have noticed something off with the woman. When he and Buster had returned home after the visit to the cemetery, Spencer had reported the episode to Erica, basically because it had been curious and because he was looking for validation that it was nothing—or that it was something. For the most part she had disregarded the matter, almost accusing him of an imagination run wild.

He thought of Mrs. O'Donnell again and kicked himself for not having asked about the tombstone he and Buster had discovered. Would such a conversation have made a difference? Would it have stopped what happened? Was there any connection to her sudden death?

"Mr. Spencer, I'm sure you are aware that a young couple was found dead near Galbally a few days back," Detective Walsh said. "Now we have another death, though not a young one, under mysterious circumstances."

Mysterious circumstances? Her son didn't say anything about mysterious circumstances, Spencer thought. His mind was in full-out thinking mode, and he needed to hear more.

"What do you mean?" Spencer said. "Her son didn't mention anything of the sort."

"You do understand we are detectives, don't you now?" Detective Walsh said, slightly indignant. "We aren't in the business of paying a visit to a death scene if it's simply an elderly lady passing in her rocking chair."

He gave another hard stare in Spencer's direction.

"Yes, of course," Spencer said sheepishly, but he needed more details. "Can you tell me exactly what you mean by mysterious circumstances?"

"I probably shouldn't be sharing this with you," the detective said, "but for all intents and purposes, Mrs. O'Donnell seems to have passed away from natural causes. Just sitting there and boom! But her eyes were wide open, they were, with an expression of fear like I've never come across before. Almost as if she had died from fright.

"Do you know the most peculiar thing, Mr. Spencer?"

The detective stared intently into Spencer's eyes, almost as if he were looking into his soul. Before Spencer could answer, the detective continued.

"There, on the wall of the house, directly across from where Mrs. O'Donnell was sitting and where she had died, was written the word "GOD," all in capital letters. You know, Mr. Spencer, sometimes it's quite interesting when people die."

Spencer felt his jaw drop as he looked at the man sitting across from him.

"Now, mind you, it's possible poor Mrs. O'Donnell was aware she was on her way out and was communicating with the good Lord before He took her," the detective said, "but the word was written in a crimson red color, with lipstick of all things. Funny thing is we couldn't find a single tube of lipstick in the entire home. Being as old as she was, perhaps that's no surprise. It certainly doesn't explain matters, however."

Spencer thought he should say something, but the words wouldn't come. And for the life of him, he couldn't recall whether Mrs. O'Donnell regularly wore lipstick or not, or makeup at all for that matter. Why the hell would she write "GOD" on the wall before she died? What if it wasn't her? Is that what the detective is insinuating? He truly felt terrible for the loss of Mrs. O'Donnell, but his emotions went well beyond that. There was definitely more to all of this.

"At any rate, Mrs. O'Donnell's being transported up north to Limerick as we speak," Detective Walsh said. "The coroner will help us get a clue as to her true cause of death, if it's any different than what we're guessing at.

"I don't want you to misconstrue our intentions here, Mr. Spencer. If we find any foul play, you are not a suspect, for the time being at least, but we'll certainly need to talk to you again. After all, you and your daughter may have been the last two people to see Mrs. O'Donnell alive. Don't be wandering too far. And you'll keep our conversation to yourself, won't ya now?"

'For the time being at least,' Spencer thought. *They can't really believe I had anything to do with this, can they?*

Danny Walsh rose from his chair, and Detective Dunn closed his notebook and followed suit.

"Yes, I understand," Spencer said, but he didn't really. He felt sick inside all over again, afraid of what he knew and afraid of what was yet to come.

"Detective, may I ask you something before you leave?" Spencer said, standing up.

Detective Walsh nodded his head without saying anything.

"When the autopsy is finished, will they bring her body back? I mean, will there be a proper funeral? She was my employee, after all, and I would like to attend."

"From what I understand her family has been in this area for generations; I'm sure there are many who would want to pay their respects," the detective said. "But that's up to her boy, of course. He seems to be her only surviving relation. Her husband and another child passed away years ago."

Husband and child passed away? Was that one of them at the cemetery? If so, where is the other one buried?

"I see," Spencer said, distracted by his own thinking. He temporarily put the thoughts out of his mind and began walking the two men off the patio in the direction of their car.

They all shook hands, and the men then got into their blue sedan and headed down the driveway to the main road. Spencer passively watched as they went, lost in confusion and sorrow and more emotions than he could stand.

As he was about to turn back toward the house, suddenly a thing or two dawned on him. He hadn't been working on a puzzle quite yet, but a piece fell into place. He thought back to the cemetery. Yes, O'Donnell wasn't an uncommon name in Ireland, but Buster had known something Spencer hadn't understood. He realized finally why Buster had stopped and made a fuss at that particular gravestone and why, more importantly, he had sat in the empty space next to it. The dog had known, and now it had come.

Spencer's mind found its way to an image of Mrs. O'Donnell sitting cold dead in her wooden rocking chair. He could see her face so clearly; he could see the desperation in her still-open eyes. His mind looked across the room to the lettering on the wall: GOD. Everything is not always what it seems. Killian had said something like that in the past.

He now thought he understood. This all seemed so insane, but the written word on Mrs. O'Donnell's wall was not of her doing. Someone else had authored the message, and Spencer was almost certain the message was meant for him. He pictured Angus sitting in a pub last night, maybe Killian's, drinking his ale and thinking morbidly happy thoughts. He had been too confused today and had let the opportunity slip away. He wouldn't next time. Next time, he would tell the detectives about Angus, tell them about his suspicions, tell them they should take a closer look.

Spencer looked around and called out for Buster. He yelled out again and again and scanned the perimeter of the yard for his dog. He heard the sound of the front door opening, and Buster came flying out in Spencer's direction. Spencer glanced over at Erica standing in the doorway. He knelt, wrapped his arms around the dog's neck, and placed his head next to Buster's.

After Killian made a left turn at the intersection and crossed the small bridge in Bansha on the road that led to the Square One, he noticed the dark sedan coming from the opposite direction. He had met the two men in black suits and dark sunglasses more than once.

After the pair of men had passed, Killian momentarily studied the car in the rearview mirror as it sped toward Bansha. He quickly realized where the two men had been, but he had no idea why. Regardless, he wished he had arrived earlier to help Spencer out if needed.

This time and for once Spencer knew more than he did, and they had a lot to discuss. What had happened to Mrs. O'Donnell was certainly hitting closer to home, and Killian could only imagine where things went from here. He thought about the relevance of her death. Had things progressed one step further?

Spencer didn't know everything, however. Last night, the second of the five green bottles had toppled from the ledge. Like the first, the bottle had been empty, nothing but shards of glass sprinkled on the concrete floor below. Forever it seemed, the bottle had swayed delicately next to the wall, like trying to make up its mind. It finally fell, floating through the air, end over end, before hitting the surface below. Three more to go. Three more to go, and Killian could only imagine when and for what reasons. When he was awake, nothing offered a clue. But he had intuition, and he had feelings. The bottles were a bad omen, and he felt that Spencer was in more trouble than could be imagined.

Regardless of where the discussion this morning went, he had one piece of advice that he would impart, and not for the first time: Spencer and Erica needed to leave. Murders, innocent deaths, or whatever, this place was becoming unsafe. He thought some more. He realized it was plausible Mrs. O'Donnell had died naturally. Chances were she had. Natural on the surface, maybe. There had to be more. After all, police detectives were generally not much interested in routine deaths. No, none of this was good.

Killian pulled into the driveway, parked, and climbed out of the seat of the car. He grabbed the right side of his lower back and gave it a vigorous rub. I'm getting too old for this nonsense, he thought as he headed to the front door of the house. Erica answered, and the two of them worked their way through the home and out to the patio. Spencer was sitting with his back to them on the edge of the deck, a brown coffee mug in his hand and Buster lying by his side.

Killian grabbed a chair from beside the round table and dragged it over beside Spencer. Buster rose and walked the few steps to Killian, giving him a quick lick on the hand and then settling back down next to his chair. Erica soon returned with two cups of coffee. She pulled up a seat next to her father and Killian.

"Mind if I join in?" she said.

"No, not at all," said Killian. "This is a discussion for the three of us. That's for certain."

Killian fixed his eyes on Spencer, who continued staring off into the distance.

"So, Spencer, I see you had some visitors this morning. Passed by them on the way over, I did. Care to tell me about it?"

Killian watched as Spencer finally turned and acknowledged his presence. The man's demeanor was calm, but Killian noticed a look in his eyes he hadn't seen in a long time. This was the same look as when Spencer had been so dogged in pursuing the runaway Shandy.

"I don't know where to start. I wish you had been here," Spencer said. "I could have used your help."

Killian looked on as Spencer again stared out into the open field.

"I apologize for running a bit late, but of course I had no idea detectives would be showing up so soon or would even show up at all. And I know firsthand Detective Walsh is not the most cordial of fellas. Anyway, it's not like there was a murder or anything on that order. I'm curious why they were here."

He wasn't certain at all about the no-murder aspect, but he would let the conversation play out naturally.

Killian listened intently as Spencer shared all of the discussion that had transpired this morning and about the trip he and Buster had taken to the cemetery. Spencer remained calm as he told every detail, but Killian could sense Erica's anxiety as she fidgeted in her chair next to them. Obviously, Spencer hadn't the time just yet, or possibly the inclination, to tell her the details of his talk with the detectives.

Killian stared into the vista and ran the palms of his hands up and down his cheeks. They all sat silent for a minute or two.

"I must say, Spencer, your deduction seems spot on," Killian finally said. "And it makes perfect sense. Something, or someone, may have its sights set on Buster."

If that were true, then who's to follow?

Buster stared up and grinned at Killian upon hearing his name and then set his face back down on the deck, resting it between his outstretched legs.

"GOD—DOG," Killian said softly as he looked down at Buster. "Not sure I would have figured that one out right away."

"Still, it's difficult to know what to think for certain," Killian continued. "But there may be some real danger here. Maybe best for you to vacate the area for the time being, at least until we have a better understanding."

"And how about you?" Spencer said in a soft voice.

"Well, I believe I'm just a bystander at this point," Killian said. "Who knows? I'll be just fine. Besides, this is my home, and I'm not going anywhere."

"This is my home now too, Killian," Spencer said, his voice raising a few octaves.

Buster raised his head and looked at Spencer.

"Saying that, Buster and I are staying, but perhaps it's better if Erica leaves," Spencer said, talking to himself more than to anyone else. "She can go to my brother's house in Colorado and stay there for the time being. Come back, if she wants, after things settle down, if they do settle down."

Spencer's answer was as Killian had expected; he knew Spencer wouldn't leave. Killian switched his gaze from Spencer to Erica. He knew the young woman well enough by now to understand this wasn't going to go down easy.

"NO FRICKIN' WAY!" Erica immediately blurted out. She had been quiet up to this point. "No way, Dad! I'm not going anywhere. I'm as much a part of this as anyone. And you guys are just guessing at things. You have no way of knowing anything. This is just bullshit!"

"Erica, we can talk about this later," Spencer said, his voice and his expression kind and loving.

"No frickin' way," Erica repeated. She rose quickly from her chair and stormed toward the house. "No frickin' way." The kitchen door slammed behind her.

"Just leave her be for a bit," Killian said as he returned to Spencer. "Besides, and it's nothing but my sense, mind you, but if you are determined to remain, perhaps it's better to stay together. Maybe Erica's right. We are just guessing at this point."

"Maybe, Killian," Spencer said in a voice that didn't mask his feelings, "but I didn't ask for your advice this time, and perhaps you should let me decide what is right for Erica."

"Of course, Spencer. I apologize," Killian said. "You know how I am. Let's forget that and talk about our next steps. If you're staying, we need to think matters through and consider what to do next."

"I think what we need to do is tell the police about Angus," Spencer said without hesitation. "That guy's a real whack job. After this, after Mrs. O'Donnell's death, do you really think he's not involved somehow? Was he in the pub last night?"

Killian decided to tread lightly. Spencer was distraught, and his suspicions about Angus couldn't be totally disregarded. Maybe Angus fit the same modus operandi as someone like the infamous Unabomber—a seemingly benign man who could pull off murders under the noses of everyone. Even their physical descriptions might have been a good match.

But Killian had no sense of Angus being involved in any of this. Not once, since the discovery of the Kelly couple at the abbey, had Angus made himself present in one of Killian's dreams. He could understand Spencer's suspicions, but he was almost certain that they were unfounded.

Still, even if Angus were somehow involved, Killian knew there was more to this. He'd wait for any information on Mrs. O'Donnell's true cause of death, but the coincidence was too much this time around. He was certain the ghost from before was back, and he just needed the time to convince Spencer. Maybe Spencer didn't need much more convincing. Perhaps he was using Angus as a method of denial against the real truth.

"I can't tell you that," Killian said. "Michael was running the show, and I didn't step into the pub even for a second yesterday. Does it make any difference—whether Angus was there or not?"

"I don't know," Spencer admitted. "I guess I was just curious how he was acting."

"There or not, I can assure you he was acting the same as he always does. With that man there are no emotions to decipher."

Killian and Spencer talked for the next hour. They hypothesized on the true relevance of the three recent deaths—or murders. If they were in fact murders and the culprit were the ghost, the Kelly couple had likely been chosen randomly, perhaps because they had a dog that resembled Shandy or perhaps because they had been at the abbey. Probably both. Mrs. O'Donnell was a different story. She had most likely been selected because of her connection to this household, to bring things a step closer to Spencer and to those he loved. Killian wished Erica had been here to listen to this part of the conversation. She needed to understand what was unfolding.

Killian could see that Spencer was still unconvinced about the ghost theory, his mind too preoccupied with thoughts of Angus. Regardless, Spencer made a promise to visit the pub that evening after they both had some time to sit on things for a while. Before meeting in Galbally they would meet at the cemetery to search for clues, to search for anything helpful to understand what was going on.

When the conversation was finished Killian made his way back to his parked car. He grabbed the handle, opened the door, and prepared to get inside. A motion caught his attention, and he looked off to his right. In the distance at the top of the hill, he could see Erica and Buster playing fetch with the tennis ball. He gave a wave in Erica's direction, and she waved back. He considered walking over and having his own private discussion with her. She needed to be brought around. He decided to leave well enough alone for today. He had a feeling she would be staying.

CHAPTER ELEVEN

The shock of Mrs. O'Donnell's death continued to weigh heavily on Spencer (and on Erica) throughout the rest of the day, and he was having trouble coming to terms with her demise. The whole thing just didn't make any sense. The young couple and their dog had been one thing, but Spencer hadn't known them. Mrs. O'Donnell was different; she had been a personal relation and someone he had cared about, or at least he thought he had. Guilt and sympathy melded into one, and he wasn't quite sure what he was feeling.

Still, decisions had to be made and actions had to be taken. The most significant concerned Erica. Spencer and she had delved into one argument after another since Killian's visit this morning. Erica was as stubborn as he was, and Spencer had acquiesced finally. He realized he couldn't physically force her to leave, and she certainly wouldn't go on her own accord. And he was okay with the verdict, because of Killian mostly. If Killian truly sensed they should stay together, for whatever reason, Spencer wouldn't argue.

Spencer decided to shut down the Square One Bed & Breakfast for the time being and for however long necessary. That judgment and that decision would obviously be bad for business, but he wasn't about to put anyone, especially complete strangers, at risk. He canceled all reservations for the next two weeks, hoping matters, one way or another, would resolve by then. Writing personal notes to the canceled guests ripped at his heart. This wasn't the way he lived or the way he ran a business. He promised himself he wouldn't let it happen again.

Erica argued that closing the inn was a drastic and hasty measure. Even after Mrs. O'Donnell's mysterious death and the sorrow it was bringing, Erica was still not on board that more was to come. She didn't believe in any murders, and she didn't believe in the return of some haunting ghost. Spencer wouldn't be dissuaded, however. Ultimately, this was his house and his business. He'd rather play it safe and not have anything else to regret or feel remorse about.

That evening, Spencer and Killian met at the cemetery as planned, but they discovered nothing more than what Spencer had seen the first time. Before they met, Killian had already checked the public records. Spencer's guess that the gravestone in question was in fact that of Mrs. O'Donnell's late husband had been confirmed.

Afterwards, they shared a few drinks at the pub. Spencer waited for Angus to show, but he never did. Spencer even popped into O'Dwyer's after leaving the Grafton, but there was no Angus. He wondered when he would meet Angus again and under what circumstances.

The next day the inn's last guests departed. Spencer, Erica, and Buster now had the house and their lives to themselves. Spencer was grateful for the peace and quiet; he had time to think and consider. Erica immediately began spending a lot of time in her room. She said she was working on some things and making plans for her future if needed, but Spencer suspected there was more. With no immediate work to be done, he let her be. She needed time to digest Mrs. O'Donnell's death, and so did he.

On the same day, later that Saturday afternoon, Detectives Walsh and Dunn made another visit, asking questions, searching for clues, and trying to piece together the curious death of Mrs. O'Donnell. Other than the lipstick writing on the wall, no further evidence to indicate a potential crime had been uncovered. The obvious conclusion was that Mrs. O'Donnell had written the word herself before she had died, but Spencer could sense the detectives weren't fully convinced. Neither was he.

Because no criminal activity had been ascertained, neither Spencer nor Erica was held in suspicion of any kind. The coroner's preliminary results showed the cause of death as a heart attack, with no indication of foul play. Spencer harbored no doubt that Mrs. O'Donnell had succumbed to a failed heart, but the cause was the mystery.

The detectives told Spencer they would continue investigating until they were sure. The case of the dead couple had been technically closed. The abbey was reopened, but Spencer assumed that was just for public consumption. Regardless, the detectives had a lot on their plates, considerably more than they were likely accustomed.

After the detectives departed, one last time Spencer considered Killian's advice that he, Erica, and Buster all leave together. Perhaps that would be the smartest move. He could start over again, somewhere, anywhere. Certainly, then they would be far away from Angus, if he were truly someone to be feared. If an evil spirit were their nemesis, as Killian insisted, well, Spencer was fairly certain a ghost doesn't travel well overseas. They'd leave later if they had to. For now, they would stay, and they would stay together.

They all made another visit to the cemetery a couple of days later for Mrs. O'Donnell's funeral. The landowner opened the gate for the day, and the derelict graveyard got spruced up a bit beforehand (by her son, Spencer imagined). It was still the most pitiful ceremony in which Spencer had ever taken part. Not only was the burial ground an eyesore, but the number of attendees was abysmal. Other than Mrs. O'Donnell's son and a scattering of relatives from two counties over, no one showed except an elderly couple from Bansha. Spencer had suspected so, and it turned out Mrs. O'Donnell had been a lonely old lady after all. He felt sad for her in both life and death and wondered why a person's journey had to be so cold and mean sometimes.

Finally, there was Buster. The dog had been hanging around the kitchen a lot, as if waiting for a Mrs. O'Donnell who never came anymore. Spencer often studied him and speculated about how much he understood. And he kept a constant eye on his pet, generally requiring him to be by his side, or Erica's, twenty-four hours a day. He had a feeling deep down that Buster knew or sensed something evident to no one else.

M rs. O'Donnell's death had shaken Erica to the core. Nobody would have called them close. And the old lady had hardly been the likable type, though Erica had found a way. But Mrs. O'Donnell had been someone she had known. At her young age knowing someone who had died was not common. She hadn't known another except for her mom.

Erica found herself crying in bed at night, crying over a cranky old lady and not knowing why. She was sure the pain would ease with time. For now, she was having a tough time understanding her feelings.

Over the last couple of days, hours spent in her room continued to occupy a lot of her time. She was depressed, and being alone was helping her to resolve the emotions, if even just a little. To distract her mind and because she was curious, Erica spent time on her computer combing for articles and firsthand accounts of the supernatural. The amount of content was superfluous and interesting, but still Erica wasn't certain of her motives or what she was looking for.

Eventually, her attention turned to the death of Mrs. O'Donnell. Had she just simply passed away, or was there more? The red writing on the wall was suspicious. Was there any chance her death was more meaningful, and not in a good way?

Online, she found a certain level of information on families named O'Donnell in the region, but the details were scattered and not enough. She hadn't come up with much. A few trips into the city of Tipperary, to the main public library and to a couple of college ones, ultimately provided what she needed to know. She left amazed each time at the plethora of information on Irish ancestry and descendants, even that specific to this county of Tipperary and the surrounding area.

The O'Donnell clan had been in this vicinity for more than a few generations; they had been here since records had been kept, probably longer. Their original name had been O'Domhnaill, the present name a derivative. The most astonishing material uncovered was the family's connection to Moor Abbey. They had definitely been affiliated with the O'Brien clan, the founders of the abbey. They were possibly relatives, or maybe just acquaintances. The details were sketchy and impossible to verify. The O'Donnells had likely been around when the last friars, and their dogs, were massacred hundreds of years into the history of Moor Abbey. Erica wondered whether they had played a part.

A lot of what Erica read was likely hearsay and impossible to authenticate, but questions entered her mind. Spencer's telling of his past escapades in Ireland focused in large part on Moor Abbey. Now, there was the possibility Mrs. O'Donnell's ancestors had had an intimate past with the same monastery. Coincidental, or did it mean something?

She was slowly coming into the fold, beginning to consider that the three recent deaths entailed more questions than answers. Was her father right, that Angus was involved somehow? Or was Killian right, that the ghost of the past had returned? Or was the massacre of the dogs at the abbey somehow the connection? Perhaps there was something to fear after all.

Her doubts remained, however, and she'd believe in a ghost, or ghosts, only when she saw one.

CHAPTER TWELVE

In two days it would be a week since the passing of Mrs. O'Donnell and almost ten days since the bodies of the Kelly couple had been discovered. Things had been quiet, and not a peep had been heard from the detectives lately. Erica was feeling more relaxed, and she sensed that her father was as well.

The weather couldn't be finer, and father and daughter decided today was a good day for the three of them to get out of the house and into nature. Around the house or elsewhere, the risk was the same in their estimation, and they needed a break from the normal routine. Mrs. O'Donnell's funeral several days ago had left both her and her father feeling somber and depressed. They needed something to relieve their doldrums.

Erica still felt that any fear of a returned ghost was likely a stretch. Her father had been on the lookout for Angus, making a couple of trips to Galbally, but the man was keeping a low profile for one reason or another. Killian said Angus hadn't shown up at the pub in recent days, making Spencer even more suspicious than he had been.

Spencer had suggested packing a lunch and taking a long mountain hike, maybe over in the Galtees, but Erica convinced him they should stick close to home. The path next to and above the River Aya went on for considerably more than a mile to the west, and other trails branched off and led into the forested areas above. The early September elements were still warm enough to allow Buster to play in the water, though Erica was certain he would gladly jump in regardless of the temperature.

The slight crispness of the late morning made Erica feel good, even with all the endless thoughts going on in her mind. As they began their walk down the trail, Erica watched as Buster cut off the path and scrambled down the small hill and through the narrow stand of deciduous trees that butted against and, in places, towered over the river's water. Like her father, Erica had become very protective of Buster lately, and she immediately called out to him. Only a minute or two later, Buster was back on the trail, a wetter dog than he had been.

"Buster, stay out of the water until we stop somewhere for lunch. Then you can play all you want," Erica said.

She looked down at Buster, who was shaking his body from tail to head until he was satisfied enough water had been shed. Erica returned his smile, knowing he understood her meaning.

"Dad, do you wanna stay on the trail or go up above?" Erica asked as she set the pace in front of her father.

"Let's just stay on the trail today, Erica. I know a good spot on the river where we can have lunch. And I'd like to see what the fish are up to."

They mostly remained quiet as they continued down the path. The sun was shining brightly, and the day grew warmer. Erica marveled at the beauty around them and thought, not for the first time, how much she enjoyed being in this country. She could make a life here, whether at the Square One or doing something else. In a way she realized this was her place. She had discovered a land she had known nothing about. And she had rekindled—no, unlocked—a relationship with her father that may never have happened otherwise. Yes, life was more than all right here, and she had no intention of leaving.

In twenty minutes they reached their destination, and Erica followed with Buster as Spencer led them down toward the water to a flat area void of brush and bushes. They took off their backpacks and placed them on the ground. Erica held on to Buster by the collar as Spencer sat down and stared into the water. Within moments the telltale sign of more than one trout feeding was evident, their mouths gingerly protruding as they sucked up the aquatic insects that danced on the surface. Erica studied her father as he stared at the water and the fish.

"I bet you wish you had brought your rod and reel, huh, Dad?" Erica said.

"Yep. Coulda, shoulda, but that's all right," he said. "I'm fine with just watching 'em today. Anyway, why don't you let Buster go now? The fish can swim somewhere else."

Erica let go of Buster's collar, and the dog sprinted into the previously calm water. Both Erica and Spencer laughed as Buster frolicked, coming out of the stream and immediately going back in. The scene was repeated over and over until Buster had had enough and finally settled down beside them.

Erica broke out the peanut butter and honey sandwiches and a bag of potato chips. She handed Buster snacks from the baggie she had brought, making him perform a trick for each one. As they finished their lunch Erica tossed a half-eaten apple into a small cluster of trees and watched Buster scramble after it.

"Mind if I take a little snooze?" Spencer said before placing a thin wool blanket on the ground. He removed his hiking boots and settled back.

"Mind or not, that looks like what you're gonna do," Erica said, snickering. "Go ahead, Dad. I think I'll take Buster a little ways further up the trail."

"Okay, but don't you go too far. I mean it, Erica. Stay close."

"We will, Dad. Don't worry."

Erica climbed up and looked down from the top of the hill. Spencer's eyes were already closed, and she was happy he was able to get some rest. She knew how hard these last few days had been on him.

Erica and Buster proceeded down the trail a few hundred yards until they found another opening that led to the river below. They made their way down to the water, and the same scene as before was repeated. Erica was amazed at how much the dog enjoyed being in the water, and he was most certainly going to need a bath once they got home. Erica picked up a random stick from the ground and gave it several throws into the water, each time Buster faithfully bringing the piece of wood back to set down in front of her. Again, he was rewarded with a snack for his stellar performances.

A slight breeze kicked up on what had been a perfectly calm day. Erica gazed up at the treetops and watched their green leaves begin to shake and sway. She couldn't imagine the reason for the sudden change. Without any further warning an unrelenting wind, the likes of which Erica had never witnessed before, violently shook the same treetops and worked its way down to the ground. The air had changed, and it was getting harder to breathe. The howling wind blistered Erica's ears. She felt cold as she gawked at the trees bowing to the river from the wind's ungodly force.

Erica pivoted her head as she just barely discerned Buster's bark through the cacophony. Her dog stood at the bank of the river, barking and growling madly at the unseen force around them. Not knowing what else to do, she ran to his side, lowered her body beside him, and draped her arms around his neck.

She thought back to one of the stories her father had shared. When he first came to Ireland something similar had happened to him on a river where he had almost drowned. Was this it? Is this how a ghost makes its presence known? She knew the answer already and tightened her hold on Buster. This thing would not have her dog, not today. Buster continued to growl and bark uncontrollably and tried to break free from Erica's grasp. She reined him in and tightened her grip on his collar. She reached her arm around into a pocket of her backpack and slipped on Buster's lead. She held tight, and then she stood up.

"Leave us the fuck alone, you piece of shit!" she shouted at the top of her lungs. She looked into the force, and she looked into nothing at all; she had no idea where it was. The wind quickened and increased in intensity until the river's water was splashing onto the bank and onto her shoes and Buster's paws.

Erica had never been more scared, and she had never felt more confident. Her long hair twisted in the wind and whipped around her face until she looked half-crazy. She shouted out again and again, with a determination unknown to her, as Buster continued his unbridled rage.

The yelling seemed to be accomplishing nothing, and Erica was beginning to have doubts. She had no idea what was to come next, and running away as quickly as possible seemed the sensible decision. She grasped Buster's lead more firmly and pulled, determined to make a quick exit up the hill. The dog would not give up his spot. Erica pulled again and pleaded with Buster, but he wouldn't move.

"Buster, stop it! We need to go," she said.

His barking and growling were incessant, and his attention was solely focused on the enemy around them. Erica gave one last pull, as hard as she could, and the dog turned his head. Then, as they were turning to run up the hill, the unsolicited visitor faded away just as suddenly as it had appeared. The wind settled gradually and returned to a small breeze again before dissipating completely. Erica threw herself to the bare ground, and the tears came freely. Her heart was pounding inside her chest, and for several minutes the adrenaline rush did not subside. Buster sat down beside her and began whimpering. He nestled his head next to hers, and his long pink tongue wetted her face. Erica grabbed Buster around the neck, and the tears continued.

After a few more minutes of trying to gather her senses, Erica heard someone calling from up above. She didn't know exactly what was going on, but she knew her father's voice.

"Erica, Erica, are you down there?" Spencer said from the top of the hill. "Erica, where are you?"

Erica wiped her face with her hand and looked in the direction of the incline above her.

"We're down here, Daddy," she answered back in as strong of a voice as she could muster.

She watched her father scramble down the narrow path toward her and Buster. When he reached them, she fell into his arms, her crying unabated.

"Are you all right? What happened?" he asked.

Erica pulled herself away from Spencer's arms. Between gasps of air she told him what had just occurred. She listened as Spencer described a similar, though not as intense, experience, and not one where he was screaming obscenities at the devil. When he was finished, Erica watched Spencer as he scanned the area around them. All was exactly as it should be: calm and serene, with a river quietly running beside them.

"I'm scared, Dad. Let's leave," Erica said.

"Shit, it's really happening now, isn't it? Yes, let's get out of here. I mean right this instant," Spencer said as he took one last look around and turned toward the trail.

They ran to the top of the hill, took a final look below, and began walking quickly in the direction of the house. Erica's hand grasped her father's as they walked, the other hand holding the lead attached to Buster's collar. Neither spoke.

They hurried along the trail. As they neared their house fifteen minutes later, they spied one of their neighbors picking up and piling rocks near the trail. Spencer waved from a distance, and Erica could tell he was trying to compose himself for the unwanted small talk to come.

"Afternoon, Brendan. Out working as usual, I see," Spencer said as they reached the man. The two shook hands.

"Hey ya, Spencer," the man said. "Brilliant day for a leisurely walk, isn't it now?"

"Yep, just playing around a bit with the dog down by the river," Spencer said. "You've met my daughter Erica before, haven't you?"

"Ah, sure, I have. Nice to see you again, Erica," Brendan said.

Erica could only nod her head and smile back.

"That sure was some kind of wind storm we had earlier, wasn't it?" Spencer said.

Erica could tell he was trying to feel the man out.

"Wind? Can't say I noticed any wind. I must have been inside at the time."

Erica knew a wind like that would not go unnoticed, inside or not. Was it just them who saw and experienced the whole thing?

"Yeah, you must have been," Spencer said, receiving the confirmation he needed.

The two men engaged in a casual conversation for a few minutes, while Erica hung in the shadows, giving her attention to Buster. Finally, she caught a glance from her father and knew they could be on their way.

"Well, we've got some work to do ourselves, so better get on home," Spencer said. "Nice to see you, Brendan. Please give our regards to your wife."

"Sure will, Spencer. Take care."

"You as well."

A few more minutes, and Erica, Spencer, and their dog were safely within the confines of the Square One. Erica had never felt so shaken in her life, except for the moment she witnessed her mother's death. They took seats and stared at each other across the kitchen table. Spencer had poured them each a glass of water, but Erica hadn't touched hers.

"Dad, can I have some of your whiskey?"

Erica had partied a bit while at university, but she didn't imbibe much here, only an occasional glass of red wine with dinner or a sip from one of her father's favorite craft beers. She was a social drinker, and the social life in Bansha left something to be desired, at least for someone of her age. Not that she cared much, anyway. But right now she needed a drink in the worst possible way.

Erica looked on as her father stood up and returned with a bottle of Jack Daniels and two shot glasses pulled from the kitchen cabinet.

"I think I'm going to join you," Spencer said. "Neat is okay?"

"Please. The more potent, the better."

Erica could tell her father was upset, but he seemed a lot more composed than she was feeling. This wasn't his first rodeo when it came to ghosts. For Erica, the convincing had come. What had just happened was more than enough. There was danger, and this thing, this spirit Spencer had talked about, was real and truly back.

Spencer filled each shot glass to the top, his hand shaking slightly, and sat back down. Erica watched her father take a small sip. He reached down, and his hand rubbed Buster's head. Erica stared at Buster for a moment or two, amazed that his demeanor was the same as always.

She had no idea whether the nasty spirit of just a short while ago had been after her, after Buster, or after the both of them. Maybe it hadn't been pursuing them at all but had only come to impart a message. She would never know for certain. She couldn't imagine how she would have handled things without her dog by her side. She threw her head back and drained the glass. Spencer refilled it.

"Don't get carried away, Erica."

Erica managed a slight smile and took only a small sip this time. The effects of the first shot were already warming her insides and had begun calming her nerves.

"What exactly did you yell at that thing?" Spencer asked with a small grin, trying to lighten the conversation and the situation.

"I told it 'Leave us the fuck alone, you piece of shit,' or something like that. I can hardly remember now."

Erica watched as a huge grin took form on Spencer's face. In seconds he was laughing as hard as she had seen him laugh in weeks. He laughed so hard it almost seemed contrived. Was he all right?

"That must have taken him by surprise. No wonder he left. Probably had to go home and take a peek at the urban dictionary," Spencer said, appearing to be completely amused at Erica's choice of words.

Spencer settled back down, and once more he twisted the cap from the bottle and topped off each glass. He then got up and placed the whiskey on the counter, signaling enough. Erica watched as he came back and stood next to the table, his normal expression and tone of voice having returned.

"Well, I guess it really has started, hasn't it?" Spencer said. "I thought it was Angus, but I was wrong...and Killian was right. Maybe we should get out of here. Maybe go to Dublin or somewhere else, somewhere away from this house and this area. I don't know, but we've got to figure this out and soon."

"Dad, I'm so sorry I doubted you. I didn't believe some of your past story, but I do now. I'm sorry."

"It's fine, Erica," Spencer said, rubbing his daughter's shoulder. "Obviously, I too was wrong about what was going on this time, so we're even."

"Still, I'm sorry," Erica said. "And I'm not sure what we should do, but I did find something out today."

She needed to talk.

"What's that?"

"You know how I have been spending a lot of time in my room?" she said.

"Yeah, I guess I did notice that a bit," Spencer said.

"The truth is, I have been doing some research online," Erica said. "I must have looked at a hundred sites. You know, how to conquer an evil spirit, how to de-haunt a house, goblin be gone. Those kinds of things. Just in case we needed to know, I guess."

"And... "

"And there is so much information you can't believe it. Much of it you can take with a grain of salt, and a lot of it is obviously BS. But there was one theme I saw repeated over and over."

"And what's that?" Spencer asked.

Erica could see a glimmer of hope in his eyes.

"You remember when I was a kid and you took us to Arizona on that overnight pack trip on horses?" Erica said. "The first time I rode a horse. Remember?"

"Yes, I remember."

"You told me that horses are intelligent and that they can sense fear," Erica said. "You told me I had to show the horse who was the boss or it would take advantage of me. Do you remember that?"

"Yes."

"I think it's the same thing with this spirit," Erica said. "And that's exactly what I read online. And that's what I did today. Cursing at it was probably of no use, but I showed I wasn't scared, even though I was. Maybe that's why it went away so quickly."

Erica looked on as Spencer set his drink down, removed his glasses, and sat back in his chair, his head pointed to the ceiling. After several moments of silence he leaned forward.

"You know, maybe you're right," he finally said. "I guess I tried the same when I was looking for Shandy, though I may not have realized it at the time."

Spencer put his glasses back on and looked through the kitchen window to the outside. Again, several moments went by before he spoke once more.

"You know something else? It seems to me this thing could have taken Shandy on more than one occasion, but it didn't. It makes me wonder whether it can't finish the job when others are around, that there is some kind of force in numbers.

"Maybe the presence of Colin and me deterred it somehow, and when Shandy was alone she was somehow able to evade it until she wasn't. Maybe it's a dog thing. Still, I was there when she died, and that theory doesn't explain how that young couple got taken. I don't know, but maybe it's something."

"Dad, there's something else," Erica said.

"What's that?"

Erica explained all the information she had uncovered about Mrs. O'Donnell and her supposed distant relatives of long, long ago.

"Why have you kept this from me until now?" Spencer asked.

"I don't know," Erica said. "I guess I was still unconvinced and wasn't sure it meant anything. It probably doesn't. Maybe I wanted to know something you didn't."

"It's okay, really," Spencer said. "I'm not sure it has any relevance. I'm sure everyone around here is interconnected in one way or another and has some association with the past."

He said those words, but Erica could see his mind was on a different page. This was new information to him, something he hadn't known nor considered.

Erica thought for a moment about dogs and abbeys and ghosts. If this thing had truly murdered Mrs. O'Donnell, was the reason because of the woman's ancestors? Maybe revenge for past horrible deeds? What about the Kelly couple? How did they figure in? This was so messed up. Her mind was spinning. She closed her eyes and tried to wish it all away.

As they continued talking and planning the early parts of their next moves, the sound of a knock on the front door echoed into the kitchen. Erica made her way through the house and soon returned. With her was Detective Walsh. Erica wondered where Detective Dunn was today, but she didn't ask. She couldn't imagine why the detective was making another visit so soon, and she could see her father was feeling the same, though he was doing his best to disguise his discomfort. Spencer and Detective Walsh greeted each other and exited to the patio at the detective's suggestion. Erica was asked to join them. She could only guess at the reason why.

"So, detective, to what do we owe the pleasure?" Spencer asked, acting as cordially as possible.

"I'm just out and about today," Detective Walsh said, business-like as usual. "Stopped by the O'Donnell place one last time before we pull up stakes. I wanted to have one last look around, you understand, and make certain there was nothing we missed."

"Makes sense," Spencer said. "Come up with anything?"

Erica knew, as her father did, the question needn't be asked; the detective certainly hadn't come out here today for lack of anything else to do.

"As a matter of fact, I did. Would you like to hear?" Detective Walsh said.

Erica did her best to hide her nervousness as the detective gave her a glance from across the patio table and returned his attention to Spencer.

"Go on," Spencer said.

"Well, I wasn't sure what I was looking for, but the matter of the lipstick has been bothering me, of course, from day one," the detective said. "The fact that we were not able to find even a single tube in the house just wasn't sitting right with me.

"Today, the last place I searched in the house was in Mrs. O'Donnell's bedroom. I looked around, not finding anything of consequence. Then, just as I was about to leave, I looked at the wall behind her bed. There, just off to the right of the bed, just up on the wall a wee bit, was a framed picture of a dog. I didn't think anything of it at first, and then it came to me that the dog looked familiar. I couldn't place it until I finally did."

Erica watched the detective as he pivoted his head a few degrees until he was looking straight at Buster, who was lying on the edge of the wooden deck, surveying the field in front of him. Spencer's eyes followed where the detective had planted his gaze.

"What?" Spencer said. "She had a picture of Buster hanging on her wall?"

"Unless I'm mistaken, and I think I'm not, yes, the picture is of your dog."

The detective reached into his black briefcase and pulled out an 8" by 10" frame encased in a transparent plastic bag. He gently placed the picture on the table in front of Erica and Spencer and sat back in his chair again. He seemed somehow pleased with what he had just presented.

Erica grabbed the picture before Spencer had a chance and held the photo close to her face. There was no mistaking Buster. Mrs. O'Donnell had clearly taken the photo right there in the kitchen of the Square One. Erica handed the picture to her father and waited for his reaction. As Spencer examined the image, Detective Walsh continued speaking.

"It seems ole' Mrs. O'Donnell was more fond of your animal than perhaps she let on."

"Wow, that's unbelievable," Spencer said. "I had no idea..."

"That's not the most interesting part; no, it's not," the detective said.

He reached into his bag again and pulled out a small transparent pouch. He held it up so both Erica and Spencer could see its contents. Inside was a tube of lipstick.

"When I pulled the picture off the wall to examine it closer, this fell to the floor. It seems to have been tucked behind the top edge of the frame, out of sight in a way. Now, I could have forensics run the fingerprints and do all of that, but it seems to me this is not a lipstick brand or type to be used by an old woman. Any idea of whose it could be?"

Erica knew right away the lipstick belonged to her; the detective was undoubtedly thinking the same. The lipstick was her brand and one of her colors. She even remembered the store where she had purchased it in Michigan. She hadn't been using much in the way of lipstick or other cosmetics since being in Ireland. She had hardly opened her makeup case at all lately. That something had gone missing was as much a surprise to her as to anyone else.

"Dad, it's mine," she said immediately.

"What?" Spencer said, looking directly at her. "How the hell would your lipstick end up in Mrs. O'Donnell's house? You've never even been there, have you?"

"No, of course not," Erica said, feeling slightly unwell and a little dizzy. "I didn't even know it was missing!"

"You can see we have a bit of a problem here," the detective interrupted and said matter-of-factly. "Ms. Spencer, we're gonna be needing to talk to you in a more official capacity, I'm afraid."

Erica's heart quickened. She grabbed a hold of the edges of her chair to steady herself. Her head was spinning, and she almost felt like she was watching the entire scene from up above the table. She could only imagine what the detective, and her father, was thinking.

Before she had a chance to respond, Spencer spoke up: "Detective Walsh, I think there's something I need to tell you."

CHAPTER THIRTEEN

After yesterday's unnerving episode at the river and the unplanned visit from Detective Walsh, Spencer felt things were spinning out of control. *Were things spinning out of control because of Shandy?* He had asked himself that very question many times since yesterday.

After she died, Spencer was able to learn a lot about Shandy. She had been living, of all places, right here in this community of Bansha. Her life must have been a happy one, belonging to a solid family of four, including two young girls who had undoubtedly loved the dog with all of their hearts. But Shandy's family wasn't and hadn't been a wealthy one. When the dog was diagnosed with cancer, her care and possible remedy would have been beyond the means of the McGregor family. The father's solution, after a lot of soul-searching, had been to put the animal down, a decision he had come to on his own without sharing with the others. Shortly after that decision had been made, Shandy mysteriously disappeared, near Moor Abbey, maybe having run away, maybe abandoned by Mr. McGregor, maybe because she realized her fate. Spencer didn't know, of course. That was a question that only Shandy could have answered.

Soon the entire McGregor family, with the father willingly or unwillingly playing his part, had begun a full-scale search for their missing dog, scouring the vicinity of Galbally and the monastery and hanging lost-dog posters in every conceivable location. By that time Spencer had already initially stumbled upon Shandy and had made up his mind to find her again.

By chance, one day Mr. McGregor, a man Spencer had never met, had showed up at the Grafton Pub for a drink following a long day of searching for his lost dog. Conversations go from one place to another, and soon the sad story of the lost Shandy had been shared with Killian. Spencer had been sitting on the opposite side of the bar counter, only a listener, only an observer. The lack of other patrons had allowed Spencer to hear every single detail of the talk between the two other men. That was when he first became aware of Shandy's cancer diagnosis and Mr. McGregor's original plan to end the animal's suffering. Spencer toyed with the idea of coming forward and telling this Mr. McGregor about his chance meeting with Shandy. But a voice inside told him to do otherwise. Spencer let this new man, this new character in the Shandy saga, leave the pub that day without saying a word to him.

After the episode at the pub, Spencer's search for Shandy had become a fair degree more desperate. He was in a race to find Shandy before the McGregors, not knowing whether the father would have his way and have the dog put down if she were found. Spencer had money; he could take the dog away from here and get her the treatment she needed. Irrational thoughts perhaps, but that is what he had told himself.

The real reason Spencer wanted to find Shandy had been half-hidden deeper in his mind, easily accessible but not quite ready to be dislodged. His subconscious knew Shandy was there because of him. She, in a way, and certainly before she died, had been meant to save Spencer, something he had failed at so many times. The world can work in mysterious ways, sometimes in ways that defy a normal existence. In this case a man had been suffering his entire life, and a dog had been sent to save him. It was as simple as that.

Spencer did not admit any of this until the very end, but he had known. He couldn't help but to have known. The search for a dog dying of cancer had nothing to do with her and everything to do with him. His first trip to Ireland and his happenstance meeting with a lost dog had been preordained. He didn't know by whom or by what, and that didn't matter. Without Shandy, he knew the deep abyss that had been waiting for him his entire life would have finally engulfed him.

Spencer owed Shandy more than he could ever repay; he owed her his life. She had died, and he had survived and even prospered. She was gone now and had been for some time, but his relationship with Shandy had not seen its end just quite yet. He had no evidence to support such an assumption, but he could feel something. Regardless, this reappeared ghost from the past was connected to her in one way or another.

Upon waking up, Spencer's head was pounding once again. He popped a couple of aspirin and got dressed after a quick shower. On his way to the kitchen to get the coffee started, his knuckles rapped on Erica's bedroom door. They weren't running late, but he didn't want to have to hurry. Spencer imagined only Buster had slept well last night, but he wasn't sure of even that. For the first hour or so, he had seen and heard the involuntary leg movements and the soft whimperings. Even the dog was on edge.

Detective Walsh's suggestion (but certainly not just a mere suggestion) that today Erica pay a visit to the Garda headquarters in Limerick only added to their growing list of problems. He could only imagine how Erica must be feeling. She had stayed fairly quiet the rest of yesterday, and Spencer had left her alone.

The detective had said the guards only wanted her statements for the record, but Spencer worried nevertheless. The detective had also disclosed that his partner Detective Dunn and some others would be back at the O'Donnell house today, dusting it once more for fingerprints. If they came up with any missed previously, the new prints would be compared for a possible match with Erica's. She would be sharing hers today at the Limerick police station.

Spencer hoped the visit this afternoon was truly nothing but a simple formality. Certainly, they would not find Erica's prints in the house, and she would soon be off the hook. He knew she was innocent, but someone had planted her lipstick in Mrs. O'Donnell's home. He also understood that the culprit wasn't a "someone." What else was it capable of?

Whether Detective Walsh had bought the details about Spencer's past adventures with Shandy was another question mark. The man had maintained his professional demeanor as Spencer shared the unlikely and improbable story. But his wasn't a story at all; it was a series of true events, but unfortunately not something that could be proven. Spencer realized the far-fetched tale could only sound ridiculous to the uninitiated ear. Still, the detective seemed sympathetic enough, and Spencer couldn't ask for anything more.

Spencer had also noticed a certain kind of affection directed toward Erica, the kind a man interested in a young lady might show. The glances from the detective were more or less inconspicuous, but Spencer hadn't missed them. He wondered whether Erica had noticed the same.

He had mixed feelings about someone having eyes for his daughter. As far as Spencer could remember, Erica had had only a small handful of boyfriends while in high school, and the relationships never lasted long. Her personality back then didn't lend itself to the development of deep relations with anyone. He realized things probably had changed while she was away at university, but he had no idea really. During those years the rapport between the two of them had been so artificial that nothing personal was ever shared, not from her side at least.

The Square One received parcels and packages regularly, generally supplies for the inn that couldn't be purchased locally. The same person, a young man from nearby Tipperary, delivered almost every package. He was handsome with an earnest, outgoing personality, and Spencer made sure to hand him a soda or some other drink each time he appeared.

Back in the early summer, when the delivery driver spotted Erica for the first time, his eyes lit up like he had seen an angel. Every time after that, whenever Spencer answered the front door instead of Erica, he could sense the disappointment in the man's eyes. His head would swivel from right to left and left to right each time, scanning the inside of the house and hoping to catch a glimpse of Erica. The two had spoken to each other many times during the course of giving and receiving packages, but Erica was either oblivious to the young fellow's admiration or she just didn't care.

Spencer decided he would no longer concern himself with Erica's social interactions. For the last two months he had been pushing Erica, in a low-key manner, to get out and mingle with people more often. He put great effort into finding social events for young people, but Erica declined each time, saying she was too busy or this or that was not her thing. At the end of the day, she seemed happy here, and that was enough for Spencer. And right now they had bigger fish to fry.

"Morning, Dad," Erica said as she shuffled into the kitchen, still wearing her red flannel pajamas and the furry maroon slippers she loved.

"Morning, Erica," Spencer said. "Coffee?"

"Please," she said as Spencer pulled the pot from the machine and filled the white ceramic coffee mug she used each morning.

"Listen, we're not due in Limerick until 3:00 p.m., so I thought we'd stop in Galbally on the way and fill in Killian on the latest," Spencer said. "We've got a lot to tell him. I've already called, and we'll meet him at the pub. Limerick's less than an hour's drive from Galbally, so we've got plenty of time. But I've got another place I'd like to visit on the way. Let's leave here in an hour or so, okay?"

Erica didn't respond.

"You all right, kiddo?"

"Yeah, I'm all right. Just tired, I guess," Erica said.

"Listen, Erica, I know how you're feeling; I'm feeling pretty much the same. I never thought I would be facing all of this again. You ready to leave, maybe head to the States? I wouldn't blame you at all."

"As I told you before, no way," Erica said calmly. "I just need to catch a second wind or something. I'm scared to death, but I'm not. We're a family, and families stay together. I'm not leaving."

Spencer sucked some wind and held his breath. He never thought he would see this day, when he would finally and completely bond with one of his children. Regardless of how all of this turned out, he had accomplished that.

Just over an hour later, the two of them and Buster were out the door, on their way to Galbally and then Limerick. As they climbed into the car, among the many thoughts in Spencer's head was yesterday's drama by the river. He had faced something similar, his debut supernatural experience, when he first came to Ireland.

That day, he was also next to a river, one much bigger, deeper, and more intimidating than the River Aya. He had been checking out the fishing prospects and had taken a careless step. That misstep immediately had him slipping down a muddy bank and into the water, where he was submerged and soon washed downstream by the river's current. He had managed to safely climb out within a minute or two, but, as he sat on a downed tree afterward to collect his wits, he was greeted by a violent wind quite similar to that of yesterday. The blast that day had come and gone quickly, and Spencer had given the matter little thought at the time, for it had been days before his first meeting with Shandy. He understood later, as he understood now, that the episode had been his first meeting with the same nasty spirit that had called again yesterday.

Spencer pushed the thought out of his head, listening to Erica as she re-lived and gave further accounts and suppositions about yesterday's events. The tone of her voice and the occasional smile indicated a mood better than that of earlier this morning.

The car reached town. Today Spencer didn't take the usual right turn at the intersection that led to Galbally. Instead, he drove through the center of Bansha. He looked out the car window as they made their way down the short distance of the main road. He enjoyed this little village, but at times he wished there were more to the small community. Other than occasional social and sporting events, there wasn't a whole lot that went on here. The smattering of stores and retail outlets was unimpressive: a few take-out places, a pub that seemed closed more than it was open, and two small grocery stores that offered little variety and seemed out of place in a modern world.

The only business of consequence was a hybrid gas station/convenience store at the near end of town, which seemed to be busy all the time. The grocery selection there was not half bad but hardly adequate for the business needs of the Square One.

Soon, just on the outskirts of Bansha, Spencer made a right turn onto a narrow paved road that in places could just barely fit two passing cars. As was common in Ireland, the overload of bushes and trees on both sides of the road obscured their view as they drove.

In only a short distance the mass of green blocking the scenery had disappeared. The tracts of fields and open farmland reminded Spencer of his very first drive across the Irish countryside, a trip from Dublin to the village of Cahir. Then, the sight hadn't been as perfectly green as he had expected, and he was surprised that while Ireland was rural in most places, humanity seemed everywhere. No matter the place, it was nearly impossible to drive even a mile or two without stumbling upon a house, farm building, or small village.

Today the elements were downright comfortable outside, and the two were driving with the car windows down. Spencer had been up and down this particular road numerous times before, and he knew what was coming next. Agriculture at its best—or at its worst—was just around the next bend, and Spencer grinned inside as he waited for the odor to permeate the car's interior.

Wait for it, wait for it. Now!

"Jesus, what the hell is that?" Erica exclaimed as the intruder, seemingly out of nowhere, entered the open window next to her and the one across from her. She quickly pulled her fingers to her nose and pinched her nostrils.

"Oh, just a little sweet smell of dairy cow, as I like to say. It won't hurt you," Spencer said, letting out a laugh as he watched Erica hurriedly roll up her window.

"Dad, shut your window! I mean it. I'm gonna puke right here, in this car, if you don't."

Erica looked pale already, and Spencer complied.

He, too, was at the point of intolerance. He laughed again, happy to pull this little surprise on Erica and lighten the mood from what promised to be a difficult day.

"Wicked stuff, eh?" Spencer said. "I thought you might enjoy a little taste, or smell, of the real Ireland."

Erica looked at her father and frowned. "Just get us the hell out of here! Please."

Spencer had spent much of his childhood around cattle, a kind of hobby of his businessman father. But those cattle were of the beef type and generally spent their time in open fields of grass. Regardless, they were dirty, lazy animals, and Spencer never cared for them much, no matter their purpose.

This particular dairy farm, just off to their right, could be seen now. He surveyed the tan, low-rise building where the milking took place. The milling black-and-white cows were crowded into enclosed dirt lots that resided around the building, feeding, drinking, and waiting until the next milking session. The mooing was incessant, and Spencer wondered how the neighbors were able to tolerate the sound and the constant noxious air.

They drove about half a mile until they were certain it was once again safe to open the car windows. Spencer watched and snickered quietly as Erica stuck her neck halfway out and gulped in the fresh air.

Another half a mile later the car pulled over in front of a blue two-story house that sat lonely on a large plot of land. To the right of the house in the yard, Spencer could see the marker.

Shandy was buried here, in this yard, and this house belonged to Shandy's original owners, the McGregor family. Spencer was sure they still lived here, the husband, wife, and two young girls, though he hadn't come across any of them in a while. Mr. McGregor had become a friend of sorts, and Spencer occasionally ran into him, or his wife, when he was in town. They were acquaintances more than friends really, and acquaintances who were never told of, or even suspected, Spencer's involvement with Shandy one year ago. The McGregors were simply the family whose dog had run away and then came back dead several weeks later. If they only knew the adventure Shandy had been on, and had led Spencer on, before she died.

Spencer would secretly stop by here on occasion to pay his respects and to share silent messages with a dog who had meant so much to him and who had changed his life.

"Why we stopping here, Dad?" Erica said, surveying the area through her window.

"This is where Shandy used to live and where she is buried," Spencer said.

"Really?" Erica said and fixed her eyes where her father's were.

"Yeah, I stop by here once in a while just to say hello," Spencer said, looking at his daughter with a kind smile.

Erica smiled back and returned her attention to the small white cross and brown plaque tucked away in the back corner of the yard.

"They must have really loved her, huh?" she said.

"I'm sure they did. She was a special dog."

"And so are you, Buster," Spencer said, turning around toward the backseat and rubbing the top of the dog's head.

Buster looked at Spencer with excited eyes and began whining and letting out the faintest of barks. He pranced back and forth on the backseat. He looked out the window and stared at the same spot as Erica. He turned to Spencer again and once more out the window.

"Settle down, buddy. There's nothing out there," Spencer said.

Spencer knew there was something out there, something that couldn't be visualized. His intuition had been correct. Buster had just confirmed the reason why Spencer had wanted to stop here today. He had had a hunch, and now he was fairly certain that Shandy still had some role to play in this saga. I sure wish dogs could talk, Spencer thought, wishing he could read Buster's mind.

They sat there for a while longer, silently and passively studying the scene. Buster, too, had quieted after a few minutes and was lying down on the seat.

"Why did you really want to stop here today?" Erica asked before they left.

"I guess I just wanted to show you this place. That's all," Spencer said and smiled again at his daughter. He would tell her the real reason once they were with Killian.

Erica shrugged, and Spencer watched as she turned and looked out the window at Shandy's grave.

Spencer started the car's engine and began driving the back roads that led to Galbally.

S pencer and Erica arrived just before 1:00 p.m., and the car came to a stop in front of the pub. Killian was outside, sweeping the pavement. He rested the broom against the wall and then ushered the two, and Buster, into the Grafton Pub. The conversation used up most of an hour, as Spencer and Erica conveyed as much detail as possible about yesterday's two extraordinary events. And Spencer apologized to Killian several times for the doubts he had harbored. They all knew now, with no uncertainty, that the ghost had returned.

Regardless, Killian didn't like any of this. Sure, the lipstick matter was a new twist, but the episode at the river was a natural progression of things in his mind. He had been certain something like this would be coming their way. Last night, the third bottle dropped.

As Erica explained her and Buster's unnerving confrontation with the ghoul, Killian thought she might be on to something. Perhaps showing no fear was a weapon that could be utilized. Still, he was certain things weren't so simple.

If the ghost did show again, they would have to match strength with strength. That would be their only chance of seeing the other side of this dilemma. Inside, he wanted Spencer and Erica to leave; he desperately wanted them to leave. No good would come from remaining. Staying here and risking everything, maybe their very lives, made no sense to him. But Spencer was Spencer, and Erica wasn't that different. The man sometimes made questionable decisions, but he wasn't to be deterred once his mind was set. They would stay, until they wouldn't, one way or another, and Killian would do whatever he could.

Spencer relayed today's earlier visit to Shandy's home, and Killian silently wondered about the dead dog. She had been a brave animal, no doubt, but could things have ended differently for her? At the end of the day, she had been suffering from cancer, and maybe her ultimate fate was the one she had been meant to suffer. Part of that fate had been to help a lost man, something she had accomplished in spades.

Like Spencer, he also wondered whether Shandy would make another appearance somehow. Buster's reaction to being near her had some meaning attached to it. They would know soon enough.

The final act of their discussion was an attempt at strategy and entered Killian's mind just as Spencer and Erica were about to leave. Limerick was full of people, and the city might be the perfect place to test a theory. That theory was a long shot at best, but testing it would be simple. And Killian realized Spencer and Erica could use a break. Some time away from this area would be good for them.

When today's meeting at the Garda headquarters was through, hopefully with a positive outcome, Spencer, Erica, and Buster would head back to Limerick a day or two later. They would hole up there for a few days. The reason wasn't to run away, not at all. They needed to know whether the spirit would be reluctant to make a return appearance while the three of them were in the middle of a bustling city, protected perhaps by the mass of other people who would be around them.

If that ended up being the case, they could have some confidence that the fight to come, if it were to happen, would take place at the Square One or perhaps close by. Killian wasn't certain whether that held any advantage.

They exited the Grafton, and Killian walked Spencer and Erica to the car as Buster followed. Earlier, he had secretly encouraged Spencer once more to pack bags and leave, but the man wasn't having it, not yet. If one more bottle drops, Killian's recent dreams might require sharing. Then maybe Spencer would be convinced.

Killian assured Erica her meeting with the detective would go smoothly, and he was glad to detect a slight tinge of hope in her eyes.

She wasn't herself, but that was to be expected. Today, she would be fine, he was sure. What was coming later was his worry.

Spencer and Erica found the parking lot at the Limerick Garda station and pulled into an empty spot. Spencer gave his daughter a comforting look after they stopped, and he put the car in park. He touched the top of her right hand softly and then opened his door.

"Buster, you be a good boy while we're gone," Spencer said, shutting and locking the car door. He worried whether it was safe leaving Buster here by himself. The dog showed his usual disappointment at being left behind, staring sadly through the window as Erica and Spencer moved away.

"It'll be all right, Erica," Spencer said as they began walking toward the police station. "Just answer the questions they ask and do what they tell you. You've got nothing to hide. But I wouldn't go into anything Shandy-related, even if it's just you and Detective Walsh. There are probably cameras and microphones everywhere."

Spencer was concerned for her, but he knew she was strong, stronger than he was. He wished they had asked him in for questioning as well, so he could be beside her. Perhaps that was something the guards were leaving for another day.

"I'll be fine, Dad," Erica said, and he knew she would be.

They walked around and in between the smattering of patrol cars parked in the lot. The vehicles were all painted white, accompanied here and there by stripes and patches of blue and yellow. The Garda insignia appeared near the bottom door panel of each car.

Stopping ten yards in front of the station house, Spencer gave the place a quick once-over. The building was less impressive than he had imagined and in serious need of an upgrade. The grungy, three-story structure of brown bricks separated by rows of dirty and opaque windows had seen better days. Not that it mattered; Spencer hoped this would be their one and only visit here.

They had hardly walked through the slow-moving automatic glass doors of the front entrance when the detective made his appearance. Spencer figured he must have been waiting for them.

"Good afternoon, Mr. Spencer. Erica," Detective Walsh said and nodded.

Erica, huh? That is a bit familiar, Spencer thought as the detective led them to a waiting room. The room was as dingy and unappealing as the rest of the place and filled with an assortment of characters. Spencer could only imagine their reasons for being here.

"Mr. Spencer, you'll have to wait here, I'm afraid. Shouldn't take any longer than a half hour or so. There's coffee over there if you'd like some."

Spencer watched as Erica and the detective walked down the hall and then disappeared into the confines of a private room. He moved over to a stand next to the wall and grabbed a cup of coffee from the pot. The dark liquid appeared to have been sitting there since this morning, but he'd take his chances. He poured in a packet of powdered milk and a smattering of sugar, just to be safe.

As he sipped the strong brew, he thumbed through the accommodation list Killian had texted to him. He contacted a couple of the places and asked whether they might stop by before the evening to check things out. When he was done he checked a phone app for the latest sports news from the U.S. and then did a little research of his own on how to deal with the supernatural. The results were mixed, but Erica might be on to something. They didn't have much else to go on.

In just over forty minutes the detective and Erica returned. Erica plopped down beside her father, and Spencer could tell from her demeanor that things must have gone well. He didn't know whether he should speak or wait for the detective to begin the conversation.

"Mr. Spencer, we're all finished," Detective Walsh said. "I must tell you that Detective Dunn and his team finished dusting the house and found no additional fingerprints. We'll need to analyze Erica's prints against the ones we found earlier, but I'm not expecting much. Erica can fill you in on the rest of our conversation."

That's it?, Spencer thought and breathed a sigh of relief. He told himself to be thankful for small miracles. At least something had gone right, for once. The three of them walked down the semi-lit hallway and out the front entrance. After they had made their way to the car, the detective continued the earlier discussion.

"I want the two of you to know Erica is not a suspect. We simply need to dot our i's and cross our t's, you understand. After all, there is no motive or hard evidence to suggest a crime has been committed. We'll most likely just chalk this up to death by natural causes, as the coroner report already states."

"So we're in the clear?" Spencer asked.

"I can't say that exactly, but I wouldn't worry too much," the detective said. "The lipstick matter is still a mystery. Let's just say it's quite possible Mrs. O'Donnell stole it—maybe I should say borrowed it—from Erica without asking. Still, if that were the case, we would have found the woman's prints, don't you think?"

Spencer had to agree. Again, he knew the true perpetrator, but he needed to look at things from the detective's point of view. Maybe Mrs. O'Donnell was wearing gloves when she used the lipstick to write the words. Why would she do that? And where are those gloves now? Did she put them back in the drawer where they normally resided, so no one would be the wiser? Why go to all the trouble? For what reason? Spencer was certain these were the same questions the detective had asked himself and his colleagues. The story had a big hole, but he was glad for today's outcome nevertheless. He wondered whether it would hold.

"That's a relief," Spencer said as he glanced over at Erica and gave her a reassuring look. He seriously doubted Mrs. O'Donnell had been a thief.

"About the other matter we discussed yesterday," Detective Walsh said, "I'm not quite sure what to make of that. I'm personally not a big believer in netherworld beings, but it's not the first time I've heard something of that sort. This is Ireland after all, and we're supposedly full of ghosts."

Spencer wasn't sure whether he was supposed to laugh at the last comment or not, but he chuckled lightly, and the other two did the same.

"Let's just say I'm going to doubt your story for the time being, even though it's obvious you two believe," the detective said. "I'm sure you understand I can't base my investigation on tales from the other side."

"By the way," he continued, "I meant to ask whether you have anyone else who can confirm what happened over those weeks you say you were chasing the small dog?"

"Yes, a couple of people, but I'd rather not give you their names unless you absolutely need them," Spencer said.

"I understand," the detective said as he pulled out a pair of sunglasses from his inside jacket pocket. "You will let me know if you have any problems or need some assistance. If you're gonna be dealing with ghosts, you might find yourself in a bit of trouble."

Spencer couldn't tell whether the man was being sarcastic or not, but it didn't matter. If the detective hung around long enough, he too might end up seeing things he wished he hadn't. He watched as Detective Walsh touched Erica on the forearm before he reached out his hand and shook Spencer's.

"Yes, we will," Spencer said. He couldn't wait to get out of here.

The detective stood in place while Spencer backed up the car and began driving out of the parking lot. Through the rearview mirror he could see the man waving goodbye as they went.

"Seems to me a certain someone has got an interest in a certain someone else, and not on a professional level," Spencer said casually, making a right turn and joining the road that ran in front of the station.

"Oh, Dad, don't be silly," Erica said. "He's just doing his job."

"We'll see," Spencer said and focused on the road ahead. "I've got a couple of places I'd like to stop before we head home."

As they drove along toward their first destination, Spencer listened intently. Erica was recounting her private discussion with Detective Walsh. She referred to it as an "interrogation." She kept using the term as if it were new to her vocabulary. She was animated and excited. When she had finished her account, Spencer knew that interrogation was a misplaced word. The conversation between her and the detective seemed to have been quite benign. But he couldn't blame Erica; her first experience as a possible suspect in a crime must have put her on edge the entire time. The effects were still evident now.

He also listened as she described how kind Detective Walsh's questioning had been. She said that he had been a real gentleman the whole time and never made her feel uncomfortable. *Hmm,* Spencer thought as he listened. Perhaps Erica was, maybe just slightly, beginning to develop feelings for Detective Walsh. Maybe she didn't even realize it yet. And Spencer was more than certain the detective felt the same. He speculated whether the detective's affection was clouding his judgment. Not likely, Spencer thought. The man seemed much too professional.

They arrived at the first of the two inns Spencer intended to visit. The place wasn't much, and they quickly left. The second place, however, was perfect. The small bed and breakfast was smack dab in the middle of Limerick and just around the corner from a large supermarket and every other type of shopping they would need. The accommodation allowed pets and even had a small backyard where Buster could get outside. Spencer made a reservation beginning the day after tomorrow. If the ghost came after them there, it would have to create a scene for all eyes to see.

When he was done with the paperwork, they all got back in the car and headed to an area just on the edge of Limerick. Spencer had one last stop before they returned home. The car pulled over on the side of a street that ran adjacent to a large white building that ran half a city block. Spencer put the car in park and rolled down the window.

"So this is where you were, huh?" Erica said.

"Yep. Not one of my fondest memories. That's for certain," Spencer said. He subconsciously touched his face and rubbed the thin groove of scar tissue. The two-inch curving line, something barely discernible to others, was situated just below his left eye and would likely remain there forever.

This hospital was where Spencer had woken one October morning, just about a year before. He had been admitted after taking a beating he would never forget. The previous night he had suffered two assaults, one from the two bigoted village locals and the second from the psychotic man named Owen. Owen had possessed stronger motivations than the first two. He had been stalking Spencer for days and had been out to steal Spencer's financial information and eventually all of his money. Why he had attempted to kill Spencer that night, however, would forever remain a mystery, for Owen met his own fate just an hour later. Too much alcohol and a tight, winding road had resulted in Owen performing a head plant through the front glass of his automobile.

For Spencer, the beatings had been a blessing in disguise. If they had not happened, he would have left Ireland the next day, never to be living the life he was today.

"Who found you that night? I mean, how did you make it to the hospital?" Erica asked.

"I don't remember all the details, and I was unconscious at the time, but apparently some friends of Killian found me lying next to the street," Spencer said. "When I woke the next morning Killian was still at the hospital. He had stayed all night."

"You're lucky to have a friend like him, Dad," Erica said.

"I know; I really am."

Spencer had been thrashed to a pretty good pulp, but none of his injuries, except for a mild concussion, had been serious enough to keep him in the hospital long-term. Killian had taken Spencer from the hospital back to Galbally the next day, and he had spent the next week or more at Killian's home being nursed back to health by Killian and his wife. When Spencer had recovered and just as he was getting ready to depart Ireland once again, he tripped upon the living Shandy for the final time and then watched her die in his arms.

A day or two later came the epiphany that would lead Spencer down a different road and to a new life in Ireland. With Shandy's death, Spencer truly had no reason to remain longer in this country. After having been absent for so long, he was afraid he had already lost his job. Not that he cared much, but, still, he knew the time to go had come. A heart-to-heart with Killian couldn't convince him otherwise, and he repacked his bags and said his final goodbyes. On the way out of town, he stopped by Moor Abbey for one last visit. He didn't know why necessarily, but it just seemed proper; so much had happened there. The night before had been unseasonably cold, and the frost was only beginning to thaw once he reached the monastery.

A misstep on the bench of a picnic table had almost resulted in a serious head injury, but he had survived, just like he had survived all that had happened to him here in Galbally.

He had never noticed the makeshift public toilet in the parking lot of Moor Abbey and was certain it was a new addition. Nature was calling, and he decided to use what was given. When he was finished and before he could step out, something drew his face to the mirror inside the outhouse. There he saw the message: *God bless you, Spencer.* The message had only stayed briefly, like subtitles on a television or movie screen, but its impact would be life-altering.

Spencer realized that what he was experiencing was likely not real, but none of his supernatural existence during the weeks before this day had seemed real either. But they had been, and maybe this was as well. Regardless, the sign he had been waiting for his entire life, the sign he thought would never come, had finally appeared. It had been a simple message and perhaps would have meant nothing to most people, but to Spencer the message could not have been clearer. Everything he had gone through here had come with a purpose. Spencer got into his car. He then turned the vehicle around and headed back to Galbally, never to leave again.

Spencer took a final look at the hospital. This was the first time he had returned since that frightening night, and there was no reason he should have until today. Even now he wasn't exactly sure why he had come this way, but he realized this place was a reminder of all of the things he had suffered and, more importantly, all that he had gained.

"How about we stop in Ballylanders and pick up some Chinese takeout for dinner?" he asked Erica.

"Chinese sounds great," Erica said. Spencer was happy to see her in a positive mood.

He rolled down the back window so Buster could stick his head out for a while, and they headed home to the Square One.

CHAPTER FOURTEEN

The few days spent in Limerick were peaceful and uneventful. Not once did anything out of the ordinary occur. Perhaps the ghoulish fiend truly couldn't perform its duties in a social environment; perhaps there was protection in numbers.

Regardless, they were days not wasted. Other than the hospital stay in the city, Spencer had never really spent much time in Limerick. Being alive in the hustle and bustle of a bigger city was a welcome change from the solitude of Bansha and the inn.

Spencer and Erica enjoyed as much of the local culinary fare as they could. They spent evenings in nearby pubs. Spencer accompanied his daughter on one shopping spree after another. And they visited a nice sampling of Limerick historical sites. Their bond became stronger.

In a local bookstore they bought a few reads on the occult and similar subjects. Erica began going through them voraciously. She finally confided to her father that she had always had some fascination with the supernatural. Privately, Spencer thought the attraction was a bit strange, but he hoped it would pay some kind of dividend when and if needed.

They arrived home at the Square One around noon. Spencer opened the rear car door, and Buster made a quick dash for the river. He had been fussing ever since recognizing familiar surroundings. Erica called out sharply and immediately ran after him, and within a minute Spencer watched as daughter and dog, the latter on the end of a lead, made their way back to the front yard. The dog hadn't even had a chance to get wet, and Spencer laughed as Erica admonished

Buster over and over again. He was in a good mood and hopeful their blessings in Limerick would continue here at the Square One.

Spencer pushed open, almost hesitantly, the front door of the house, and they stepped inside. Spencer went directly upstairs, and Erica covered the first floor. Ten minutes later they met in the kitchen and walked out onto the patio. They had scoured everything and everywhere near and far. All seemed to be normal. They returned to the kitchen.

"Well, I guess the damn thing is not up for any fun unless we're around," Spencer said jokingly.

"Yeah, I guess not," Erica replied. "Maybe it'll stay that way. God, I hope it stays that way."

"Me too, Erica."

"If you're getting hungry, I'll make us some lunch," Erica said. "You okay with sandwiches?"

She began rummaging through the grocery bags she had brought in earlier and pulled out some bread and lunch meat.

"That'd be just fine," Spencer said. "And I shall do my part and get our stuff out of the car."

Spencer opened the patio door again and looked back at the whining dog standing behind him.

"Buster, I know you wanna go out, but you stay in here with Erica for now. We can all go out later after lunch."

Spencer reached the car and began removing their luggage. He set the bags on the ground and wondered how to bide his time here with no guests. He decided he would get an early start on the list of winter projects he had organized. The inn's web page and social media sites also needed some improvement. He would leave that work to Erica.

Spencer picked up a couple of the bags and lifted his head to the sky. He studied the depth and darkness of the building and bulbous clouds to the west. He hadn't checked today's weather forecast, but some late-afternoon rain might be in store for them.

Back in the house Spencer set Erica's bags in her room and then went back downstairs and outside for his own. He came back up the steps and walked through the open door of his room, placing his bag on the brown ottoman in front of the cushioned chair in the corner. Nature was calling, and he opened the door to the en suite bathroom. He flipped on the light switch and headed to the toilet. Spencer caught his reflection in the mirror as he passed by and instinctively turned his head. He stopped and stared directly ahead. A moment or two was enough, and he felt himself move backward, almost involuntarily.

He stepped out of the bathroom and sat down on the edge of his bed. He stared blankly at the half-open bathroom door for several minutes. Finally, he stood up, walked to the bedroom entrance, and hung his head out in the direction of the stairs.

"Erica, come up here. There's something you've got to see."

A round five that evening the rain made a visit. The inclement weather started as only a drizzle. The clouds gathered in strength and number and soon portrayed an ominous attitude. Within an hour the rain unleashed from the skies at a level neither of them had seen in months. The roof of the house amplified the sound as the relentless deluge pounded away. Soon, the wind was gusting and pushing violently against the windows. Lightning flashed as day gave way to night, and thunder shook the Square One.

After a simple dinner of pasta, garlic toast, and salad, they sat in Spencer's study, and he again broke out the bottle of Jack Daniels. They finished off the last remnants. Spencer then twisted open a bottle of Irish whiskey, a gift from one of the inn's guests this past summer.

Neither held back tonight. The nerves were frazzled, and the storm outside, now in full force, wasn't helping matters. Their unwelcome adversary had paid a visit while they had been gone, and they could only guess where it hid itself now. Was it still in the house? Could it come and go as it pleased? What waited for them next?

"Dad, what do we do now?" Erica asked. She reiterated the same question she had already asked several times today, and Spencer could see the alcohol was starting to get the best of her.

Spencer was standing near a four-pane window, but the water pelting the glass and the darkness of the evening obscured everything outside. He could hear the wind whistling and howling and could feel its voracity, as the entire house seemed to vibrate, stop, and vibrate again. He tapped on the window with his finger, leaving a mark in the condensation. He turned and gave Erica his attention.

"Erica, as I said before, I don't know. I wish I had an answer for you. I don't. But we've decided to stay, right?"

"Right," Erica replied meekly.

"So, that's what we do for now," he said. "I have a feeling we'll know what to do when the time comes."

Earlier in the day Erica had nearly fallen over when she came up the stairs and opened the bathroom door to see what was written on the mirror. They hadn't seen with their own eyes the message inscribed on Mrs. O'Donnell's wall, but they imagined it must have been quite the same. This time, however, the order of the letters was reversed: D O G, in large, evenly spaced capital letters written in what was obviously red lipstick. Unlike before, the meaning of this message was more than obvious.

Spencer had asked Erica whether she had another of the same lipstick, or at least one of the same color. She hadn't. She only possessed two others, one brown and the other maroon.

They were dealing with a spook that was not only able to sneak in wherever and whenever it wanted but also one that could somehow physically possess and carry objects. And the thing was capable of deeds much more heinous, like murdering an innocent couple and an old lady whose only crime was to be unfortunately associated with this household. Maybe. Spencer imagined any coming battle would be easier if the spirit were strictly focused on Buster, but he had no way of knowing the plans of a sinister being.

Like Killian had suggested, Spencer, too, was now feeling that Erica was meant to stay. The spirit could have taken her, and Buster, down by the river. It had every opportunity, and no one else around to interfere. But it hadn't. There was a reason. He knew that much. The lack of fear she had shown was one element, but Spencer sensed something deeper.

At the same time, he considered the stupidity of staying at this house any longer. Yes, that was the word—stupidity, plain and simple. That a real danger was present was more than evident now. Killian had been pushing him hard, and Erica might even agree at this point. They should leave. He filed the thought away and would revisit it in the morning.

As the rain and wind continued their onslaught outside, Spencer and Erica sipped at their drinks and sat watching a streamed comedy video Spencer hoped would take some of the edge off. Buster seemed completely unaffected by and disinterested in the storm outside and lay in a corner, half-asleep.

About an hour into their movie, the lights, in the study and throughout the house, suddenly flickered. Five seconds later they all went out, and the TV screen soon followed. The house was in total darkness.

"Dad, what's going on?" Erica said.

The fear in her voice was obvious, and Spencer felt the same, though he wasn't about to show it.

"I'm sure it's nothing, just caused by the storm," he said reassuringly.

Spencer stood up and tried to adjust his eyes to the surrounding blackness. Once comfortable enough, he made his way through the dark to a cabinet and pulled open a drawer. He removed a flashlight and clicked it on. Power going out was not an uncommon occurrence, and Spencer kept a flashlight in almost every room.

"I'm gonna check the breaker box just to be sure," Spencer said as he sprayed the flashlight in the direction of the study's open door. He shone the light briefly on Erica to make certain she was okay.

"You're not leaving me here alone!" Erica said adamantly, and she too stood up. She moved to where Spencer was standing, and he felt the slight pull as she inserted two fingers over and into the backside of his belt.

The two of them, with Buster right behind, climbed the stairs to the second-floor hallway. Once there, Spencer opened the small steel door on the wall and used the flashlight to examine the black switches within, running his fingers over each one of them. None had flipped to the off position.

"Probably a power line went down from the wind," Spencer said as he closed the door until it clicked shut. "I'm sure the electricity will be back up soon."

"It better," Erica said.

Spencer could only see the outline of her face, but, from what he could make out, his daughter didn't look well at all.

"In the meantime let's grab the lanterns. I think they're downstairs in the closet," Spencer said.

He kicked himself for not having the backup generator in proper working order; he had been planning to do just that this coming week.

The house would get chilly soon, and he thought they should start a fire. Thankfully, there was a pile of split wood and kindling sitting next to the fireplace. He wouldn't need to go outside in the dark and in the rain.

Before they reached the bottom of the stairs, the lights returned with no warning, and Spencer silently let out a long exhale in relief.

"See, told ya," Spencer said, showing Erica the big grin she needed to see. "Just the storm."

He wrapped his arms around his daughter and gave her the hug she also needed.

They stepped back into the study. Spencer looked at the now-blank but lit screen of the television set. He hoped some little girl's voice wouldn't materialize and tell them, "They're here."

Spencer and Erica drank one more shot each of the whiskey and finished watching the movie that had been cut short. When the show was over, even though the evening was still rather early, they decided to call it a night. At Erica's insistence they went to bed with the doors to their bedrooms open and the hallway light on. Buster began the night at his master's bedside as usual, but later on Spencer saw and heard him several times roaming back and forth between the two rooms. He was sure the dog was aware of more than they could understand.

Spencer read ten or fifteen pages from a book he had been working on. He couldn't concentrate. He inserted the bookmark and returned the novel to the nightstand. He wasn't hopeful, but he decided to try. He tossed and turned under his sheets, listening to the relentless rain smacking the roof above him and wondering about the electricity. Was it nothing but the storm? That was the logical conclusion, but nothing was logical these days. Was the thing still in the house? He finally concluded Buster would be up in arms if that were the case. He fell asleep eventually and dreamed of things that couldn't be remembered.

They woke the next morning to a bright and beautiful day. Outside, the signs of the previous night's storm were everywhere: gigantic rain puddles all over the yard and driveway, and broken twigs, branches, and thick limbs scattered about as far as the eye could see. Even a few uprooted and fractured trees could be seen in the yard and beyond. Spencer was certain the garden on the backside of the house was destroyed, but hopefully not beyond repair.

Spencer knew what they would be doing today and hoped there wasn't any serious damage to the house or property. He would go out later and check on everything, maybe check how high the Aya had risen from all the rain.

Coffee and breakfast were in order first, and then Spencer would call Killian to tell him the latest. A call to Detective Walsh would then be made. No crime had been committed, but someone or something had intruded this home. If the detective wasn't a believer yet, Spencer hoped the writing on the bathroom mirror might persuade him. They needed all of the help they could get.

This morning, and last night in bed, Spencer had indeed revisited the thought of leaving. He knew it would be the smart move, but he couldn't will himself to pull the trigger. Not yet, unless Erica insisted, and he knew that wasn't likely. And they needed to at least hear what the detective, and Killian, had to say first.

Killian showed up at the Square One before Detective Walsh did. No bottle fell from the wall last night, but that didn't necessarily convey a meaning. Besides, a different sort of dream had taken its place. As soon as the phone conversation with Spencer was complete, Killian wasted no time in getting out here. This morning there was much to see, hear, and, most importantly, tell. He understood that his presence might surprise the detective, but what difference did it make? They were in this together.

Spencer and Killian made their way to the patio. They brushed off small twigs and other debris from the seats of the chairs and sat down. The field in front of them looked like partial swampland, but the water would recede quickly on this warm day. Erica soon joined them. She brought along a pot of coffee and poured the steaming liquid into the mugs. They all sat back for a moment and enjoyed the warmth of the morning sun. The cleansing, yet devastating, rain brought the fresh smell of sweet air. Killian sat back and breathed deeply for a few moments before he spoke.

"By the way, Spencer, there's a fairly large tree down near the road entrance at the bottom of the hill. You're going to have to break out the chainsaw to take care of that one, I'm afraid. The road is a muddy mess. Passable. Just barely."

"Yes, my afternoon is going to be a full one, cleaning up this disaster," Spencer replied. "Probably tomorrow and the next day as well."

"I'd give you a hand," Killian said, "but I've got a bit of the same at my own place, I do. That certainly was some kind of storm."

"And the last thing we needed, especially after seeing what we saw," Spencer said.

The small talk soon ended, and the three of them ventured up to Spencer's room.

"I'll be damned," Killian said as he stared at the red lipstick on the bathroom mirror. "It's exactly as you described on the phone."

They made their way back to the patio. Killian stood on the edge of the deck, looking out into the open. In a minute or two he returned to his seat and sat down.

"You know, I was thinking on the way over here that perhaps the three of you should come stay at my house for a while. It's no longer safe to stay here. Only the good Lord knows what will happen next. And the wife would love to have a dog around the house for a spell."

"I appreciate that, Killian," Spencer said, "but running won't resolve this problem. Running away will only prolong things. Besides, I'm not about to put you and Elizabeth in possible harm's way. We're going to stay right here, unless Erica has other thoughts."

They both glanced over at Erica, who was gently shaking her head back and forth. *They might change their minds in a minute or two,* Killian thought as he shifted his attention back to Spencer.

Killian then listened as Spencer and Erica went into every last detail from the previous day and night. Killian told them the power had gone out in several other areas as well, so the chance of their nemesis having been present was unlikely. Next, they discussed how to deal with Detective Walsh when he arrived. Killian concurred the man was a possible ally, and they concluded they would relate to him anything and everything he hadn't already been told.

"Spencer, and Erica, I had a dream last night," Killian said with some hesitation after the previous conversation was finished. "It was all a bit murky, but you need to hear it, even though you might not like where it may lead."

"A dream, huh? Dreams are for those who sleep, and I can't count myself among them, not lately at least and certainly not last night. What was it, Killian?" Spencer said.

"I dreamt that you, and you alone, had a meeting of sorts," Killian said, getting right to the point. "It was a premonition more than a dream, I'm sure. I even remember the exact date and time: two days from today, on Thursday, at half ten in the evening. At Moor Abbey of all places."

"What the hell is that supposed to mean?" Spencer said and stood up.

Killian had assumed this foreshadowing wouldn't go over well. He looked over at Erica as she sat on the edge of her seat. He couldn't tell whether she was excited or frightened, maybe both.

"It means what I said. This thing, this spirit, wants you, and only you, to make an appearance. I believe it has something to tell you, something to show you. That's all I know."

"You've got to be kidding me," Spencer said incredulously and paced back and forth on the deck before stopping. "You've got to be frickin' kidding me!"

"Dad, you can't do that!" Erica said. "We already agreed no one should ever be alone."

Killian watched the tears well up in the young woman's eyes. *Why do I always have to be the bearer of bad tidings?* Killian wouldn't blame Spencer for not partaking in a potentially dangerous encounter.

"I know, Erica, and I agree," Spencer said, reaching out for his daughter's hand. "Killian, you can't be serious about this. You've been pushing me so hard to leave, and now you suggest this, based on some dream!"

Killian glanced up at Spencer and could see the man's mind weighing the pros and cons. And he knew Spencer. And he knew he would go to the abbey.

"Spencer, I realize I have been telling you to go, and you should. I haven't changed my mind on that one, not one iota. With the monastery, I'm not saying what you should or should not do. That is your decision. I'm just telling you what I have seen."

Killian hadn't changed his mind. He did want them to go, or, at the very least, come and stay with him. But he was aware that the dream of last night was not one to ignore. Following through might be the only way to see the end of this thing, the only way for life to return to normal, and the only way for Spencer and Erica to stay in Ireland. The alternative was for them to leave and never return. This was a risk-and-reward proposition with no clear path forward.

Killian looked on as Erica rose from her seat, picking up the coffee pot and turning toward the door that led to the kitchen. She knew what her father would do. The building moisture in her eyes was now running slowly down her cheeks. She used her elbow sleeve to wipe her face, and she walked off the patio without a word.

Killian and Spencer sat silently and stared down the road as a large 4WD made its way toward them.

CHAPTER FIFTEEN

The detective looked the mirror up and down. Spencer could get no sense of what was happening in the man's mind; he was impossible to read and barely spoke as he examined the situation.

After Killian had excused himself and left for home, Detective Walsh spent the next thirty minutes or more examining a setting similar to what he had seen before. He put on latex gloves and covered not just the mirror but the entire bathroom from top to bottom and corner to corner. He then went into Spencer's bedroom and did the same. He snapped photos one after the other, never distracted from the task at hand.

Spencer assured the detective he hadn't used the bathroom since the discovery. The "crime" scene was still fresh, and Spencer and Erica marveled at watching a police officer doing his work.

When all was done Detective Walsh hadn't discovered much or anything at all. No case of red lipstick was found in the bathroom or nearby.

Spencer was dying to ask the man what he truly thought, whether there was any chance a human being was not the culprit, but he knew the comment would have seemed more than a little inane. He kept his mouth shut.

There were no subtle jokes like the other day at the Limerick station house, and Spencer could see that Detective Walsh was all business. He was a policeman. An intrusion had occurred in this house, and he wasn't about to let this go without further effort. He had an obligation and duty to follow the matter until something or nothing was found.

The next day a two-person team arrived from Limerick. They were junior detectives getting their feet wet, the best the Limerick Garda could do with limited resources and at a place that was barely on the cusp of being a crime scene. The two scoured the house, every nook and cranny, checked for fingerprints in the bathroom and throughout Spencer's bedroom, and asked Spencer and Erica countless questions, most of which were unnecessary and a bit too imposing. They were nothing if not overzealous in their work, but Spencer realized they were trying to prove their worth.

The rookie detectives also came up empty. In Spencer's room there were no fingerprints other than his own and those of Erica, and no case of red lipstick was found in the house. The scene was much the same as Mrs. O'Donnell's place: a strange and mysterious occurrence with no clue as to motive or perpetrator. Detective Walsh showed up later in the day and told Spencer his superiors had taken a healthy interest in the not-so-coincidental occurrence of two similar events. He was to stay on the case.

Spencer knew that meant they would be seeing more of Detective Walsh, for which he was grateful. He imagined the detective felt the same way, but perhaps for different reasons. Spencer was certain now that the man had eyes for Erica. From the glances exchanged it was becoming more and more apparent that perhaps Erica might be feeling something as well. He wondered where things would go once this chapter of their lives was a closed book.

By the end of the day, Spencer had finally convinced Erica they had to do what they had to do. She had no problem staying here, but she was adamantly against the idea of a midnight visit to the abbey. Spencer had persuaded her, and he now hoped he wouldn't regret the decision.

That evening, Killian joined Spencer and Erica for dinner at the Square One. With their nerves frazzled, Spencer and Erica drank more than they should have. Before Killian left for home, however, a plan had been formulated.

The night in question was only a day away. They would all gather at Killian's house first, just in case and because of Erica's insistence that she remain close to her father. They would have a meal together and then wait. When the appointed time arrived, Spencer alone would walk from Killian's to Moor Abbey. Though the decision made everyone uncomfortable, especially Spencer, they were determined to follow Killian's premonition as closely as possible.

Spencer again worried they might be putting Killian, and his wife, in some kind of danger, knowing that the ghost had now found a way to enter Killian's subconscious. But Spencer would most likely have the full attention of the spirit at the abbey, and that would keep everyone else safe.

The three of them debated long and hard whether they should inform Detective Walsh. The man still showed no pretense of believing in the supernatural aspects of Spencer's stories of the past, and the latest evidence hadn't persuaded him, though they weren't sure what he was thinking.

They decided to tell him. Spencer made the phone call early the next morning, and the detective, after several moments of indecision, said he would loiter around Galbally that evening just in case he was needed. Spencer knew the man's decision was simply to humor them more than anything else but also perhaps an opportunity to be near Erica. When the time came the detective would either become a believer or he would end up thinking they were all bonkers, depending on how things played out at the abbey.

After the phone call Spencer continued his work of cleaning up the remnants of and destruction from the storm. The activity kept him physically busy, but it didn't stop his mind. He had faced this spirit more than once in the past, but this time would be different, completely on the ghost's terms. He couldn't begin to imagine what was in store for him.

They gathered at Killian's that evening. Spencer's scheduled get-together with a ghost was only a few hours away. Dinner, an Irish barbecue of sorts, was served outside in the patio area. They certainly weren't celebrating anything, but they had to eat, and the weather was cooperating. Spencer was glad the elements were being kind; the meeting of later would be more tolerable that way.

He picked at his food as he glanced around the patio. He wasn't in the mood for conversation, and the others let him be for the most part. The detective had joined them, but Erica was more or less ignoring the man this evening. Her concern for her father was evident, and Spencer felt better having her nearby before the big event. She ran inside to fetch him another beer, and Spencer sat back in his chair. Killian approached.

"How ya doing, Spencer?" Killian asked. "I know this can't be easy."

"Oh, as well as can be expected, I suppose," Spencer said. "I sure hope we've made the right decision."

"As do I," Killian said. "Honestly, I don't know what else we would do. Perhaps it will turn out to be nothing. Perhaps my vision was incorrect. It wouldn't be the first time."

Spencer stared at his fingers as he fiddled with one of his shirt buttons.

"I don't know whether I want it to be right or wrong," he said. "Anyway, part of the process, right?"

"Yes, part of the process, Spencer," Killian said.

Spencer looked at his good friend and smiled. As before and as always, he would be lost without him. Although not recently, Spencer had sat in this very courtyard more than a few times. Here, along with the pub, is where Spencer had listened to Killian's sage advice about Shandy and about a broken man who needed fixing. Here is where Spencer had shared details about his life with a man who was willing to listen. Spencer had taken a lot of the advice Killian offered; he had ignored some as well. Their last related conversation at this place, almost a year before, did not end well, with Spencer blowing up at Killian's persistence and know-it-all attitude. But Killian did know it all, and Spencer had never met a man so in touch with the realities of this world—and a world beyond.

Erica returned with her father's drink and set it down on the small table next to him. Spencer picked up the glass and gulped down a large swig, hardly tasting it. This would be the last one for the evening; he needed to be in total control of all of his senses for what was to possibly come.

Detective Walsh had been helping Killian's wife Elizabeth clear the dirty dishes and remaining food. Spencer watched as he came back outside from the house and pulled up a seat near the rest of them.

"Mr. Spencer, I'll be in the area somewhere, probably near where the road meets the abbey. Not too close, though. I haven't decided yet, but I won't go until you're already there. You have your mobile, but don't forget about the beeper I've given you. All you need to do is push the button once, and it will alert me."

Spencer tried to read Detective Walsh. Was he buying into all of this, or was he here because of his affection for Erica? Either way, he was here, and his presence made Spencer feel just slightly less anxious.

"Please call me Spencer. I think we've come far enough in our relationship for that."

"Certainly, Spencer. And you please call me Danny."

Spencer smiled at the detective. He was beginning to grow slightly fond of this man. Underneath the detective's rough and serious demeanor was a gentleman at heart. And there was no denying his rugged good looks. Naturally, Erica could easily fall for a guy like this. He wondered if she would.

"Spencer, there is something else I have been meaning to ask you, if you don't mind," Detective Walsh said. "And I'm asking this as a friend, not as an officer of the law."

The last thing Spencer needed right now was some interrogation-type question, but he had no reason to refuse.

"Sure. What is it?"

"As I told you before, I'm not a believer in ghosts, not in the least bit," the detective said. "And I won't be until I see one with my own eyes. I'm here this evening maybe just out of curiosity, and I'm certainly not expecting to see my first ghoul.

"But for the sake of argument, let's suppose there is a ghost, one responsible for the things that have happened. I guess I'm still not quite understanding the motive, assuming there is one, that is."

"Boy, if we knew that, this all might be a lot easier," Spencer said. "I think I told you before that the damn thing is angry about my messing around in a world where I didn't belong. That's the best I, or any of us, can come up with."

"It all seems a wee bit over the top, if you ask me," the detective said. "I mean killing a couple unknown to you and then your employee, just to exact some revenge for nothing really. It doesn't add up, not to my mind at least."

Spencer also went on to tell the detective about another theory, the one related to the O'Donnell ancestors and their relationship with Moor Abbey. He told him of the dogs that had been massacred there. However, that theory had been put to rest for the most part. Both Killian and Erica had done a fair amount of research, and there was no evidence to connect either Sean or Claire Kelly. Their families had both originated in Northern Ireland, about as far away from here as a person could go and remain on this island. There was no explainable reason for their deaths.

"I really don't know anything for certain, Danny," Spencer said. "We're just guessing here, and your guess is as good as mine."

But Spencer thought he might know. He had formulated one more theory as of late, one he hadn't shared with anyone. The Shandy who had come back to visit him that last time at the Square One, months after she had died in his arms, had been a ghost. He was certain of that now, even though she had looked and felt real and would have seemed that way to anyone else.

Spencer speculated perhaps that Shandy was the one who had done something wrong, something not allowed in the spirit world she had entered. Maybe she had broken the unwritten rules of the dead by presenting herself to Spencer, especially in a form true to life. And perhaps since that time she had been, in a way, on the run, running from the reaper just like she had when she was still alive.

Maybe all of this, all that had happened recently, was simply a ploy by the ghost to force Shandy's appearance again. Maybe it knew if Spencer and his family were in jeopardy, Shandy would intervene and try to save them. And then the spirit would finally have a chance to corner its quarry.

But why hadn't he seen Shandy? Why hadn't she shown herself, even once? Maybe she was waiting until she was truly needed. Maybe he would need her tonight. Spencer knew this supposition was all a stretch. His theory was merely a theory, and probably not a good one, but it made more sense than anything else.

Detective Walsh asked a few more questions, and Spencer did his best to answer. He realized there was no way to make the detective believe until he actually saw a real ghost. Maybe he would this night.

They all chatted for a while longer, plotting a strategy that didn't exist. They adjourned to inside the house and sat mindlessly watching the regional news and some other programs until the time came. The clock was just short of ten when Spencer got up from the sofa and made his way to the front door of the house. He placed one hand on the wrist of the other to stop the shaking.

Erica's head was bowed as she stood silently in front of her father. Suddenly she grabbed Spencer and threw her arms around his waist. He held her for the longest time, whispering into her ear that he would be just fine. She broke from his embrace and squatted down to pet Buster, trying to avert her attention from the reality of the situation. Not another word was said. Killian and Detective Walsh busied themselves with nothing in the background until the father-and-daughter moment was finished.

Spencer bent down and gave his dog a rub on the head. Buster began sidestepping to the right and to the left and began whining. He turned a full circle and stopped. He stared up at Spencer and barked. Two more barks soon followed.

"It's all gonna be fine, buddy," Spencer said. "You stay here and take care of your sister, make sure she doesn't get in any trouble."

He scratched the dog's head one more time, stood up, stepped outside the door, and began a slow walk toward the abbey. Ten yards out he turned around once to wave goodbye to Erica as she stood at the doorway. She was holding onto Buster's collar as the dog continued his antics. Detective Walsh was already in his car, waiting and watching Spencer go.

CHAPTER SIXTEEN

Spencer arrived across the road from Moor Abbey and studied the structure from a short distance. No, he hadn't liked this place for a long time, if ever. Now he recognized how much he hated and despised it. Why does it have to be here, of all places? Maybe nothing would happen at all. Again, he couldn't decide which was better.

He looked in the darkness for any approaching headlights as he began crossing the road. When he reached the other side, he did a double check for any parked cars and any sign of life. All was quiet, and he was alone. The air was still and heavy, and a half crescent of moon shone in the sky to his right.

Ghosts appear and then go away. Ghosts appear and then go away. He couldn't get the phrase out of his head and wondered whether it came from a song or whether it was something he had conjured up on his own. If there were a ghost, he did hope it would go away, go away once and for all and out of their lives forever.

Spencer still had time until 10:30. He smoked on a lone cigarette he had placed in his front shirt pocket. He stood ten yards this side of the abbey entrance and smoked the entire cigarette this time, joking to himself this one might be his last. Somehow, it didn't feel like much of a joke.

He turned around at the sound and lights of a car sneaking up from behind and to his left. The vehicle sped by quickly on the way to somewhere. He watched its taillights disappear in the darkness as it went across the bridge and rounded the bend in the road. Out of habit, maybe, he turned around and examined the other side of the road from where he had just come. His eyes stuck on the picnic table, sitting on its lonesome and partially visible in the black of the night. His eyelids closed for a brief moment, and his mind flashed to the scene of Shandy dying here.

Spencer erased the thought and proceeded to the entrance of the abbey. He peered inside to the black hollowness of the empty monastery. All he could make out was the tower in the middle. He had already given this some thought, and there was no way he was going inside. If this thing wanted to meet him, it would be outside, where he hoped some form of escape might be possible should things go awry. He veered to the left and made his way around the left perimeter of the abbey. He arrived at the rear of the structure and rested his body against the railings of a wooden fence. His nerves were on edge, and he seriously contemplated high-tailing out of here.

He pulled his wrist up to his face and looked at the time: 10:20. He was ten minutes early. He waited for those ten minutes and ten more. Except for the occasional passing of cars on the other side of the abbey, nothing disturbed the quiet, and no otherworld entity appeared.

Maybe Killian was wrong for once, Spencer thought. He gave his watch another look, waited five more minutes, and began heading back toward the road. He felt relieved in a way, but also slightly disappointed.

A light breeze kicked up and made its presence known. Spencer halted in his tracks and did a 360-degree survey around him. He took another step, and the wind strengthened. The air became cooler, and Spencer could have sworn the night had become a few shades darker.

It was here.

He smelled something sulfurous-like and, for some reason, cast his eyes at a thick oak tree off to his left in the distance, not more than a hundred yards away. A single blackbird escaped out of the tree's mass of branches, flew just above his head, and then shot straight upward to the tower of the abbey. He watched the bird settle on the ledge of an opening in the tower and stare down at him. It abruptly departed and soared back to the tree, its wings motionless in the glide to its destination. Spencer followed the bird with his eyes. Behind the tree he could see a dark swirling of matter taking form, almost like a whirlwind gathering strength on the prairie.

He stood motionless and in awe. The twisting shape seemed to gather power and began to move toward him. He had sensed and felt the presence more than once before, but this was very different. Spencer hesitated, considering what he should do. If he tried to run, he knew it might be over. Show no fear. He wished he weren't alone. Where was Detective Walsh? He dislodged the backpack from his shoulders and threw the bag on the ground. He spread his legs wide apart and displayed the most defiant posture he could muster.

In what seemed like a moment, the wind was ripping at an incomprehensible level, and the beast was directly in front of him. Then, and very suddenly, the wind died completely, and the mass of dark matter spread out and filled with a bright light. Black specks danced around within the illumination. The menace was before him, and around and above him, and even seemed to have permeated the ground on which he stood.

He tried as he might to look into the dark nothing. Its depth seemed immeasurable. For a reason unexplainable, an indescribable feeling gnawed at Spencer's soul. At that moment Spencer realized, although he didn't understand why, that this day was to be the day that marked the end of him. He would now cross to somewhere else, maybe to an astral plane, maybe to nothing at all. Maybe to heaven, maybe to hell, maybe to someplace in between.

Maybe coming to Ireland wasn't such a great idea after all, he half-joked in his mind, relinquishing himself to the sad ending he knew was coming. He calmly sat down on the soft grass below him, waiting to be taken.

Really? This is how I go? Thoughts of his life slipped in and out of his mind. He should have done better. He could have done better. He sat there, waiting. The ending didn't come. Not yet.

Instead, a vision appeared within the mass of nothingness. He couldn't make things out at first. Spencer stood up. He squinted his eyes and peered into the illusion. There in front of him was the young couple who had perished. Their dog was off in the background, but Spencer couldn't make out what she was doing. First, the couple were laughing and touching one another tenderly, and then they were lying still next to each other beside the River Aherlow, their bodies nothing but lifeless forms with eye sockets but no eyes. The dog, now just a skeleton of white bones, was lying at their feet.

The altered reality vanished in a heartbeat and was replaced by one of Mrs. O'Donnell sitting and rocking back and forth in a wooden chair. Then her eyes grew large, and the fear she exhibited was like nothing Spencer had ever seen. Then the rocking ceased, and she sat in her chair without moving. Her eyes remained open, but she was no longer. Still, those eyes of no life stared passively at the red writing on the wall across from her seat. Spencer stared at the wall and the word of crimson. He read the letters in reverse order.

Next, a vision of Buster appeared. He was splashing in and out of the water as Erica threw a stick over and over again. Then Spencer's dog was lying on the ground, his throat cut wide open and blood seeping endlessly to and settling deeply on the ground below him. White maggots squirmed around the wound and made their way up through the dog's nose. They poured out of his eye sockets like toothpaste being squeezed from a tube.

Finally came a joyful Shandy playing with some children next to the picnic table. She was jumping here and there, dodging the youngsters as they chased her. Soon, she was running across the road. A large thump pierced the scene, followed by a car coming to an abrupt halt. A man with an obscured face was holding the dog's battered body in his arms, and Spencer knew the man was himself. The man placed the dog in his car and drove away to somewhere.

A stream of tears began to flow from Spencer's eyes as the final vision fluttered out of his sight. He closed those eyes and bowed his head. This is all my fault, he thought, and waited for the end.

Suddenly, he felt like he had been kicked from behind. Spencer's eyes flew open, and his body began to move forward as the force slowly sucked him into the light and into the darkness. He tried to stop his movement. He couldn't. He planted his feet firmly on the ground, as hard as he possibly could, but he couldn't stop the force. His body scooted ahead, inch-by-inch, foot-by-foot. He was almost there. It would be over soon.

He wanted to speak. He wanted to say goodbye to Erica and to his other two children, with whom the repairs hadn't been fully made. He wanted to say goodbye to Buster. He couldn't find the words.

He heard Erica's voice.

"I love you, Dad," she said.

"I love you, too, Erica," he said. He knew she wasn't there.

He knew her voice was just his imagination, just some trick from the ghost that had brought him here. He was alone, with only the pain of his lifetime for company. He started choosing his confessions, wishing he could have been a better man, a better husband, a better father. It was too late now. It was too late.

Make me a rock. Cover my eyes. There's nothing more for them to see. His head bowed, and he forced his eyes shut. He let himself go.

A sound, one he barely discerned, snapped Spencer out of his stupor just a moment or two later. His eyes popped open once again, and he looked into the mass. The swirling particles had stopped but remained levitated as if time were standing still. He heard the sound again and looked down and to his left. Right next to his leg stood a barking and growling dog, hysterical with anger.

Spencer fell to the ground and watched as Buster's ferociousness reached a level beyond imagination. The dog rushed to the edge of the mass and stopped. He bellowed at the spirit, indignant and full of rage, his white teeth gnashing in the darkness and saliva flying from his mouth. Buster ran back to Spencer, as if to check on him, and then back at the spirit. His furor was unabated, and the scene seemed never-ending.

Spencer held his head in his hands and cried out in anguish.

In a split second everything was completely calm, as if nothing had been there and nothing had happened. Spencer sat on his rear, his arms angled back and his hands flat on the ground, supporting his body. He looked at the backside of the dog standing in front of him, who in turn was staring at something no longer there. Quiet pervaded. A sense of dizziness and heaviness overtook him. His arms gave way, and his body fell to the grass. Buster immediately rushed over and began licking Spencer's face, crying and whining. Buster settled down next to his master, and Spencer felt the dog's head come to rest on his chest.

A sharpness sounded way off in the distance, like a crack of thunder during a building storm. Spencer tried to lift his head but wasn't able. It didn't matter now. Whatever had been there was gone. He might live to see another day.

Spencer reached over and gently caressed Buster's head and scruffy mane.

"You big, wonderful mutt," he softly spoke to his companion and managed a small chuckle.

They were only there for a minute or two, but it felt like an eternity to Spencer. He could hear a voice in the distance, soon accompanied by two others that seemed further back. Buster jumped up at the sound.

"Mr. Spencer, are you all right? Are you all right?"

Soon the detective was standing over him, and Spencer looked up at the man's face. He heard running footsteps near the road coming toward him. Erica and Killian appeared beside Detective Walsh.

"Spencer, are you all right?" the detective repeated.

"Daddy, Daddy, what happened?" Erica said as she got on her knees above her father's head.

Spencer focused on the sobbing face above him, and he knew things were going to be all right.

"Yeah, I'm okay," he said, sure he wasn't.

He lifted himself off the ground and immediately fell to one knee. He felt the detective's hand reach under his bicep and pull him back up.

"Maybe I should sit down," Spencer said.

"Sure thing, Spencer. Let's get you over to where there's a proper seat," Detective Walsh said.

Near the entrance of the abbey was a steel bench. The detective continued to assist Spencer until he was sitting down on his own. Spencer didn't know what to say as he barely registered the three bodies moving around him. Buster's face rested on Spencer's leg.

After a few minutes he felt better and more composed. He explained to the three everything he could remember, although the experience was very much a blur and must have seemed more than nonsensical.

When Spencer was finished the detective told everyone he hadn't stayed as far away as he had planned. He had planted himself on a small hillside overlooking the abbey, so he had a perfect view of what was happening below.

"Spencer, even in the dark, I was able to see you quite well, especially because you didn't go inside the abbey," he said. "But I sure didn't see a ghost or spirit or anything you have described."

"You'll have to take my word for it," Spencer said, not caring right now whether anyone believed him or not. "Or you can ask Buster."

He reached down and petted his dog's head.

They all knew what had happened was true. The detective had not only seen Spencer and every action he had taken but also the delirious scene Buster had created. If Detective Danny Walsh hadn't been a believer before, Spencer was certain he was now.

They all stood and sat there for a while until Spencer felt he was able to head back. Detective Walsh insisted Spencer was in no shape to walk to Killian's house, and he soon took off down the road to collect his automobile. As Spencer, Killian, and Erica watched the detective trotting away from them, Spencer could feel Killian's eyes on him.

"Are you really okay, Spencer?" he asked.

"I think I am. I don't know for sure."

"Spencer, I'm very sorry," Killian said. "Your coming here tonight was a mistake. And I was obviously duped by this freckin' ghost. It planted that vision in my mind and in my dream to get you here alone, so no one could help you. Maybe you're the real target after all. I should have known better."

"We all should have," Spencer said.

"And perhaps it's Buster who has the power against this ghost," Killian said. "Regardless, it's clear to me that the time has come for the three of you to leave, and I mean pronto. This thing might have killed you tonight if it weren't for Buster. You won't be as lucky the next time."

"I agree, Dad," Erica said without hesitation, her face still wet from tears. "The Square One isn't worth our lives. We'll find another place—you, me, and Buster."

Spencer couldn't argue, and he too had no interest in staying here. They would pack the house tomorrow and head for Dublin, hopefully far enough out of reach from this bringer of death. Once Buster's papers were in order, they would leave for the States.

Killian told Spencer he would look after the inn and keep the place safe. He'd help Spencer put it on the market or just do some general upkeep until they returned. Spencer looked at his friend and knew the next sentence didn't need to be spoken: He would never be coming back here.

As they sat there waiting for Detective Walsh, Spencer asked Erica how on earth Buster managed to get out of the house and ultimately save him.

The outside entrance to Killian's kitchen had two doors in the same place, one the main and the other a lightweight screen door that allowed air to enter the house. The screen door was made of a wood frame and another straight section that ran horizontally across its center. Above and below the wooden piece in the middle were two windows of wire mesh. The screen could be cut easily with a sharp knife or the teeth of a large dog.

Buster had digested the situation, and when he was alone, found a slight tear in the bottom mesh. The loose piece was enough for him to grab with his mouth, and, in one quick motion, Buster created a hole large enough in the screen for an easy escape. No one knew he was missing until they did.

At least that is how they imagined the dog had accomplished what he did. No one would ever know for certain. Things would have turned out very differently if he hadn't.

The detective returned with the car. They shared their decision with him, and he concurred. Erica was still a person of interest, slightly, in the death of Mrs. O'Donnell, but there was nothing legally forcing her to stay in Ireland. The detective said he would explain her departure somehow, and he also said he would even try to help with Buster's paperwork if possible. Spencer studied Detective Walsh briefly and could see the melancholy in his eyes.

Yes, this man was beginning to grow on Spencer, and he thought it a shame that a possible budding romance would have no chance now.

As they began to leave, Spencer turned around for one last look at the abbey. The scene was dark and quiet, like nothing had happened at all. As he was about to face the opposite direction, his eye caught a slight movement at a line of trees near the backside of the structure. Spencer squinted, trying to figure out whether he had seen anything. It was there again, half hidden behind one of the larger trees. He could tell now it was a person, and that person was staring back at him. Facial recognition was impossible, but Spencer could make out the trench coat and the tweed cap.

"Angus, you piece of crap! What the hell are you doing here?"

The others turned around and scrambled back to Spencer.

"Spencer, are you all right? What happened?" Killian asked.

"Angus! Angus was right there!" He pointed in the direction of the tree line.

The other three strained their eyes, trying to make something appear. Whatever Spencer had seen was no longer there.

"Are you sure?" Detective Walsh asked.

"Of course I'm sure," Spencer said, but he wasn't. "He was just there a second ago."

"Dad, let's get you back to Killian's," Erica said.

Spencer shrugged, took one final look, and went with the other three to the parked car. Buster hadn't left his side.

When they got back to Killian's home, no one knew what to do or what to say. They all sat around in the living room, lost in thoughts and barely speaking. The television screen flickered with motion in the background, but Spencer hardly noticed. No one's voice penetrated his senses.

His mind returned repeatedly to the scene of a short while before, and he couldn't clear his head no matter how hard he tried. He needed someone to help him, to explain what he had just been through, to tell him he was okay. Erica sat next to him, but even she remained quiet for the most part. The time was very late already, and Spencer excused himself after thirty minutes and said he was tired. Buster followed him to the bedroom. Spencer slept like the dead that night, and his dreams told him he was.

CHAPTER SEVENTEEN

K illian stood silently a few steps behind Erica as she knocked on the door of the bedroom where Spencer slept. She rapped softly once and received no response. She knocked again, this time a little harder, and then nudged open the slightly ajar door.

"Are you awake, Dad?"

Killian's eyes followed Erica as she stepped into the room. He stopped at the doorway and peered in.

"Dad, I brought you a smoothie. I know you're not crazy about them, but they're good for you."

Killian looked on as Spencer rubbed his eyes with the back of his fists and slowly lifted the comforter from his body. He struggled to slide his legs over the side of the bed. He smiled at Erica and gave a glance in Killian's direction. Buster rose from the floor and greeted Erica with a grin and a wagging tail.

"Thank you, Erica," Spencer said. "Just set it there on the dresser. I'll get to it later."

"Did you get any sleep?" Erica asked.

Killian gazed at his friend. Spencer looked dreadfully tired.

"I'm not sure. I think so, but my dreams were so crazy," Spencer said. "Maybe I'll get in a nap later today. How's everyone else doing?"

"Oh, I don't think anyone got a lot of sleep last night, but we're fine," Erica said as she stood in front of her father as he sat. "Dad, you don't look so good. Are you okay?"

"I'm fine. Just tired and worn out, I guess. And those dreams..."

Killian entered the room and sat down on the bed close to Spencer.

"Spencer, Erica's right. You don't look very well," Killian said. "I don't think you're okay at all.

"Erica, go ask Elizabeth for a thermometer, please. If you can't find her, I believe there's one in the medicine cabinet in your bathroom."

Spencer's face was mostly void of color, and his cheekbones were gaunt. Killian didn't like what he was seeing. He raised his left hand and placed it on Spencer's forehead.

"You're burning up, man!" Killian said. "Lie back down in the bed, and I'll fetch you a glass of cold water."

Spencer offered no resistance and did as he was told, and Killian got up from the bed. He left the room and caught Erica just as she was coming out of the bathroom.

"Erica, your father has a high fever, and I don't know what else. Go take his temperature, and I'll be in shortly with some water and an ice pack. There are some extra pillows on the shelf in the hallway closet. Grab a couple of those, would you please?"

Killian went to the kitchen and filled a glass with cold water. He grabbed an ice pack from the freezer and made his way back to the bedroom. *What's going on?*, he thought. *This is no doubt related to last night.*

"Yep, he's got a fever, and a pretty nasty one. Borderline emergency-room type," Erica said as Killian walked back into the room.

Killian took the thermometer from Erica and gave it a quick look. *This is no good.* He handed the water to Spencer, who took a large gulp and gave the glass back. Killian reached over and placed the ice pack in Erica's hand, and she gently positioned it on Spencer's forehead. She fluffed the pillows and arranged them so her father was more comfortable.

"Dad, we should get you to a hospital," she said. The worrisome look on her face was telling, and Killian was feeling the same.

Spencer remained quiet, his eyes half-closed. Killian couldn't tell whether he was simply tired or whether the fever was already having its way.

"Erica, I don't disagree with you, but you must realize that's not a good idea," Killian said. "If he goes to hospital, he'll be alone at times and we can't have that. Not after what happened last night. I know a doctor up Bruff way. I'll give him a ring. There are still a few doctors in these parts who don't mind performing a house call."

"Thank you, Killian, and I know you're right," Erica said. "But I'm really worried now. Could you call right away?"

The concern on the girl's face was clear. Killian hoped she wouldn't cry again; she had done enough of that. He gave her a quick pat on the shoulder and walked out of the room and into the hallway.

The doctor was fortunately making his rounds throughout the county today, and Killian arranged the visit for just after noon. He checked on Spencer one more time before heading to the Grafton Pub to make certain things were in order. His son had taken over duties yesterday evening, and he wasn't always the best at cleaning up properly once the last inebriated customer had left for the night. Killian needed a break from the house anyway, and Elizabeth decided to join him. She had some grocery shopping to do while he was busy at the pub.

After Killian and Elizabeth arrived home a couple of hours later, the doctor from Bruff showed up within ten minutes. He came and left. Yes, Spencer had a high fever and was certainly out of sorts, but a diagnosis was not forthcoming. Spencer showed no additional signs of a cold or the flu, and the doctor left the house unable to tell them anything further. He told Killian to keep Spencer comfortable and well-hydrated and to keep an eye on the fever. If anything changed, he was to be called right away.

After the doctor departed Killian reentered the bedroom. Erica sat on the bed next to her father, patting his forehead with a wet, cold cloth. Spencer had been awake during the doctor's visit, but he had gone to dreamland now; Killian hoped those dreams were not once again a replay of last night's event.

Buster was lying still next to the bed. He had only been outside once since last night, and the food and water Erica had set on the floor for him remained untouched. Killian marveled at the uncanny nature of dogs and their fierce loyalty to the ones they loved. A thought for another day perhaps, but he would talk to his wife soon about getting a dog of their own.

"Erica, I need to head back to the pub," Killian said. "I'm late in opening as it is. Elizabeth is here if you need anything, and I suspect the good detective will show up sooner or later."

"Sure, Killian. We'll be fine," Erica said.

He could see her spirits had picked up a bit since her father was able to sleep.

"Give me a ring should you need," Killian said and walked out of the bedroom.

Killian's stay at the Grafton Pub ended up being a rather short one. Elizabeth had called him just a couple of hours after he had left. Spencer was still asleep, but his temperature, which had been stable and had even gone down a bit, was on the rise again. Killian called the doctor, and the man was again on his way to the house. Killian's son showed up at the pub to take over a few minutes before five. The regulars were beginning to pile in one after another. As he left, Killian told his son to keep a lookout for Angus.

When Killian arrived home Elizabeth and Erica were changing the bed sheets, gingerly rolling Spencer to one side and then the other to dislodge the wet sheets and replace them with new ones. Spencer had begun sweating profusely soon after Elizabeth's call.

"How's he doing?" Killian asked his wife upon entering the room.

"Not well, I'm afraid," Elizabeth said. "His temperature is above even where it was this morning."

Killian stared down at his friend. Spencer was either asleep or perhaps unconscious. Erica had just finished wiping his head down, but the fresh pillow was already becoming saturated.

"Dr. Byrne should be here shortly," Killian said. "We'll have a decision to make depending on what he says."

Killian had given the situation a lot of thought throughout the afternoon. Sure, he and Erica could take turns staying with Spencer at the hospital, but Buster would have to remain here regardless. Everyone staying together would be impossible. Spencer's going to the hospital would make things complicated, something Killian hoped to avoid.

And though she had objected, Killian had convinced Elizabeth she needed to head for her sister's in Tipperary. He would not put her at risk any longer after what had occurred last night. After she was gone, he knew he needed to keep Spencer, Erica, and Buster together. They would only take Spencer to the hospital should his situation become dire.

Dr. Byrne appeared within thirty minutes. He was adamant that Spencer be taken to the emergency room if his temperature ticked up even a half degree higher. Killian couldn't argue, and he wasn't about to let Spencer die here in his house. They would figure something out, maybe even sneak Buster into the hospital if necessary, maybe say he was an emotional-support dog. In the meantime Dr. Byrne would notify the hospital in Bruff to possibly expect an emergency visitor later in the evening.

Killian walked Elizabeth out to the car and gave her a hug and kiss before she left. He hated having his wife gone, but he knew it was better this way.

He made his way back to the house. Once in, he pulled from the refrigerator the meal Elizabeth had prepared for him and Erica.

The detective hadn't shown up today. He had called and said he was simply caught up in too much work. He promised to stop by in the morning and said to let him know if Spencer's condition worsened.

Killian reheated the food and brought a plate in for Erica. She thanked him, but he could tell she wasn't going to eat her dinner. She sat in the chair next to her father, letting nothing distract her as she kept her eyes constantly on Spencer. Except for the sweating and deep breathing, Spencer showed no sign of being part of this world. After Erica removed the thermometer from underneath Spencer's armpit, she gave Killian the okay sign with her eyes. Spencer's temperature was still stable.

"Erica, I'll be out in the living room. Let me know if you need anything," he said. "You really should try and eat something, you know."

"I will, Killian. Don't worry."

Killian turned to walk out the door.

"Killian."

"Yes," he said, turning to face her again.

"Is my dad going to be okay?" she said and with her sad eyes looked into Killian's face for the answer.

"Sure, he is. He'll be fine, he will. I've seen him go through worse and come out shining. He is one stubborn man, and he's certainly not going to let a little fever get the best of him."

Killian could see his attempt at optimism wasn't hitting home. He had no idea what was in store for Spencer. He watched as Erica removed the ice pack from Spencer's forehead and wiped the same area with a damp cloth.

"Killian, why is all of this happening?" Erica said as she replaced the ice pack. "What did my father do to deserve all of this?"

"That's one I have no answer for," Killian said, and he didn't. "I've seen a lot of things in my day, but nothing quite like this. You may know I'm a religious man. I believe God has a plan for all of us. Why He is putting your father through all of this misery, I can't say. But there is a reason for everything. Perhaps we will understand that reason someday; maybe we won't. The Lord performs his work in mysterious ways, but I'm certain you've heard that one before.

"One thing I do know is that your coming to Ireland was meant to be. Your father had been lost in so many ways, but he found a life here that was making him quite happy, I believe, until the latest of course. You three children were the last part of the puzzle. He tells me things that perhaps he doesn't know how to share with you. If you hadn't come Spencer's life would never have been complete. God sent you back to him, and we're all going to get through this together.

"Let's keep the faith, Erica."

Killian patted Erica on the leg before leaving the room. He was glad to see a small smile on her face for the first time today.

Killian cracked open a new bottle of Scotch and plopped down in his favorite leather chair. He wasn't hungry either, and his food sat on the kitchen countertop, getting cold. He took a small sip of his drink and felt the warmth enter his body. He thought about what Erica had said a few minutes before.

What did Spencer do to deserve all of this? Nothing, nothing at all. Sure, the man had, or did have, a long list of issues and problems, but his character was true and beyond reproach. He was one of the finer men Killian had ever known. Killian closed his eyes and silently said a brief prayer. He needed God's help on this one.

When Killian had finally gotten to sleep last night, unnerved from all that had happened at the abbey, he knew the dream would come, and it had. The fourth bottle had met its fate just like the three before. This time, when the bottle shattered, its contents splattered everywhere, bright crimson blood showering the floor and dripping down the white surface of the wall. *Would the fifth bottle drop after Spencer passed away in this very house? He had to get better; he had to.* Killian did his best to discard the thought from his mind, and he threw back the contents of his second drink.

Shortly thereafter, Buster emerged from Spencer's room and wandered over to the front door without looking at Killian. Killian studied Buster for a second or two and grabbed the dog's lead from the sofa. Together they stepped outside. When Buster had finished his business, Killian sat down on the steps leading to the front door. The night was beautiful and clear, with stars and a partial moon lighting the sky. He gently caressed the dog's ears as Buster looked off into the distance.

I wonder what's going on in that head of his, Killian thought. Buster knew things they didn't. Killian possessed the art of getting into people's minds. The same trick didn't seem to work so well with animals.

Killian watched as Buster stared out into the darkness in front of them. For a good five minutes the dog didn't twitch a single muscle or make a single sound, his focus complete and without interruption. Killian looked on in amazement at an animal that appeared more as a statue than a living being. Buster dropped his head and swiveled around. He walked up right next to Killian's face and began smothering him with licks and kisses. At that moment Killian knew that Spencer was going to be all right. Killian gave Buster a quick peck on the head. They walked back into the house, and Buster returned to the bedroom. Maybe the fifth bottle wouldn't drop after all. Killian sat down to have his dinner.

"And how is our Mr. Spencer doing this morning?" Killian asked as he pushed open the door with his shoulder and then set the plate of poached eggs and slightly burnt toast on the nightstand.

"Not too bad," Spencer said. "Erica said I wasn't in the best of shape for a while, but I don't remember much."

"You hungry?" Killian asked.

"Not really," Spencer said. "But I'd take a refill on the water and maybe some coffee."

"Sure thing," Killian said. "And I'm certain Erica will have this food sliding down your throat as soon as she's out of the shower."

"I don't doubt it," Spencer said as he handed Killian the empty glass.

"Were you able to sleep last night?" Killian asked.

"Slept like the dead," Spencer said, "but I'm glad I'm not among them. I'm not quite ready just yet."

Killian chuckled and went over to the blinds. He pulled the draw cord to open them, and bright light showered every corner of the room. He turned back to Spencer.

"It's another beautiful day out, but it's best you stay in bed, for today at least," Killian said.

Last night Killian had fallen asleep in front of the television before finishing his third glass of Scotch. Around midnight he was awoken by voices down the hall. When he walked into the room, Spencer was sitting up in bed having a conversation with Erica. Buster was lying next to him, resting his head on Spencer's leg. A sight for sore eyes, it was, and Buster had been correct. The fever had broken about an hour before, and Spencer's face color was already returning to normal.

"I'm sure you realize that your departure for Dublin will have to be postponed a few days," Killian said. "You're in no shape to be traveling right now."

"I know. I'm not so sure how keen I am about leaving, but I suppose it's best and something we have to do," Spencer said.

"Yes, Spencer, you have to go. That's one not even up for debate."

Killian watched as Spencer planted his eyes on the scene outside the window and took in the new morning. He would miss this man, more than he could imagine, much more than he felt the first time Spencer had threatened to leave Ireland. They were much closer now, friends who understood each other and who could almost read each other's thoughts.

"Anyway," Killian said, "Erica may have told you already, but today or tomorrow she's planning to do a thorough cleaning of the Square One and properly pack everything the two of you need to take. The rest can be sent later. Detective Walsh will accompany her. And I heard Detective Dunn will go with them as well, though I'm not sure why or how things were explained to him. They'll be safe if they're together, and you, Buster, and I will be safe here in the house."

"Yeah, she mentioned it to me this morning," Spencer said. "I guess there's no other choice, but I'd rather go with them so we're all together."

"Everything is a bit of a risk these days," Killian said, "but we'll make it work. Why don't you eat your breakfast and then get some rest? I'm going to call the doctor and tell him about your miraculous recovery."

Killian laughed as he said the last bit. Spencer's fever breaking was miraculous in a way, but Killian had had a feeling, even before Buster had told him so. He wondered what else Buster had to tell, and he wondered whether they would get through the next couple of days with no issues.

CHAPTER EIGHTEEN

As Killian, Spencer, and Erica were finishing breakfast the next morning, Detectives Walsh and Dunn knocked at the front door. Spencer wiped his mouth with a napkin as Killian stood up and made his way to the entrance of the house.

Physically, even though only one day and a couple of nights had passed, Spencer was basically feeling back to his old self today, except for some dragging weariness. He was thinner than usual, and Erica forced him to eat every last bite of his morning meal.

He wasn't so sure about his mental condition. His dreams, at least those he could remember, were anything but sweet. The experience of the other night, including the terrible visions he had seen, haunted him when his eyes were closed. Even last night he had seen the hideous picture of Buster over and over again. But when he was awake he felt fine for the most part. Consciously or subconsciously, he was having some success in blocking things he didn't wish to relive. He wasn't so sure about Erica, but her mood was certainly better today than it had been. He wondered about Buster.

Over breakfast, Spencer decided he felt well enough to tag along on today's outing. Neither Killian nor Erica objected, based on the promise that Spencer would do nothing more than "tag along." He would remain in the backseat of the car with Buster as the other three did what was necessary in the Square One.

The safety-in-numbers theory convinced everyone they should stick together. Still, Spencer worried about Killian, leaving him here alone without any support.

"Spencer, I told you once, and I'll tell you again: This is my home, and this is where I will live or die," Killian had said. "If this spirit wants to make mincemeat of me while you're gone, so be it."

Spencer realized they would be leaving Killian alone for good anyway once they all left for Dublin. Since shortly after meeting him for the first time, Spencer always thought of Killian as invincible. He didn't know why necessarily; there was simply some resilient strength that exuded from the man. Spencer knew no one was invincible against this damn ghost.

Over the last few weeks Spencer had wondered about the spirit and why it had taken so long to come back and haunt them. Maybe because of Buster? Maybe because of Erica? He didn't understand completely, but he did in a way. A supernatural being probably had an eternity to do what it wanted and when. He was certain its time frames were not measured in a way understandable by lowly humans.

The damn thing might be in a hurry this time, especially if it understood their plans of leaving this village and this country. Only this final day remained until they were gone for good. They just had to get through today, and then all would be well, he hoped.

The five of them piled into Spencer's SUV. Things would be a little tight, but the luggage rack on top would take care of any extra belongings that needed to go. Detective Walsh would drive, and Spencer silently laughed to himself as Erica took the other seat up front. He would give her a hard time later. For now, he was glad to find a small piece of humor in something.

Thirty minutes later the vehicle pulled up in front of the Square One Bed and Breakfast. Spencer looked out the car window at the place he loved. This inn had meant and still meant so much to him, and the sorrow he felt in leaving this house hit hard as he studied the structure up and down. He feared he would never see it again, or this country, or his dear friend Killian. He wondered where he, Erica, and Buster would ultimately end up. There was much to contemplate, but now wasn't the time. Now they needed to get ready and get out.

Detective Dunn opened the rear door and stepped out. Buster whined as the door shut behind the man. None of them had talked about ghostly things on the drive over, and Spencer wondered how much the detective knew about the situation and the reason for their sudden departure from Ireland. Not that it mattered any longer; Spencer couldn't care less at this point who knew what about anything.

Erica and Detective Walsh joined Detective Dunn at the front of the car. Spencer watched as the three of them made their way to the house entrance. They opened the door and disappeared inside. Erica came out five minutes later and told her father that all was well and that no return visit from the spirit was evident. Buster begged to go with her as she headed back to the house.

"You gotta stay here with me, buddy," Spencer said to Buster as the dog continued to show his frustration at being left behind. "Sorry about that, but you can blame this one on me."

Spencer glanced in the direction of the River Aya. He would likely never fish there again or play with Buster in its clear, welcoming water. He turned around at the sound, and through the back window he could spy a tractor slowly moving through a field above. The sudden departure of the Spencer family would surely be the talk of the town for a while. This is so messed up, he thought as he turned back around and then pulled out a treat for Buster from the seat pocket in front of him.

After a half hour of sitting in the car, Erica came out with a box full of perishable items from the refrigerator and freezer. Detective Walsh soon followed with another box full of other food. They opened the rear door and placed everything inside.

"We've still got a ways to go, Dad," Erica said after she came around to Spencer's open window. "I need to clean out the refrigerator and the freezers so we can unplug them before we leave. There are so many things I want to take, but I know we can't take them all. Just two suitcases each, I promise. And one duffel bag for Buster's stuff, of course. Killian can come later and get the canned goods if he or Elizabeth wants them."

"I'll leave it to you," Spencer said. "Just don't forget my fishing gear if you find space."

Spencer owned a lot more than would fit into two suitcases, but Killian had promised to ship whatever was left behind, the things Spencer truly needed, at least.

As the two of them waited in the car, Spencer made a double check of the accommodations in Dublin. The reservation was made for a week at a busy downtown hotel that accepted pets. He was confident they would be safe there. They'd extend the reservation if more time were needed to get Buster's papers for importation in order. The airline's requirements would be another hurdle. He had no idea how much time would be needed to get everything done. He would remain wary and vigilant until they were out of the country.

Erica came out again with more boxes. Spencer could see she was handling most of the work now, as the detectives wouldn't know what or what not to pack. He could see the two of them out on the patio, talking, and Detective Dunn smoking a cigarette. Spencer was glad they were here. They too were likely incapable of fighting a nasty spirit on their own, but Spencer knew he and Erica were in good hands nonetheless. He hoped so.

As Erica left and once more was out of sight inside the house, Spencer could feel himself growing sleepy. The event of that night and the subsequent sickness had taken a toll on him. His mind and body were beginning to feel heavy and listless all over again. He placed his head against the back of the seat, Buster lying on the space next to him with his head on Spencer's right thigh.

He awakened in what seemed only a few minutes. Buster was standing on the seat with his head poking out the window. He wasn't barking but rather just staring to the outside. Spencer worked his fingers into the inside corners of his eyes and ran them down the bridge of his nose. He leaned forward and wrapped his head around the right side of Buster to have a look.

He hadn't seen her in a long time, except for the vision shared by the spirit the other night, but there was no mistaking what he and Buster had their eyes on. Spencer studied his old friend with her long wiry coat of white hair and a wide patch of brown that ran down her back from head to tail. She was sitting on the porch of the front door at first, but she was not looking in their direction. She jumped off, and her nose sniffed the ground and the yellow daffodils sitting in the dark brown planters. She sauntered around to the corner of the house and ran back to the porch. Buster was calm and seemed mesmerized, and Spencer was feeling the same.

"I'll be damned," Spencer said softly.

As he was about to call out Shandy's name, the door opened, and out came Erica. Spencer looked at Erica momentarily and quickly shifted his eyes back to the porch. It stood empty.

"Got this one, and then the three of us will be back out with the rest," Erica said as she reached the car. "That should be about it, but give me a little more time. I wanna do one last walk-through before we lock up. Maybe you'd like to go inside once to say goodbye?"

"Yeah, maybe," Spencer said. "I'll be in before you lock up. Take your time. We're in no hurry."

Spencer couldn't wait for Erica to leave. He had to see whether Shandy would reappear.

Once Erica was inside the house, Spencer and Buster stared at the porch, letting nothing distract them. But Shandy didn't show.

After five minutes their eyes became tired, and Spencer leaned back on the car seat, dejected.

"Buster, you were my witness this time, so I know I wasn't seeing things," Spencer said, tousling Buster's head. "I wonder what she wanted."

Buster's eyes told Spencer that he hadn't been imagining or hallucinating. *Why did Shandy show up today of all days?*

Spencer let his head fall back again on the headrest and passively stared in the opposite direction, across the green growth that led to the River Aya. Before his eyes could focus Buster scrambled across the car seat and stuck his head out the window. To Spencer's amazement, Shandy was sitting motionless on a patch of bare ground. This time she was returning the stares of Spencer and Buster.

Buster whimpered, fidgeted, and agitated, desperate to get outside and investigate this newfound oddity of a dog he had never met before. At this meeting, however, Spencer was certain Shandy wasn't a dog at all but rather the ghost of a dog that he once knew and loved.

Buster settled down somewhat, and the two of them stared intently in Shandy's direction. Again, Spencer wanted to call out her name, but he wasn't sure he should. He let the silence dictate what would come next. Shandy didn't move a muscle the whole time and just sat silently watching Spencer and Buster. Her eyes didn't even blink, and she seemed to possess no emotion at all.

Voices carried from the direction of the patio, and Spencer turned to see the two detectives and Erica talking and looking in the direction of the car. He wondered whether they could see Shandy. He moved his eyes back to the spot. Shandy was gone. He stared at the spot for another minute, willing Shandy to return, hoping Shandy would return. She didn't.

Now that the surprise had worn off, if even slightly, Spencer's head drooped, and he became lost in thought. He hadn't seen this dog for such a very long time. She came for a reason. She knows something. *She came to warn me, or maybe ask for my help.* Maybe his new theory about her—that she was the one potentially in trouble—was correct. Regardless, Spencer was certain that somehow things were not yet complete.

Spencer was startled and looked up and to his left.

"Dad, do you wanna go inside the house before we lock the doors?" Erica asked as she stood at the open car window across from him.

"Sure. I think I will," he said.

He opened the car door for one last visit to his home. He snapped a lead on Buster's collar before getting out.

CHAPTER NINETEEN

Three weeks had come and gone since the Tractor Run and the subsequent discovery of the bodies of Sean and Clare Kelly a day later. To Spencer, it seemed like only yesterday. Time can fly even when you're not having fun. With any luck, things would all come to a close today.

Spencer woke very early the next morning, even though they didn't plan to leave for the three-hour drive to Dublin until around eleven. He had received another decent night of sleep, even though his mind remained full and the dreams wouldn't stop. On the ride back from the Square One yesterday and through dinner, Spencer had contemplated whether to tell anyone of his vision of Shandy. But what he had seen wasn't a vision at all; he knew it had been real.

After the evening meal last night, he had sat in the living room with Killian, each sipping a drink, Spencer neat bourbon and Killian Scotch and water on the rocks. Erica had been out on the patio with Detective Walsh. The detective hadn't returned right away to Limerick with Detective Dunn; he was undoubtedly set on spending as much time with Erica as possible.

Today the detective would be driving them to Dublin in Spencer's car and spending the night there with some relatives before coming home. They would all have dinner together somewhere. Spencer was more than grateful for the man's assistance.

As Spencer and Killian had sat there enjoying some quiet time and the company of one another, Spencer decided to reveal the episode with Shandy. And he decided to share his supposition that perhaps Shandy was the true target of the menacing ghost. Like so many times before Killian had been nonplussed at news that would have been unbelievable to any other person. Spencer realized that Killian had seen enough of the Spencer-Shandy escapades to let nothing surprise him.

And though Killian was a man of God, Spencer knew his friend also believed in the supernatural world and had believed long before Spencer had stepped into his life.

This time, however, Killian's oracle-like powers hadn't provided the necessary insight; he couldn't make heads or tails of what Shandy's appearance meant. He did agree that Spencer's new theory might deserve a small amount of merit. Shandy's appearance at the Square One could have been a plea for help or a warning of some kind. Or perhaps she simply wanted to say goodbye to Spencer before he left Ireland forever. They decided together that the latter was most likely the case and that the chances of anything else happening were remote. On the way to Dublin everyone would be in the car together. Once they arrived, there would be safety within the confines of the bustling city. Spencer hoped they were correct.

Finally, they had discussed Spencer's supposed sighting of Angus at the abbey and any possible meaning. On this one, Killian had serious doubts, and Spencer had to admit he more or less felt the same. He saw Angus because he wanted to see Angus. There was no other explanation. Just a throttled mind playing tricks on him. None of it mattered any longer, and he would let the subject rest.

Spencer cleared his mind and began pouring a second cup of coffee. He glanced up at hearing the footsteps of Killian making his way into the kitchen.

"Coffee?" Spencer said.

"Yes, Spencer, thank you."

They relaxed at the kitchen table and stared at the lifting steam rising from their cups.

"Well, I guess this is it," Spencer said. He really couldn't get his head around the fact that this was his last day in Galbally and in this part of the country.

"Yeah, I guess this is it, isn't it now?" Killian said. "Listen, today's a difficult day for us all, but what choice is there? You know and I know this has gone much too far. Whether you can ever come back here or not, I can't say. There are no other options right now."

Spencer hated the idea of leaving, but he knew Killian was correct. His heart was telling him there was a chance he could come back, but his head told him otherwise. This terrible spirit that was ruining his life would be waiting, whether six months from now or years from now. He contemplated again whether the damn thing was capable of following them across the open ocean.

The two talked for another thirty minutes, mostly just casual banter, interspersed with moments of sincerity between friends before they parted. Near the end of their conversation, Spencer got a bit of a shock, although there wasn't much that could surprise him these days.

Spencer listened as Killian explained the dreams of five green bottles and the significance of each up to this point. Killian then explained that the fifth bottle was still in place, as far as he knew, because the dream had not come again. Killian remarked that he felt strongly that he had seen the end of the strange dream, and that could only mean one thing—that Spencer, and everyone else, had made it through the worst and most likely had clear sailing ahead.

Spencer sat back, feeling relieved and thankful once again for Killian's uncanny insight into matters others could never even hope to understand. As he stared at the table, he noticed the document he had set down earlier.

"Oh, before I forget," Spencer said, sliding the paper across the table. "I appreciate your help with this."

"Not a problem, Spencer," Killian said. "I'll get you the best price I can, whether from me or someone else, and then wire the money to your account."

Along with everything else, Spencer would miss his car. Killian had said he was even considering buying and keeping the car for himself, but for now they both needed to sign the title and give Killian ownership.

As Killian was setting down the pen on the kitchen table, Erica came into the room with Buster at her side.

"Boy, you guys are up early," she said. "Couldn't sleep?"

Spencer rose and poured a cup of coffee for his daughter.

"I actually did all right last night," Spencer said as he handed the mug to her, "but when it was over it was over."

"That's great, Dad. I'll make you guys some breakfast if you're hungry," Erica said, "and then I'm going to repack my bags. Sorry, Dad, but you're on your own if you want to do the same."

"No problem," Spencer said. "I am a bit curious what you packed for me."

"By the way, Danny called and said they'd be here around ten-thirty," Erica said.

"They? Who's they?" Spencer said.

"Didn't I tell you?" Erica said. "Detective Dunn is coming as well. He's just going to follow us and make sure we safely make it to the motorway. Then he'll turn around and drive back to Limerick."

"Not a bad idea. Not a bad idea," Spencer said, ignoring the fact this was the first time he had heard Erica call Detective Walsh by his given name.

Spencer looked over as Killian got up from the table.

"I'm gonna be passing on breakfast, Erica. Thank you, anyway," he said. "I've got some paperwork at the pub I need to go through this morning. I'll be back before ten. Don't be leaving on me before I return."

"No chance of that, Killian," Spencer said.

His sorrow resurfaced, and he wished he could join Killian to experience one more time the little village that had factored so heavily in his life. He also wanted to have a final beer, even a morning one, with his friend at the Grafton Pub. But there was no point in taking chances, and he would stay here with Erica and Buster.

Maybe they'd take a quick drive through Galbally on their way out.

Killian left, and after breakfast Spencer and Erica busied themselves with their belongings. Spencer opened the duffel bag with Buster's things and found his fishing rod neatly snuggled in its case. He pulled the rod out, the same one he had been using for years, and stared at it. Maybe I would have never come to Ireland in the first place if not for you, he thought. Fishing in Ireland had been the excuse for venturing here on his initial trip. That excuse had been only partially true, and the real reason for coming here had run much deeper. Someone had once told him "to expect the unexpected," and his adventures in Ireland had exceeded all of his expectations, both good and bad. *Why did it have to end this way? Why does it have to end at all?*

He placed the rod back in its case and organized the rest of his things.

The two detectives showed up right on time a few hours later, and Killian was already back. The bags were loaded into the car, and then Spencer and Erica did one more run-through of the house to make certain they hadn't forgotten anything. When they were done, they all gathered out on the front porch. One of many moments Spencer had been dreading was here.

"Killian, I don't know what to say," Spencer said as they stood facing one another.

"Nothing needs to be said, Spencer. And this isn't the last you'll be seeing of me. You have my promise on that one, you do."

"Yes, I suppose you're right," Spencer said and forced half of a smile.

He reached out his hand. As Killian took it Spencer grabbed his friend and wrapped his arms around him. The embrace lasted until both were uncomfortable and was finished off with pats on the back as both let go.

Spencer stared at Killian's face, and, for the first time he could remember, saw a semblance of tears forming in the man's eyes. Spencer tightened his facial muscles. There would be no crying today, except from Erica, who was standing to the side and already wiping the moisture from her cheeks.

Spencer looked on as Killian gave Erica a hug and then knelt to Buster's level.

"You take care of these two, Buster," Killian said. "I'll be counting on you, I will."

Spencer watched as Killian rubbed the dog's head a last time and stood back up. Spencer gave Killian a fake punch in the shoulder, and they all walked over to the parked vehicles. The three people and one dog got into Spencer's car, and Detective Dunn got into his own. Killian stood nearby. As the two vehicles pulled out of the driveway, Spencer opened the window and slowly waved his hand back and forth. Killian was right: No words were necessary. Spencer adjusted his baseball cap. He reached into a shirt pocket and put on his sunglasses.

They were driving to Bansha through the Glen of Aherlow on the same road Spencer had driven so many times over the past year. From Bansha they would duck southeast to the village of Cahir, where they would say their farewells to Detective Dunn. From there they would join the M8 and then the M7 motorway that led directly to Dublin. Spencer wished they could stop by the Square One just one more time before leaving.

As the two cars navigated the contours and curves of the winding road, in the first vehicle Detective Walsh and Erica chatted in the front seat. Spencer had begged off any driving today and was fine in giving the responsibility to the detective. He sat silently in the backseat with Buster, barely aware of the conversation up front, and stared out the window at the passing scenery he knew so well. He recalled the first time he had driven this way, getting lodged more than once behind large tractors that were hogging almost the entire narrow roadway as they moved from one field to another.

Today, Spencer didn't care much about farm tractors. He had other things on his mind and was feeling rather melancholy, knowing and realizing that today was likely his last trip down this road. More than anything, he worried about Killian. *Would he be all right?* Maybe he'd be safe now that they were gone. He wondered whether he would ever have a chance to see his friend again.

At about the halfway point to Bansha, the car began a gradual halt. Spencer came out of his daydream and guided his eyes up ahead. The cars on this side of the road were backed up about ten deep, and Spencer could see a similar situation in the opposite lane.

"What's going on?" Spencer asked as he leaned forward and looked out the front glass.

"No idea," Detective Walsh said.

Spencer felt the car come to a full stop, and he watched the detective place the vehicle in park.

"Let me go check it out," the detective said. "I'll be back in a minute or two."

Spencer looked on as Detective Walsh opened the door and exited the car. He first went back to Detective Dunn's vehicle, had a brief discussion, and then walked by and forward to the beginning of the line of cars.

"Any idea what's going on?" Spencer asked Detective Dunn soon after he appeared next to Spencer's open window.

"No, not yet. We should know soon," the detective said.

In a few minutes Detective Walsh returned.

"Seems a large tree is blocking the road. The man who owns the land next to the road was felling the tree and made a slight mistake in calculations. More than a small mistake, I'd say. Thank goodness he didn't kill anyone. Idiot!

"Anyway, the tree took down a power line, but there's a crew already here. We won't be able to pass for a while. They'll start sawing up the tree soon, but it'll take some time to remove the line."

Spencer poked his head out the window, looking for the downed tree. He could see the power company's truck parked on the side of the road ahead.

"So we just wait?" Erica asked.

Right then, the sound of a chainsaw or two polluted the air. Spencer sat back in his seat and rubbed his hands up and down his face and then over the top of his head. This wasn't the first time he had seen something like this, but why today?

"Yes, we just wait," the detective said. "Shouldn't be any longer than an hour or so. Or we could look for an alternate route."

Spencer watched as several of the waiting cars began to back up and head in the direction from where they had come. There were other ways to get to Bansha, but they would all take some time.

The four of them discussed matters and decided they would grab some lunch and eat on a beautiful hillside that presented spectacular views of the Galtee mountain range on the other side of the valley. The place was popular, generally full of tourists and locals, and they would be sitting out in the open at one of the many picnic tables populating the setting. They would be safe there, and Spencer would have a last chance to enjoy one of the many things he loved about this area.

The turnoff to their destination was just less than a mile behind them. By the time they were finished with lunch, surely the road would be cleared and they'd be able to proceed to Dublin.

They made the right turn and began meandering up the curving road to the spot. Four or five cars from the other direction whizzed by as they went. A good sign, Spencer thought as he counted the cars. They reached the top, and the two vehicles pulled into a couple of vacant spaces. There were numerous other cars and at least a dozen people, some sitting at picnic tables, some snapping pictures of the Galtee Mountains, and some heading up one or the other of the two hiking trails that ran to the backside of the forest above them and exited at another parking area up the road.

Spencer had been to this particular place more than once over the last year. The vista was spectacular, and the trails were perfect for a hike or a run. He was slightly dubious about the tree having fallen earlier and whether it meant anything, but he was certain they were safe here.

All of them marched down to a picnic table that sat just twenty yards below the parking lot and the overlook. The sandwiches purchased at the mom-and-pop convenience store at the road turnoff were quickly eaten, and any apprehension about being here disappeared. Even more cars had shown above. At the table next to them sat a family, and a young couple were talking and enjoying their lunch at the one next to it.

Erica and the two detectives climbed back up to the overlook to take some pictures. Spencer relaxed on the bench, with Buster lying next to him. He took in the beautiful mountains far off in the distance and tried to make out some of the areas where he and Buster had hiked in the past. More memories about this land called Ireland formed in his head, and he threw out the bad ones and concentrated on those that were good. He wanted to leave this place on a positive note.

A voice called out from above.

"Dad, turn around," Erica said.

Spencer obliged as Erica lifted her phone and began snapping photos.

"Have Buster stand up, and you stand up too, so I can get some good shots," she said.

Spencer didn't feel much like having his picture taken, but there was no point in resisting. When his daughter was satisfied, he wandered over to the edge of the hillside with Buster for one last look. Almost an hour had passed already, and they could be on their way soon. He reached down and petted Buster's head as he stared into the distance. *I'm gonna miss this place,* he thought.

The ring of a mobile phone barely penetrated his ears, and he thought it had to be Detective Walsh's. He must have left his number with one of the crew members, asking, perhaps insisting, to be called once the road was clear. Police usually get what they want.

Spencer took a last look across the valley, turned around, and headed up to the parking lot. He could see Detective Walsh and Erica talking above him next to his car, and the other detective was off to the side having a smoke. Spencer stopped and reached down to tie a loose shoelace, placing the end of Buster's lead under the sole of his other shoe. He stood back up and glanced above. One of the car doors was open, but the three were no longer there. *I wonder where they went all of a sudden?*

Spencer reached the top of the small hill and walked to the parked car. Nobody was anywhere. He did a quick check of the inside. Opened bottles of water sat on the dashboard, and Erica's handbag was on the floor of the vehicle. The car keys were on the front seat. He grabbed them and stuffed the keys into his pants pocket.

He shut the door, and his head pivoted back and forth as he scanned as far as he could see. He walked over to Detective Dunn's car and saw the man's lighter and a pack of cigarettes on the passenger seat. He looked around again. There were plenty of people within his view, but not the three for whom he was searching.

He hesitated, wondering what was happening. *Where the hell could they be?* He was truly puzzled and equally concerned.

Spencer tightened his grip on Buster's lead. The two of them took off and ran up and down the asphalt pavement of the parking lot. Spencer shouted Erica's name, ignoring the strange looks he was receiving from people he didn't know. Nothing. Panic overcame him. He ran to the trailhead and yelled her name again. He yelled out the names of the other two. He and Buster scampered up the trail a hundred yards. Above, further up the trail, Spencer could see an older gentleman coming down toward him and Buster. They ran up the path and met the man halfway.

"Did you see a young woman and two men come this way?" Spencer asked through panting breaths.

"No, can't say I did," the man said. He appeared to be well into his seventies and was decked out in typical hiking attire, with a trekking pole resting in his right hand. "Haven't seen another soul for a good ten minutes. You're a stranger, are ya? Something wrong, is it?"

"No, it's nothing," Spencer said and looked beyond the man and further up the trail, hoping to see a sign, any sign, of Erica and the two detectives.

"You're planning to follow this trail up and search for those three, are you now?" the elderly man asked.

Spencer's attention swung immediately back to the man, who, with that one simple sentence, had suddenly become quite peculiar.

"I don't know," Spencer said. "And what do you mean? You just said you hadn't seen them."

"If you go, tread lightly, my dear sir. Tread lightly."

The man stared blankly at Spencer for a moment or two and headed down the trail toward the parking area.

Spencer looked on as the man went and said, "Hey, what do you mean? What are you talking about?"

The man continued down the trail and did not look back. He rounded a small curve and disappeared from their sight.

Spencer had run into another oddball of an old man about a year before, on the same day he had suffered those terrible beatings in Galbally, the beatings that had sent him to the hospital. That man had foretold, in a way, Spencer's future and had insisted that Spencer didn't belong here and that he should leave. *Was this the same?*

Spencer pushed the thought out of his mind and contemplated what they should do next. Yes, he and Buster could follow this trail up, but the path was only one of many possibilities of where the three could have gone. And this wasn't the only trail. Several more broke off from it at various points along the way. Erica and the two others could be anywhere.

Time was wasting, and Spencer didn't have the luxury of evaluating the discourse of another amateur soothsayer. He and Buster hurriedly ran back down the path toward the parking lot. Strangely enough, they never passed the old man as they trotted along, and he was nowhere to be seen once they reached the bottom of the trail.

Spencer was panicked and not thinking straight. Buster went where his master led him. They ran several hundred yards up the paved road, to where the mountain trails exited on the other end, where the other parking lot was. From there, Spencer could see even more trails, some of which went off in completely different directions. How could they possibly know where to search? He asked anybody who came along and anybody he could find in the parking area. Spencer and Buster ran back down to the original parking area and looked and searched everywhere once again. They walked half a mile down the road in the direction of the turnoff they had taken earlier today. His daughter and the two detectives were gone.

CHAPTER TWENTY

S pencer sat sideways in the driver's seat of his car, almost as if it were an unfamiliar place. His face was buried in his hands as he bent over with his elbows resting on his knees.

"My girl, my little girl," Spencer said as he rubbed the lower palms of his hands into his eyes. How could he have let this happen? He should have known better.

Buster had been patiently standing next to Spencer since he had sat down. Spencer stepped out of the car and got on his haunches next to Buster. Spencer was beside himself, and his heart was heavy, but Buster's touch was light, as if the dog understood what was happening and perhaps what needed to be done. He felt the warmth as Buster's tongue grazed his cheeks. The clarity of the dog's breath forced Spencer to pull himself together. His head rose, and he looked at Buster.

"Fuck it," he said. "Get your shit together or it will be too late!" He was talking to himself, not to his dog.

He slapped himself hard on both sides of his face, his cheeks turning a deep red.

"Get your shit together, man."

Spencer grabbed Buster around the neck and placed his face next to the dog's. As they sat and stood there, heads touching, an idea appeared in Spencer's mind as his muddled thoughts began to clear. The idea wasn't his at all; for the last five minutes Buster had been trying to tell Spencer something. He hadn't been listening.

Spencer rose, turned, and threw the door closed. The dog knew something, and that something was likely up ahead and in the forest above. The old man of a short while before had hinted at the same, and Spencer finally understood.

Spencer threw his trust to Buster and let the dog lead him back to the trailhead. Spencer studied the path above them. He was in the biggest hurry of his life, and he could only hope this route was truly the right way. And he could only rely on Buster, who had begun quickly pulling him up the winding dirt trail.

His hand subconsciously touched his pants pocket, and Spencer felt the outline of his phone. He stopped and pulled it out. He tried to call Killian, but the signal was weak, and the call wouldn't go through. Spencer hurriedly sent a text, hoping it would reach Killian and make some sort of sense. He had no time to wait for a reply and stuck the phone back into his pocket.

Spencer wasn't hysterical just quite yet, but he was getting close. The thought of losing his daughter Erica was tearing him to pieces inside. He could hardly stand it.

"Get with it, Buster," he said to his companion.

Spencer couldn't return the dog's smile as Buster looked back at him.

"Get going, Buster!"

The lead in Spencer's hand tightened, and he stumbled as Buster started and then picked up the pace. They ran full out for what seemed like a mile but was only a few hundred yards.

Spencer was physically in fairly decent shape, but the incline of the trail, at the rate they were going, had him heaving for air.

"Buster, stop!" he said.

Buster complied, and Spencer bent over, his open hands resting firmly on his knees. He knew he couldn't keep up.

"You go, boy," Spencer said as he unhooked the lead from the collar. "I'll catch up. Go now. Find Erica!"

He had realized just then that Buster, if there was any chance of saving Erica, was likely more important than he was. His dog knew what he didn't.

He watched as Buster scrambled up the trail. Within thirty seconds the dog rounded a bend far up ahead and went out of sight. Spencer stood straight and waited ten more seconds while he sucked in as much air as he could. He began a sprint in pursuit. He veered to the left around the same bend and continued to where the path straightened. As far as he could see there was no Buster. He ran stronger, determined to keep the pace. His chest pounded until he was certain it would explode.

As he scampered around a third bend, Buster came running back down the trail toward him. When Spencer reached the dog, Buster turned and led him further up the path. When they reached the top of the incline and of the mountain, Buster halted at another trail that broke to the right. Spencer stopped for a second to catch his breath and began following Buster down the side trail. In a short distance they reached an overlook that provided an expansive view of the open valley below. Several miles off Spencer could see the city of Tipperary.

He had been to this exact spot a couple of times previously and had never liked it. The place was pretty enough, but the setting was disturbing. At a particular tree, and to both sides of it, was a memorial of sorts to some young woman who had passed away. Pinned to the tree were messages from friends and family and photographs of the beautiful girl. Wilted flowers of no color and that needed replacing drooped lifelessly at the base of the tree. The scene was quite beautiful and touching, but a certain sadness hung in the air. When Spencer had been here before, he had wondered how the woman had met her demise. He had never taken the time to research the matter. Her name was there in plain sight, and he was certain he could have found the answer online.

He sure didn't like being back here today. Was there some significance he could only guess at?

Spencer looked down at his dog. Buster returned his stare and then whined and barked.

"What are you trying to tell me, Buster?"

He followed the dog's eyes into a dense patch of forest that broke suddenly with the open grass in which they were standing. Spencer fastened the lead back to Buster's collar and felt the tug. He followed Buster to the right and to the edge of the woods. They stopped and looked within.

Spencer could hardly believe the blackness on the other side, and he hesitated. The dog wanted them to enter a place where, undoubtedly, something evil awaited. That much was clear to Spencer. And he also knew that going forward provided the only chance of finding Erica and the detectives. He took out his phone again. There was no reply from Killian. He tried to call once more. Nothing. Spencer returned the phone to his pocket and again felt the pull of Buster's lead. They'd have to do this on their own.

Erica sat on the flat surface of the trunk of a tree that seemed to have been freshly cut. A heavy mist hung in the air. It came and went and came again, over and over as the eerie whiteness methodically moved between the trees and through the dark forest. She knew Danny and Detective Dunn were nearby because she could hear their muffled murmurings somewhere. She couldn't make out what they were saying or where they were. The words and voices were in front and in back of her and seemed to swirl around in a circular motion with no credence given to rhyme or reason.

Still, she felt incredibly calm, almost as if she had been sent here for a reason. *I wonder where they are,* she thought.

She was calm, but she also felt dazed and disoriented. She tried to think back as to how she got here. They were, all three of them, standing next to the car when something happened. But nothing happened. She remembered everything going black, just for a moment, just for a split second. The next thing she knew she was situated right here, sitting right on top of this tree trunk.

Erica looked behind and could see an opening on the other side of the trees. There was a sharp, defined edge where the forest stopped, and behind it were sunshine and brightness. She went there and tried to leave, but she couldn't. An invisible barrier, a boundary in front of where she stood, blocked her way. She desperately pushed with all of her might, but the air took her hands and gave them back. She tried again and again, but she wouldn't be let out.

Unfazed by the strangeness of this place and not knowing why, she sighed and made her way back to where she had begun. As soon as she returned to the tree trunk, she heard a voice, but not that of either detective. She cast her eyes back at the opening. She wondered why she wasn't surprised that Spencer and Buster were there, just on the other side. Erica could see them staring into the void. She could see her father with Buster's lead in his hand, holding the dog back and preventing him from entering where she was. She could see Spencer speaking to Buster, but now she couldn't hear anything; she couldn't hear the words or a single sound they were making.

"Dad, Dad, I'm right here! Daddy!"

Erica yelled at them again, but even her own voice didn't penetrate her senses. She ran to the opening and yelled louder. Still, there was no sound. Her mouth was working but not her ears. *Why don't they see me? Why don't they hear me?* She again tried to go out, to join Spencer and Buster. It was of no use. Erica scanned the ground and found a rock that fit snugly in her hand. She picked it up, backed up ten yards, and tossed the rock with all her might. The stone penetrated the barrier and immediately disappeared.

Erica walked back to the edge, and a movement below caused a shift of her eyes downward. She knelt and got on her knees. Buster was right there, just on the other side of the invisible wall, his long, angular face inches away from hers. She reached her arms out and tried to grab him, but she couldn't. But, this time, she could plainly hear him for some reason, hear his whimpering as he peered into the void and looked directly at her. *He can see me! Yes, he can see me!* She was sure, but she wasn't.

"Buster, I'm here! Come here, boy."

Erica cried his name over and over again as she stared at Buster on the other side, trying her hardest to will the dog across the barrier.

Her exhilaration was short-lived, her expectations destroyed. She watched in disappointment as her father pulled on the lead and forced Buster five yards back. Buster resisted and tried to surge forward. Spencer held the loop tight.

Voices from behind startled Erica and fell into her ears. She switched her direction for only a few moments and looked on as the two detectives made their way up an incline in front of her and off to her left. She turned back to the opening. It was gone and so were Spencer and Buster.

"Erica, you okay?" Detective Walsh said, panting for breath as he neared the top of the hill.

She stared for a few seconds longer at where her father and Buster had been. She collected herself, looked in the direction of the detectives, and, oddly enough, felt normal for the first time since entering this world that was not real. The flirting fog that had been present was completely removed. She headed toward them.

"Yeah, I guess so. What the hell is going on, Danny?"

"Wish I could tell ya," the detective said as he stood in front of Erica, his breathing heavy. "We were all there next to the car one moment, and then two seconds later the two of us are sitting on our arses in the middle of this God-forsaken forest. I'm glad we found you."

"I'm afraid, Danny. I'm really afraid," Erica said. The words trembled from her mouth.

"Me as well, Erica," Detective Walsh said.

She could feel the detective's arms around her. She placed her head next to his chest and could feel and hear the thumping of his heart. She hoped he was real.

"Detective Dunn's a bit out of sorts, I'm afraid," Detective Walsh said under his breath as he held Erica. "Hasn't been making much sense, but he seems certain he knows a way out."

Erica shifted her head in the direction of Detective Dunn, who was standing maybe fifteen yards away and paying them no attention. He didn't look well at all. His face was as white as a fresh sheet of typing paper, and he looked as if he had literally seen a ghost.

She could see the sheen on his forehead and the drops of perspiration slowly rolling down his temples and cheeks. She imagined he hadn't exerted himself like this in a very long time. Unlike the rest of them, Detective Dunn was wearing his formal work clothes. His black dress shoes were undoubtedly making his life more than miserable in this environment.

She looked up at Detective Walsh, her eyes moist with tears threatening to fall.

"My dad and Buster are right over there," Erica said.

She pulled away from the detective and pointed to where she had seen them. She studied the spot and saw nothing but an endless stand of trees.

"What are you talking about? Where?"

"They were there, just a minute ago," she said while continuing to stare at the spot. "Maybe I'm just imagining things, but I don't think so. I know I saw them. I know they were there."

Erica startled at the sound of the voice and looked in the direction of the other detective.

"I don't know what you saw," Detective Dunn said as he spoke for the first time and looked anxiously in all directions, "but we need to get out of here. It's coming. I know it is."

He fumbled in his jacket pocket for the pack of cigarettes that wasn't there.

Erica wanted to ask what "it" was, but she already knew. They all knew.

"I agree," said Detective Walsh. "I don't know what's happening here, but we're in some trouble, I believe. We need to get out right now."

"Let's head in that direction," Detective Dunn said. "I'm certain that's the way back to the parking area."

He was pointing in the opposite direction of where he and Detective Walsh had climbed up, and he was already moving.

"But, but, we should go where my father was," Erica said.

"Harry, hold up a second," Detective Walsh said and, for the first time, used his colleague's given name in Erica's presence.

The detective placed his hands on Erica's shoulders and looked at her with loving eyes.

"Erica, I'm not sure what you think you saw, but your father is not here. He can't help us, not right now. We just need to get out as quickly as possible. Let's go with Detective Dunn. I think he's right."

Erica turned, the detective's hands falling from her shoulders, and again glanced at the place where Spencer and Buster had been. She was still standing next to the tree trunk where she had been sitting. The detective reached out his hand, and she reluctantly took it. As they began to move and follow Detective Dunn, she removed a pink handkerchief from her back pocket and placed it on the top of the tree trunk.

Buster yanked harder on the lead as Spencer momentarily stood his ground. The dog was dead set on entering the forest directly ahead, and Spencer knew resisting, even for another second, was only foolhardy. He understood they had no choice. Erica and the detectives were somewhere within, and if he didn't act quickly, it may be too late.

Buster pulled again, and this time Spencer followed. Once they left the openness around them and entered inside the trees, a completely different world greeted them. They ventured maybe twenty yards in and stopped. Spencer couldn't imagine a forest darker, so dark that his eyes had difficulty adjusting from the bright light of only moments before. Wisps of white mist floated through the air. The imagined bamboo forest next to the cemetery that now held Mrs. O'Donnell had been one thing, but it was nothing compared to this. There were no bamboo trees here, only tall and straight spruce, so thick with limbs, branches, and greenish-blue needles that barely a space was evident between them. And they seemed to go on endlessly.

The dread and gloom he felt right now were real. He knew no good would come from this day. He glanced down at Buster, who showed no fear at all, although Spencer had no idea about the inner workings of his dog's mind. *Why can't I be brave like him?*

He wasn't sure why he did it. Spencer walked back to where they had entered. He tried to place a foot outside to where they had been. He couldn't. Nothing was stopping him from doing so; it just couldn't be done. At that moment he realized their fate was sealed in a way, and he knew for certain Erica and the detectives were somewhere inside this forest. *I will be brave, damn it! I will save my Erica.*

Spencer again tried to step out, and the result was the same. He stooped down and ran his hands over Buster's head and face. Buster let out two loud and sharp barks.

"Come on, boy. Take me to Erica," Spencer said.

Buster hurried forward and then cut sharply to the right. No trail existed, but the dog knew where to go.

Spencer began jogging behind Buster and passed right next to a lone tree stump. His eyes swung down at the very last moment, and the color of pink against the tan flat wood of the decapitated tree easily caught his attention; Buster had missed it somehow. Spencer yelled at his dog to stop, and he pulled up. He reached down to pick up the handkerchief. He examined the delicate cloth, not knowing what to make of it until he saw the embroidered initials: ECS. A small smile appeared on Spencer's face.

He held the handkerchief to his cheek and then to his nose, feeling its soft texture and the scent of laundry detergent. He lowered it down to Buster's nose.

She was in here somewhere, someplace, and they were on the right track.

CHAPTER TWENTY-ONE

The three of them traipsed through the forest endlessly. Erica instinctively pulled her phone from her pocket to check the time. She quickly realized and remembered that the damn thing hadn't been working since they had gotten into this mess. *Damn, why don't I wear a watch?* She guessed it had to be at least mid-afternoon by now, but she had no way of knowing for certain. Glimpses of the sun were only sporadic, and its positioning each time seemed to make no sense whatsoever.

Erica felt they were getting nowhere, and the parking area was no closer than it had been at the start. Aimlessly wandering up and down hills, across small gullies, and through an eternal forest of darkness and green was all they had accomplished at this point. They were all getting tired, and she was dying of thirst. She knew if they had to stay in here for more than a day or two, if there were in fact days to count, death would be their only salvation; a ghost, if one existed, wouldn't even matter anymore.

They stopped for a breather, and Detective Dunn showed his displeasure. Twenty yards ahead he glared back at Erica and Detective Walsh with a look of consternation on his face. The sweat had completely soaked through his white dress shirt, and he was becoming stranger by the minute. Only a short while before he had removed his suit jacket and necktie and left them hanging on a tree limb. Detective Walsh had grabbed the jacket and given it back, insisting it would be needed later. When the dark of night came, if it came, if they were in here that long, cold would come with it.

Detective Dunn had been staying in front of them the entire way, generally just barely within sight of Erica and Detective Walsh. They had tried and tried to convince him to even the pace, so they were all together. He wouldn't listen and remained undeterred as he charged forward into the relentless forest. He wasn't all right.

"So, what do we do? This is going nowhere," Erica said to anyone who would listen.

"Erica, we just need to keep moving. We'll find our way out eventually," Detective Walsh said.

Erica could tell the man wasn't convinced by his own words. She had learned from her father long ago that when lost, it was best to stay put. And she knew Spencer and Buster were searching for them. *Why didn't I stay where I was?* Did it matter now? They would never find their way back there anyway.

She turned her gaze to the other detective. Detective Dunn seemed lost in his own little world, staring forward as if plotting where they would go next. He had been more or less silent the entire way, and he wasn't about to participate in the present conversation.

"Is he all right?" Erica said as softly as she could.

"Sure, he'll be fine," Detective Walsh said. "He's not much of a gabber to begin with. And he's scared, just like we are. In a bit of a shock, I'd say."

"Are you sure he's leading us in the right direction?" Erica said. "I mean, we really don't seem to be making any progress."

"Your guess is as good as mine," Detective Walsh said. "If you've got a better idea, now's the time."

Erica didn't have a better idea. She let her head drop and tried to think. *What would Dad do now?* She turned and looked behind her, hoping she would see her father and Buster appear out of nowhere.

Erica was more than afraid, and she still hadn't fully wrapped her head around the predicament they were all in. Still, she felt calm and couldn't figure out why. They had been sent here for a reason, and she was certain the reason had an ending that would be no good. She also realized that if there were to be any chance of escaping from this unreal world, the responsibility would be hers. She would be strong, for herself and for the other two.

She heard a rustle and turned to see Detective Dunn rush a few yards forward. He stopped and fixed his eyes on something in the distance.

"Look, look," he said, pointing ahead. "I can see some light out there, right in the direction we're headed. I told you I knew where I was going."

Erica and Detective Walsh ran forward until they were beside him. Soon, they were sharing in the excitement of his discovery. Yes, there was a light, almost like another opening in the trees similar to where Spencer and Buster had been standing earlier. Erica smiled and crossed her fingers. Maybe there was a way out of here.

Detective Dunn did not hesitate and sprinted off without saying another word. In no time he was out of their sight.

"Harry, wait! We need to stay together," Detective Walsh said. He took Erica's hand, and they took off running after Detective Dunn.

Within a minute or so the light became brighter, and they could see that beyond the trees was a grassy meadow. The opening wasn't necessarily a way out, but it was something and a reprieve from the eternal darkness. Erica and Detective Walsh ran to the edge of the field, the wild green grass up to their knees. The bright sun above stung Erica's eyes. She briefly scanned the expanse, and her attention was soon forced to the middle of the meadow, where stood a lone tree, the largest oak tree imaginable. The tree was so large that it didn't seem real. And in front of that tree stood Detective Dunn, with his back toward them.

They watched as he turned around and began waving them forward with his right hand. The tree, and its massive limbs and broad green leaves, towered above him, making him look almost insignificant. His hand wouldn't stop its motion as he beckoned the other two to join him.

"Come on. This is the place. This is going to be the way out," he said.

Erica looked on, bewildered. She didn't know what to say or think.

The crown of the tree began gently waving back and forth, as a slight breeze settled on its top. Detective Dunn stopped waving and faced the tree once more. He stared at the giant for a few moments, seemingly admiring it, seemingly mesmerized by its presence. He then pivoted back around until he again was focused on Erica and Detective Walsh.

"Hurry, now," Detective Dunn said, eyes and a smile so warm and inviting that they weren't at all natural.

He had taken off his jacket again and thrown it on the ground next to him.

"Don't be afraid," he said. "We can become like they are."

Erica couldn't imagine what the man was talking about or what he meant. She grabbed Detective Walsh's arm as he began to move in his colleague's direction. This wasn't right. She was certain.

"Don't go," she said. "I have a bad feeling about this."

"What do you mean?" the detective said, with an expression similar to that of his friend. "If this is the place, then this is the place. We need to join him now."

Erica's heart dropped. She was certain she had mentally lost one of her companions already, and now this man, the man she had grown so fond of, was well on his way to suffering the same. He had been fine until this very moment.

Erica screamed at him: "No, we are not going! Don't you see what's happening? We are not going!"

The wind flew out of the trees from the other side of the meadow, concentrating into a circular funnel, not unlike a small tornado but horizontal instead of vertical. Suddenly, a flock of blackbirds, appearing out of nowhere, lit from the branches of the giant oak. They flew way above its top and began a large and orderly rotation in the air. The dark birds flew around in a circle as a group and in perfect unison, never descending below their pattern and never flying further up into the sky.

The funnel cut across the field, never disturbing a blade of grass as it went. In front of Detective Dunn it stopped and turned vertical. The velocity increased within until the thing was hardly visible to Erica's eyes.

She pleaded with Detective Dunn to run. She screamed and hollered, but to no avail. He simply stood there, transfixed by the motion in front of him. She looked at Detective Walsh, who remained still, gawking ahead. She yelled out loudly again, but the air was noisy and unfiltered. No one would have heard her anyway.

In a second the funnel moved forward. It hesitated for only a moment and then quickly engulfed Detective Dunn. Erica couldn't see what was happening at first. The detective had been there, and now he wasn't.

She saw him. His body was in the air. He hung suspended, facing their direction, the funnel swirling around him. Erica wanted to turn away as Detective Dunn looked down helplessly at her, terror screaming from his eyes. She was too shocked to move or say anything. All she could do was watch the depraved spectacle before her.

A moment or two passed. The funnel dropped from the sky to the ground, and then it vanished in the blink of an eye. Still, the detective remained suspended. A sickening screech blasted out, impossible to tell from where. Erica threw up her hands, covering her ears.

Detective Dunn's body bulleted backward and hit the oversized oak tree with such force that it shook the ground on which Erica stood. His body rested momentarily thirty yards up, adhering to the trunk as if stuck by glue. Then, a sudden collapse and the body fell to the ground below.

His lifeless limbs did not move an inch, and it was clear to Erica that Detective Dunn was no more. She watched as the blackbirds descended from above and landed around his body. There were thousands of them and many more; they couldn't be counted in a lifetime. The commotion caused was dizzying. The first of them took a step and then a hop. The sinister bird spread its wings and closed them. It jumped onto the right leg of the detective. The others followed, first slowly, then quicker and quicker, and then at a frantic pace. Soon, the body was covered in a mass of black. The insatiable pecking began.

Erica covered her eyes in horror and fell to the ground, unable to look any further.

"Take a look at that now, will ya?" Detective Walsh said.

Erica had been mostly oblivious to his presence. She looked up at him, amazed at his calmness as he continued studying the sickening scene in front of them. He showed no expression whatsoever.

"Looks like my good friend Harry Dunn has become a feast for carrion crows, he has. I wonder if he tastes good."

Erica had seen—and heard—enough. She stood up and grabbed the detective's hand. She pulled him back into the trees, and he begrudgingly came with her. As the air chilled around them, she hoped it wasn't too late.

They ran away from the meadow as fast as they could, through the darkness of the forest, for a good five minutes or more. When Erica felt some semblance of safety and no immediate danger, she pulled up. She searched around, her eyes pivoting in all directions, to make certain. She waited and listened for a few moments before saying anything.

"Are you still with me, Danny?" she asked the detective in a soft voice and through labored breathing.

The detective didn't answer but simply looked back in the direction from where they had come. He didn't seem tired or winded, almost as if he had acquired some superhuman strength from the anomaly that had penetrated his being. She had to get him back to normal—or hope he would get back to normal—or there would be no way out of this. The entire time they had been running, she could hear him murmuring, mostly nonsensical gibberish she couldn't make out.

"You know, we should go back for his body," the detective said suddenly. "His mum will be angry with me if I don't bring his body home."

He was still lost, and the inane comment shook Erica. She didn't have time for a conversation of nonsense.

She again studied the forest around them. Things looked no different than before, just a plethora of dark and green and not much else. She did, however, have a slight sense of where they had come from. They would head that way now, hopefully back in the direction of her father and Buster. Again, she wished they had stayed there in the first place. Things would have been different then, and Detective Dunn might still be alive.

Erica turned once again to check on her partner. He hardly seemed cognizant of her presence, but twice more he suggested they return to the meadow, to get the body.

She didn't recognize him; there was something very different. The kind brown eyes she remembered had a look she had never seen before. They pierced through her when she looked into them. They were not the eyes of Danny Walsh, and they were not the eyes of a human. Erica wanted to cry, but she wouldn't let herself.

Without notice, Detective Walsh plopped down to the ground. He pulled his knees to his chest and wrapped his arms around them. He sat there looking in the direction of the meadow.

"What are you doing?" Erica said. No response.

"What are you doing, damn it?"

This time she grabbed his left shoulder and shook, willing him to look up at her.

He didn't. The detective did not move or say anything.

"Get off your sorry ass and move!" she said.

She raised her foot and delivered a quick blow to his thigh. He didn't even flinch. Her foot flew forward again, only harder. Finally, Detective Walsh looked up at Erica and slowly pushed himself off the ground until they were at eye level with one another.

"Danny, we're in big trouble here. Do you understand me?" Erica said. "You need to understand."

Detective Walsh glanced once more in the direction they had come from and turned back to Erica.

"It's a shame what happened to Harry Dunn," he said. His face lacked any emotion. He spoke the words as if this Harry Dunn person were just a casual acquaintance or someone he had read about in the newspaper.

"Yeah, the man had his whole life ahead of him, he did. His whole life," he continued.

The detective's words, though not of much sense and from a man who wasn't even close to being fully there, hit Erica like a ton of bricks. She had been too busy trying to save the two of them to give any real thought to what had happened to Detective Dunn: She had just seen a man murdered right in front of her eyes and then eaten by a flock of countless blackbirds.

A vision flashed of Detective Dunn's body, likely nothing but a pile of bones by now, assuming that what they saw had been real. More images flew around in her mind, and she shook her head in an attempt to clear them. Her teeth pressed down on her lower lip to stifle the tears that longed to be released.

"We need to go," she said, forcing herself to be strong.

Erica grabbed the detective's hand, knowing he wouldn't budge otherwise. He was like an anchor tied to her now, and running with their hands locked would only slow them down, but she would not leave him.

Erica took the first step and heard a sound. One more step and she heard the sound. The slight aural penetration from the woods off to her right was subtle and almost indiscernible. The rustling of debris on the forest floor entered her senses, and she saw a patch of white and brown pass through the only visible opening. She stopped and waited, her heart beating so hard she was sure it could be heard by anyone, or anything, nearby. Except for that thumping heart there was only silence, and she was sure that whatever was there had also stopped.

"Get the hell away from us, you miserable prick! Leave us alone!"

Angrily screaming obscenities had worked once before, but she wasn't too sure this time. Erica stood motionless for another thirty seconds, with Detective Walsh thankfully doing the same. Only quietness pervaded, but she had heard enough. She wasn't about to stick around for a moment longer.

Off they went again, with Erica pushing herself to the limit and literally pulling the detective along with her. When she sensed safety again she slowed the pace. She had no idea where they were or what they should do. She would keep moving.

They walked for another hour or more, difficult to tell how long. They had gone a long way, but they had gone nowhere. At least it seemed that way. She released the detective's hand and let her own hands fall to her side. She hunched over. The tears she had been fighting finally found their way out. She could see no way out of this.

As Erica was about to let herself go and fall to the ground, she felt an arm drape over her shoulder.

"Erica, we'll find a way out of here. I know we will."

There was no conviction in his voice, but she was glad to have him back, if he was back. Still, there was no hope; she was certain of that. At least she wouldn't have to die alone.

She threw herself into his arms and felt the warm embrace. They held on to each other, and he stroked her long hair with his right hand. Neither spoke. The embrace wasn't long, but it was long enough for Erica to feel some renewed energy. She broke free from his arms, knowing they needed to keep going, knowing they had to try.

After a short discussion, together they decided and agreed on a direction to take, though they both realized one was likely as good as the other. They took off and for another thirty minutes bumbled through the woods, in circles maybe. How would they possibly find a way out? *Daddy,* Erica thought, *I need your help. Dad, please help me.* She knew he was not coming.

Erica looked up at the sky, hoping to find the sun to use as a guide, but it wasn't there. What difference did it make? She was no backwoods navigator, not even close. But she did sense that night would be on its way soon; they had been in here a long time. When night did come, there would be no chance.

They climbed up a small incline, and for a second a glimmer of hope and a sliver of light appeared. The light expanded, and the hope vanished. Erica knew where they were. They sneaked up to the edge of the tree line. Standing in the middle of the meadow was the humongous oak tree. There were no blackbirds and no Detective Dunn, not a single trace of either. But this was the same place as before.

The sound could be heard building, and in no time the wind came whistling from the forest on the other side. Erica looked at

Detective Walsh and his sad, defeated eyes. Somehow she managed a small smile, and she took his hand. She felt his warmth and his strength and thought about what could have been. They huddled together at the gathering storm.

CHAPTER TWENTY-TWO

After all of this time in Ireland and after all of the things that had happened to him here, Spencer recognized that time and chance could make or break a situation and perhaps even save a life. Or maybe watch one end.

He and Buster had been traipsing along in this unforgiving and unrelenting forest for what seemed like days. He knew the hours that had passed couldn't have been more than a few, but he wasn't certain. For whatever reason, his watch had stopped, and his phone wouldn't function at all.

There was still a sun in the sky above, but it was hard to track through the towering trees. He caught a glimpse and stared into the yellow sphere, wondering how they would fare without the light it provided. Not thinking, he pulled out his phone to check the flashlight. *Why won't anything work?*

Buster seemed to be on the trail the entire way, but the path was not a physical one. Spencer hadn't seen one actual trail since entering this strange place. He questioned whether Buster was following a scent or whether the dog was relying on some animal-type intuition. Regardless, he felt they had gotten nowhere. He could have sworn they were moving around in circles half the time; any sense of orientation was lost in this forbidding environment. Even the sun seemed to dodge around the sky. He looked for and found it again, but the damn thing was in a completely different place from just a few minutes before.

Still, even with all of the obstacles, time and chance would be his today.

Spencer used his forearm to knock a small branch out of the way as they sneaked between yet another pair of trees. The branch swung back before he got through and clipped his head. His face and his hands were covered in scratches and torn skin. He was tired and would have done anything for a drink of water.

Buster, on the other hand, showed no evidence of weariness. His senses remained acute, and his energy seemed to pick up the longer they went.

Like Buster, Spencer's resolve remained firm, but he was beginning to doubt they would ever find Erica and the other two. On the slope of a hill, they came across a small open space sheltered within the trees. A treeless area was a rare find, and Spencer decided to take advantage. He signaled to Buster and planted himself on the ground. He looked at his phone again, hoping to finally get a signal and wishing it to finally work. Disappointed, he placed the device back in his pocket and wondered where Killian was. If he ever needed his friend's help, today was the day.

Spencer yelled out to Erica once more and felt the scratchiness in his throat. His voice was becoming hoarse from the constant calling of her name. Buster sat down with Spencer. Spencer reached into his pocket and dislodged a smoke. He savored its taste and aroma, for this would be his last. When he was done he emptied the remaining contents onto the ground. He then crumpled the vacant pack into a ball and returned it to his pocket. A minute or two more passed, and Spencer flinched as the dog rose and pulled on the loop in Spencer's hand.

"Geez, Buster, give me a break. Let me catch my breath, would ya?"

The dog was undeterred and pulled again on the lead. He barked at Spencer and turned in the other direction.

"Okay, okay," Spencer said, standing back up.

They began walking again. Only ten or twenty yards to their right, where there was another narrow break in the woods, a welcome sight came into view. Spencer studied the open field below them, a hundred yards away at the most. Buster surged forward, wanting to go quickly, but Spencer was more cautious. He reined in the dog, giving him only a foot or so of length on the lead. They moved slowly down the hill, Spencer watching each step and avoiding any sound that would give away their presence. He had no idea what was ahead, but something was telling him to proceed deliberately.

He stopped, bent down, and held Buster's head in his hands. He looked deeply into the dog's dark eyes.

"Buster, we need to be quiet. No barking, no nothing," he said softly, desperate his dog would understand and comply.

As they came closer to the opening, Buster pulled sharply to the right, forcing Spencer to bounce off a small bent-over tree. He winced in pain, and his right hand immediately swung to cover his left arm just below the shoulder. The small protrusion, only an inch long and the remnant of a branch long disappeared, had stabbed firmly into his skin.

"Shit," he said under his breath. "Buster, wait a second."

He studied his arm, watching the crimson blood slowly spread and stain his shirt. The pain was subtle, and the bleeding not profuse, but the injured area needed some pressure. He searched his pockets, looking for something to stem the flow. His hand touched the pink handkerchief. He hated to use it for this purpose, but he knew Erica wouldn't mind.

After a few minutes, satisfied the bleeding had slowed enough and basically stopped, Spencer and Buster began moving forward again. Soon, they were at the edge of the open expanse. Spencer peered out from inside the forest. He gawked at a tree smack dab in the middle of the meadow, a tree so large that it defied reality, at least a reality in Ireland, where he had never come close to seeing something of this enormous size.

The wind had been nonexistent until now and remained that way where they were standing. On the other side of the field, however, directly across from them and at the border with the forest, Spencer could see the spruce trees violently waving back and forth, the top of one pushing against the one adjacent. The wind would switch course, with the tree tops pushing at each other in the opposite direction. He felt as if he were watching some sort of dance routine. The ferocity of the accompanying and building sound permeated his eardrums. He knew what was happening. He stood there mesmerized nonetheless, and he couldn't pull his eyes away.

Spencer looked down as he felt the nudge on his leg. Buster was there with his head firmly pressing into Spencer's outer thigh. He exchanged glances with Buster and then saw the dog turn to the left and to the far end of the field. Spencer's eyes followed, and there stood his daughter and Detective Walsh, holding each other tight in what seemed an embrace of defeat and closure and finality.

The time for being quiet ended, and Spencer yelled across at the two of them. His brittle voice could hardly get their names out. A sudden movement caught his attention, and his head pivoted to see the dark gloom emerging from the other end of the forest. Soon, it seemed half the meadow was filled as the force began making its way toward Erica and the detective.

A description of what he was experiencing—and seeing—would have been difficult. The outer circumference was as dark as the night, much darker than the forest behind them. Inside was much the opposite, bright as a strobe and punishing to the eyes if looked at directly. In the narrow circular band between the two extremes hung a mix of the two, almost like sheets of rain sliding down a window pane or a tattered black drape that only concealed a portion of what it was supposed to.

Inside the illuminated center danced specks of black everywhere, bouncing off one another and the black circle that kept them within its boundaries. And in the very center, up high, were two considerably larger spots that took the form of a dark star with only two vertical points, the edges of which dilated and pulsated continuously and constantly.

Spencer followed the moving storm as it made its way, and then he glanced over again at Erica and Detective Walsh. For a moment he thought of Detective Dunn, wondering where he was. He had seen enough.

He had to do something and quick. He began running towards them. In an instant his body met the ground below, as if he had run into a brick wall. Not understanding but still undeterred, he picked himself up and tried again, this time proceeding slowly. Yet, he couldn't penetrate the solid wall of nothing that was holding him back. He tried every direction, even behind them, but the result was the same. He was locked in a small rectangular space with no way out.

As his fists continued pounding on what was nothing but thin air, he realized he had forgotten about Buster in his haste. He looked down to see his companion still standing next to him, staring up at him, waiting for Spencer to do what needed to be done. Spencer had no idea, but he had to try, or Erica and the detective would be doomed. He reached down and unhooked Buster from his tether.

"Buster, go! You need to go. Now!" he said and gave the dog a push on his hindquarters.

Buster easily busted through the barrier that wasn't there and was instantly galloping across the empty field toward the gloom and toward Erica and Detective Walsh. The dog passed directly under the outsized tree along the way, and Spencer's dread elevated, fully expecting some anomaly to drop down from one of the giant branches and scoop up Buster. Nothing happened, and Spencer let out a small sigh of relief. Buster would be to Erica in only a few more seconds.

Frantic with fear of the fate he expected for Buster and Erica, Spencer tried again to escape his enclosure. He wouldn't be let out. He pounded and pounded to no avail. All he could do was watch.

Spencer's eyes focused again where they should. There was no sign of Buster. The moving cloud of nothingness was where he expected, however, now having stopped directly in front of its two intended victims. He could see Erica screaming and yelling, and it was clear to Spencer that she was seeing exactly what he was seeing.

She took the detective's hand and began pulling him back toward the tree line. Before they could make it their hands unlocked, and the man's body went horizontal and into the air, his stomach facing the ground and his head pointed toward the creature. He was being sucked forward. Spencer watched as Erica grabbed the detective's legs and wrapped her arms around his ankles. Her force caused the body to drop to the ground, but Detective Walsh continued to be pulled away from the trees, Erica along with him, as she held on for dear life. Spencer hollered her name.

Suddenly, the pair stopped moving forward. Spencer was dumbfounded for only a moment. His dog appeared out of nowhere and moved in on the spirit. Buster scurried to the edge of the being and then backed away, like a lion trying to dodge the lethal horns of a water buffalo. But in this case it was impossible to tell exactly what Buster was evading. Buster's barks and growls came incessantly as he maneuvered from one spot to the next.

The diamond-shaped eyes changed their angle and focused on Buster. Spencer could see the rage building within them. Screeches from within the gloom made him dizzy with their ferocity. The eyes changed shape, and the intensity from them sharpened. Spencer knew what was coming next. There was nothing he could do to save his dog.

Without warning, Spencer found himself on the edge of a sharp cliff. The dark forest and the open field, and what had been happening only moments before, were gone. Below, he could glimpse everything, and he could see the white water of the raging river splashing through the rust-colored canyon walls. Near a flat surface of stone that led to the river's edge, he could see Detective Walsh struggling in the water, his hands grasping the solid ledge in an attempt to pull himself out. Erica stood bent over on the rocky slab, thrusting her hand into his and trying to pull him to safety. She struggled and pulled, but the detective was like an unmovable object anchored in the water. His weight forced Erica forward. She crept closer to the edge, only to have Detective Walsh lose his fight with the current. As his hand became unclasped from Erica's, her feet slipped on the wet, smooth surface. She was soon bobbing in the river, right behind the detective.

Spencer yelled out their names and let his eyes follow the water down. He could see where the river ended as it ran off a precipice, a massive waterfall of bubbling white foam. He looked down below to where the river dropped. There was no water, only a black void of empty space. Spencer cried out Erica's name once more and began looking for a path down the steep hillside. Rocks and pieces of earth rolled off the cliff as he moved his feet.

As before, he was stuck in place, some invisible barrier holding him prisoner on the rocky outcrop. He tried and tried in each direction, but he couldn't move from his spot. He could do nothing but look on as the scene below unfolded.

Erica and Detective Walsh drifted helplessly through the rapids, their heads above the current, just barely. Only a few hundred yards or so remained before the river's end, where it poured into the emptiness below.

Spencer noticed a movement about fifty yards further down. Buster scampered to the side of the river and looked upstream to where Erica and the detective were flailing in the fast-moving current. The dog pranced back and forth on the bank. Even over the roar of the river, Spencer could hear Buster's whining as the dog tried to decide his next move. As Erica floated closer, Buster placed his front paws in the water. Spencer could see and hear Erica calling out to the dog, telling him to stay away. As she arrived, Buster splashed into the river and was soon swimming next to her, willing his head above water as the current grabbed at him.

Spencer watched as Erica reached out and touched Buster. She placed her head next to his, seemingly understanding her end was coming soon, and his. All three of them drifted toward the river's finish. In a moment or two their lives would be complete and over. The detective went over the falls first, soon followed by Erica and then by Buster. Spencer looked on, helpless, as all three, one after another, slid over the edge and into the blackness that waited below to consume them.

Spencer screamed out their names as they left his sight. He pounded to escape his enclosure, but his efforts were useless. He fell to his knees and to the ground; his cries of anguish were only heard within the confines of the invisible chamber.

He lifted his head, and the tears streamed down his face. His head shifted to the left and then above him. On a ledge twenty yards up the cliff wall stood Angus. Spencer lowered his head in defeat, not being able to bear the incessant laughter pouring from the mouth of Angus.

In an instant, Spencer was returned to the edge of the meadow. He used the back of one fist to wipe the moisture from his eyes and his cheeks, lost as to what had just happened. The wind was gone, and the scene was one of complete calm. He got up from his knees and surveyed the situation. He could see Erica and Detective Walsh still where they had been. They seemed to be recovering and had begun to stand up and move around. Buster was in front of them. He was running back and forth, confused. The spirit had departed, and all that remained in the field was the large oak tree.

Spencer yelled out to the three of them, urging them to run and to leave. His voice carried nowhere. They were all milling around, as if half-dazed. He could see Erica speaking something to Buster, but her voice was muted. Detective Walsh was simply standing there, staring into the sky above and mumbling words not spoken.

Something shook Spencer, and he felt the presence once again. He turned his attention to the oak tree. A shadow formed, enveloping the ground in front, and from behind the tree, out it stepped. Spencer could never have imagined that the Grim Reaper, if that was what this was, would have an appearance similar to what he had always read and seen.

The spirit had revealed itself. The dark brown robe extended from the top of the reaper's head to a length that stopped just at its feet, though there were no feet, really. The hood of the robe held something, maybe a head, but the appearance was only of a black empty space. There were no eyes, no features, only darkness. From the wrists of the robe extended something, almost like human hands, but Spencer couldn't be sure. The right appendage held a tool, a long steel pole of sorts.

Its brilliance was blinding, reflecting the sunlight in all directions and sparkling like a polished gemstone. Spencer squinted his eyes. The long blade had no point, but its large and sharp tooth-like edges were unmistakable.

The spirit began deliberately making its way toward Erica and the detective. Buster was gone. Spencer again called out as loud as he could. They stood motionless as the anomaly approached. He wondered whether they could see what he was seeing.

Spencer, bewildered, looked on as Buster once again appeared and hit the spirit from the side, his teeth tearing at the robe. The reaper stumbled slightly from the dog's force. Buster was quickly on the other side now and immediately pounced once more. This time the monster was ready, and with one swift extension of its arm-like appendage sent Buster soaring for fifteen yards, maybe more. Spencer listened to the sorrowful whimpering of his dog as Buster lay motionless, the dog's body obscured by the tall grass of the meadow.

The spirit moved in. Soon, as before, it was standing directly in front of Erica and Detective Walsh. Spencer could see and hear Erica berating the thing. She was on her knees now, with the detective next to her, neither of them making an effort to escape.

The robed being stood looking down. The spirit's tool of death moved forward until it was gently touching the forehead of the man kneeling below. Detective Walsh seemed almost in a trance and didn't move a muscle. The spirit turned to Erica and did the same. She was quiet, as if resigned to her fate. Spencer cried out again, begging her to run. She didn't move. He understood he was about to witness the unspeakable, the unthinkable, something a parent should never be forced to even contemplate.

The thing turned in the direction of Buster and pointed the tool. Spencer was certain the beast was signaling the order of death. He knew he would be the last, as it should be, as it could only be.

The serrated edges of the saw moved back and forth in the air, as if the spirit were tuning up for what was to come. Spencer knew death for all of them could come fast or slow, but it would be certain and final.

He closed his eyes momentarily as the reaper again placed the tool at the forehead of Detective Walsh and moved it down to the man's exposed throat. Spencer's last shout in vain only echoed back at him. He tried to turn away; he couldn't. The tears rolled down his cheeks.

As the cutting commenced and the first thin stream of red blood began to seep from the pale white skin of the detective's throat, Spencer's dull and defeated attention was interrupted by the sound of a dog growling. He looked over to where he had last seen Buster. Spencer threw his attention back to the spirit, the hood now looking backward and down, and the tool no longer cutting. At the base of the robe, Spencer could see a flurry of white and brown. The robe was being tugged down as the ghost swiveled its head, first looking behind to the right and then to the left. The beast turned around and raised the weapon in its hand.

The saw swung swiftly across the robe, just missing Shandy as she dodged away. The weapon pivoted back and forth, from side to side. Shandy was always one step ahead. A roar shook the earth as the beast became enraged.

The reaper suddenly stopped its motion and seemingly pondered the barking and growling dog below. In one quick movement dirt flew up from the ground and into Shandy's eyes. The stunned dog stood still for only a moment. The moment was long enough.

The saw swung backward and began its descent toward Shandy. Just before the arc was completed, just before Shandy would be no more, the beast toppled to the side as Buster struck, his muscular body sailing through the air and knocking the spirit over. The dog sprang back and was soon on top. He began to tear at the robe with gnashing teeth, pieces of dark cloth and white foam from Buster's mouth flying everywhere.

Buster jumped from his perch and joined Shandy at the end of the robe. They pulled on it with all their might, but the robe would not give. The spirit rolled over, its hands desperately grasping for the saw on the ground. The hands groped and groped and found their target, but it was to be a few seconds too late. Shandy saw her chance, and she knew what to do. She instantly ran to the head, pulling the hood backward from whatever was beneath. Another jerk from Buster at the end, and the robe fell from the being, almost as if there were nothing to hold it back.

Spencer stood amazed. Before his eyes was a skeleton of sorts, but a skeleton that was indescribable and different from anything he had ever seen. The spirit cried out, as if in agony over an ending it likely never expected. Spencer held his head and covered his ears from the incessant and pitiful screeching. Still, his eyes did not move from the scene.

Shandy and Buster had backed up and were cautiously studying their quarry, safely out of reach. As Spencer watched, his eyes unflinching, the remains turned from white to black and then to ash, covering the area below. A final screech pierced the atmosphere.

Spencer heard the cawing and threw his focus to the giant oak. A group of twenty or more blackbirds escaped from the limbs and branches and rose high into the sky. They circled the open meadow once or twice. In perfect formation, the dark birds departed from the field and headed to a destination unknown, the noise of their voices incessant as they made their way.

Spencer ran forward, no longer held back, until he reached Buster. Shandy was gone, but he had not seen her leave. He knelt and threw his arms around his dog, and Buster reciprocated with an indulgence of wet kisses and affectionate whining. Spencer stood up and looked down momentarily at the empty robe and the pile of dust. He wanted to say something, throw some insult at the evil being, say how much he hated this wicked thing. The words wouldn't come.

The two of them ran over to Erica and Detective Walsh. They were still on their knees and obviously stunned. Spencer looked down at his daughter and held out his hand. She took it and let herself be pulled up. Her wide eyes pleaded for some understanding, but they weren't crying.

"Daddy, you're here. I knew you would come. I knew it," Erica said.

She hugged her father so hard Spencer could barely breathe. He wrapped his arms around her and held on, never wanting to let go.

Detective Walsh remained silent and almost seemed incoherent. He didn't even get up from his knees.

"Baby, are you okay?" Spencer asked as he loosened his grip and looked down into her shocked eyes.

"I think so. What happened? You saved us, Dad. You saved us," she said.

Spencer knew full well it wasn't he who had saved them. The credit went to the dog he loved and to another dog he had once loved and still did.

Erica finally let go, and Spencer looked on as she got on her knees and draped her arms over Buster, kissing his head over and over while Buster did his best to do the same.

Not sure why, Spencer looked up from the most gratifying scene he had ever experienced. His eyes veered to the tree line, just where he and Buster had entered the meadow. Shandy was standing there. She looked back at him once and then turned and disappeared into the forest.

CHAPTER TWENTY-THREE

"**D**ad, it's time to go."

The words slid smooth and supported like bone. They entered Spencer's consciousness, one word at a time, one after another, until the sentence was formed and complete. He heard her voice, like a voice from a dream, and then looked around in all directions, trying to make sense of a reality that shouldn't be.

What had just happened? Why was he back here all of a sudden? Were they all okay? His eyes drifted towards the sloping hillside above. Erica and the two detectives were standing and chatting near the parked cars, acting as if the world was somehow a normal place.

Spencer stood up from the picnic table and studied the looped end of Buster's lead in his hand. He followed it down, making sure it was real. On the other end sat his faithful companion. He managed a small smile as the dog stared up at him.

"Dad, did you hear me? They say the road is open now, so we can leave."

Again, the words came.

Spencer still wasn't sure. Could he have been sitting here this whole while? Could the trauma he had just experienced have been some cruel joke his imagination was playing on him? Or perhaps a journey to another dimension that was or was not real? Again, he wished dogs could talk.

He reached down and placed his hand on the left half of Buster's rib cage. The dog let his discomfort be known, but he didn't move away. Spencer gently rubbed Buster's side and gave his apologies.

Spencer searched his memory for more answers. Everything that had happened in that lost forest and in that meadow was completely fresh in his mind. Still, he questioned the reality. He stood there, running down the history like a movie in his mind, trying to splice each piece together.

He used his hands to check the condition of his face. He traced the contours of his chin, cheeks, nose, and forehead with his fingers. Where there should have been cuts and scratches and maybe dried blood, there was nothing. He then remembered the broken tree limb stabbing his arm. He looked down at his left shoulder; the beige button-down shirt had no tear or any stain of blood. It seemed as crisp and clean as when he had put it on this morning. He smoothed his hand back and forth over his upper arm. There was no pain. The wound that should have been there was not.

What the hell is going on?

He thought some more and recalled Erica's handkerchief. His hands went from one pocket to the next until he found the soft cloth. He pulled it out and did a careful examination, the embroidered initials staring him in the face. The handkerchief was spotless and neatly folded, just like when he had initially found it on the tree stump. *Where's the damn blood?*

Spencer felt truly confused, his head cloudy inside and his thoughts bumping into one another. Doubts and more doubts.

His wristwatch caught his attention as he continued studying the handkerchief. He watched the second hand move forward, one increment after another. He moved his eyes to the hour and minute hands: 12:45 p.m. The time was only a few minutes later from when he last remembered looking, when he had turned from the view of the Galtee Mountains and had begun heading up the hill to the parking lot with Buster, right before the others had disappeared. He had been gone for hours and hours, but he hadn't been gone at all.

Buster's tender ribs and the handkerchief were something, but they weren't enough, not nearly enough. *Maybe I have gone crazy.*

"Dad!"

Her voice dragged him from his thoughts.

"Okay, Erica, got it. Got it... We'll be up in a second," Spencer said.

He just barely got the words out. He looked up at her.

"And you're not going to believe who is up here," Erica said, a big grin beaming from her face.

"Who is it?" Spencer called back.

Before she could answer Spencer saw the familiar face of Killian staring down at him. Spencer wasn't sure whether he should be surprised or not, but seeing his friend never disappointed, especially right now.

Why would he be here? Did he actually get my text message? Spencer forced a small smile in Killian's direction and waved without saying anything. *I wonder what he knows.*

"The text!" he said under his breath as the light switched on in his head.

He removed his phone from the front pocket of his pants, relieved to see it working properly again, just like his watch. His finger pushed the texting application. He examined the phone closely for a few moments and smiled inside. The confirmation Spencer needed was there, and he wasn't insane after all.

He put the phone back in his pocket and realized how parched he was. He felt he hadn't had a drink of anything for days. He took a bottled water from the tabletop and swallowed hard until the bottle was half empty. Spencer sat back down and poured a generous amount into a cupped hand. Buster lapped the water up greedily, the dog's pink tongue devouring the liquid within seconds. Spencer poured some more until the bottle was empty. He waited for Buster to come between his legs. He held Buster's head in his hands and looked him in the eyes.

"You know, and I know, but I'm not sure anyone else does. Let's keep it that way for now, buddy."

Spencer studied Buster until he was sure the meaning was clear. Anyway, dogs can't talk, he thought as he gave Buster a quick pat on the head and rose from the bench.

"Let's go, Buster," he said.

He grabbed the empty water from the top of the table, and the two of them began making their way up the short distance of the hill.

"Mr. Spencer, I just had a call a few minutes ago. They say the road is open and back to normal. Shall we get going now then?" Detective Walsh said as Spencer reached the top of the hill and the parking area.

"Yep, no reason to hang around here any longer," Spencer said, his poker face masking what he was feeling inside. He turned his attention to Killian, again wondering what the man knew. Just in case, he would play it safe.

"So, Killian, to what do we owe the pleasure?" Spencer said jokingly.

"Oh, you know me, Spencer. Just couldn't bear being away from you," Killian said, continuing the levity.

"Actually, I took off for Bansha just a short while after you left this morning, and it seems I ran into the same roadblock. I had a feeling the lot of you might be up here."

Spencer knew now that Killian had received his text. His excuse for being here seemed more than lame. Spencer realized it was probably the best the man could do on the spur of the moment. What did it matter anyway?

The other three were half-listening as they made their way to the two parked cars. Detective Dunn got into his. Erica pulled open the rear door of the SUV, and Buster jumped into the back. She and

Detective Walsh took their places in the front. Spencer walked over to the passenger side, to where Erica was sitting. The detective started the car and rolled down the window for them.

"Give me a few minutes with Killian, and then we'll be on our way, okay?" Spencer said.

"Sure, take your time. We'll still make it to Dublin before dark," Erica said as she looked at her father, a cautious joy emanating from her face. "Looks like we're gonna make it out of here without any problems, doesn't it, Dad?"

"Yes, we're going to be just fine, Erica."

He peered into her eyes, searching for any clue or awareness of what she had just been through. There was nothing. He glanced at Detective Walsh, looking for the same. Nothing. Spencer patted Erica's forearm and walked back behind the car to where Killian was standing.

"Shall we take a little walk?" Spencer said.

They strolled fifty yards or so over and next to a Christ the King statue that overlooked the valley below and faced the Galtee Mountains. The statue was easily taller than three men and had been erected long before Spencer was born. He wondered whether Christ, or something like Him, had anything to do with their narrow escape from the clutches of death.

"So, I guess you got my text, huh?" Spencer asked.

"You wanna tell me what's going on?" Killian said, ignoring Spencer's question.

"I wish I could, but it's all a blur right now. And it would take more time than we have. But it was something, Killian, really something."

Spencer explained as much as he could in the limited time available. He couldn't possibly include every single detail or even come close. He knew none of the story could make any sense, and it generally didn't. Still, just getting everything out and sharing with his friend made him feel better and slightly less burdened. Even Killian might have a tough time believing this one, but Spencer knew he wasn't crazy.

"Are you all right?" Killian said. "How about the others? They don't seem any the worse for the wear. In fact, they seem perfectly fine, which is a bit peculiar to say the least, especially after what you wrote in your text. What's really happening here, Spencer?"

"Killian, I wish I could tell you, but I can't. Not right now. Erica and the detectives were there, but I don't think they even realize or remember what happened. I really can't tell you why. I can't explain it."

"Are you sure it was real?" Killian asked.

Spencer felt the man's eyes penetrate his own. He had seen this same stare from Killian a million times over the last year.

"Yes, there's no doubt in my mind," Spencer said. "I know it was real, and I have proof."

This time, he would give Killian no reason to doubt him. He pulled out the handkerchief from his pocket and handed the cloth to Killian. He explained its relevance and then told Killian about Buster's rib injury.

Spencer watched as Killian dropped his stare and gave his attention to the ground below. He gently nudged small pieces of gravel around with the tip of his shoe. He raised his head and looked out into the mountains. He spoke again without turning to Spencer, the handkerchief resting in his right hand.

"Spencer, are you sure you're okay?" he said. "I understand that you are believing what you are believing, but Erica's clean handkerchief and a supposed injury to Buster's ribs, which he could have gotten anywhere, hardly explain a thing."

Spencer's face tightened, and he squinted his eyes. He had not been expecting this reaction, but it was natural. Not even Killian could be expected to believe a tale so warped and quite literally out of this world.

"You got my text, right?" Spencer said. "Do you think I would send something like that just out of the blue? Why would I do that?"

"Spencer, I don't know why you sent that text, but you've been under a tremendous amount of stress lately with all that's happened. I'm sorry, my friend. I don't know how to say this, but perhaps you might consider seeking some help once you're back in the States."

This was the very first time Killian had ever doubted him, and Spencer felt slightly betrayed. Yet he understood, and in a moment or two, Killian would also understand.

"Killian, you have your phone with you, don't you?"

"Yes, of course."

"Humor me and pull it out, would you please?" Spencer said.

Killian did as he was asked and held the phone up.

"Now, go to the text I sent you," Spencer said.

Spencer waited patiently while Killian thumbed through his phone until he got to where he should be.

"Okay, now what?" Killian said.

"First, what time is it right now?"

"Spencer, why are we doing this?" Killian said. He glanced at his phone again and then up at Spencer. "Anyway, it's 12:59."

"Now, what's the time you received the text?"

Killian looked at the device in his hand and studied the text. A few seconds passed, and Spencer watched as the man's eyes grew bigger, his jaw dropping noticeably.

"Jesus, Mary, and Joseph!" Killian said. "I can't believe what my eyes are seeing!"

Spencer didn't say anything in return or show any reaction, but inside he reveled in this small victory.

For the first time Spencer could recall, he was looking at a Killian who was stunned. Killian stood there, shaking his head back and forth, not believing what he had just seen. The text had been sent at 1:42 p.m., forty-three minutes from the present time. None of this seemed real or remotely possible to Spencer, but it was. He couldn't even begin to understand the time warp that had just presented itself—and he never would—but the evidence Spencer needed to convince his friend was indisputable.

Spencer suddenly realized that this proof of what had happened would be disappearing forever in less than an hour from now, but he had seen the proof, and Killian had seen the proof, and that was enough. Spencer promised himself he would never delete the text.

"You know, Spencer, I'm gonna be missing you. I truly am," Killian said. "But you can't leave soon enough. This old man needs a respite from all these shenanigans."

"You and me both," Spencer said, and they both managed a smile and a small chuckle.

They hypothesized for a minute or two longer, but Spencer knew they would never find the answer. Still, the look on his friend's face told Spencer that Killian's interrogation was not complete and that he needed to know more.

"You said you were there when Erica and Detective Walsh were about to be doomed. How about Detective Dunn? Where was he?" Killian said.

"I have no idea," Spencer said. "I didn't see him, not even once, and I never had a chance to ask Erica while everything was going on. Maybe he wasn't there with the rest of us."

"Strange," Killian said as he ran his fingers up and down his chin. "What saved you?"

"Buster. And Shandy."

"Shandy?"

"Yes, we would have been goners if she hadn't shown up," Spencer said. "It's all so unreal, Killian, but she knew what to do. She knew how to save us."

Spencer kept his eyes on Killian, who was lost in thought and still attempting to put all the pieces together.

"It makes sense, doesn't it now?" Killian finally said. "She showed up at the Square One that day to tell you she was still looking out for you. It was a warning, after all. She knew what was to come. And she appeared when she was truly needed, just like the ghost knew she would."

"Yeah, I guess so," Spencer said, staring at the ground and taking no celebration in the fact his theory had been proven correct. The motives of the little terrier that had now saved his life more than once would forever evade him.

"Is the thing dead?" Killian asked.

"I think so, but who knows for sure?" Spencer responded. "I don't know anything anymore."

Killian turned and directly faced Spencer.

"You still need to leave, you know?" Killian said. "There are no guarantees."

"I know, for now at least," Spencer said.

"Will you tell the others?" Killian asked.

"Yeah, Erica maybe. When the time is right. Maybe not. I don't know yet."

"Are you sure you're all right, Spencer?" Killian said.

"Honestly, I have no idea. It's going to take some time for me to process everything. I doubt I'll sleep much tonight," Spencer said, his voice trailing off as he pondered the nightmares that would surely come.

They stood there silently staring at the mountains on the other side of the valley, both out of words to speak. After a few moments they turned and headed back toward the others.

When Spencer and Killian reached the parking area, Erica and Detective Walsh had gotten out of the car and were standing on the edge of the overlook, talking quietly and looking at the picturesque countryside below them. Detective Dunn puffed on a last cigarette next to the open door of his dark sedan.

"I apologize for the delay," Spencer said to the detective as he and Killian approached. "I guess we're ready to head out."

"No problem, Mr. Spencer," the officer said as he exhaled a voluminous cloud of smoke through his nose. He dropped the spent cigarette on the pavement and stamped it dead with the sole of his black shoe. "It's nice to have a quiet day and just drive and relax a wee bit. It sure is pretty here."

Just then, a group of birds drifted down from the forested mountain behind them. They flew ten or twenty yards over the heads of the three men, rose high into the blue sky above, and headed in the direction of the Galtee Mountains, cawing loudly and without interruption as they went.

"Damn blackbirds and their noise," Detective Dunn said as he watched the flock soar away. "Never cared for 'em much myself. Always looking for a free meal somewhere."

"Yeah, I'm not a big fan either," Spencer said, speculating as he followed the birds on their journey to somewhere far away and to a place unknown.

Spencer and Killian made their way over to Erica and the other detective. Goodbyes were said a final time, with Erica giving Killian a last huge embrace. Spencer promised Killian a phone call once they were settled in their Dublin hotel. Spencer jumped into the back seat of his vehicle and took a seat next to Buster, his right hand coming to rest on the dog's head. He stared out the window at Killian driving away. The thoughts were endless, but Spencer knew with all certainty that the dreadful ghost was finally dead and out of their lives for good. And he felt certain there was no longer a worry about leaving Killian here alone.

Spencer would leave this country, for the time being. He knew they would be back.

As they drove away down the hill, the conversation in the front of the car barely registered. Spencer was dreadfully tired. He briefly glanced out the window and by chance noticed a man walking along the narrow shoulder of the road, just to their left. The man's head was pointed to the ground as he walked, and his face couldn't be seen. Spencer knew who he was.

Spencer placed his head against the back of the seat and was sleeping well before they reached Bansha. His dog Buster was asleep beside him.

Killian went over the small bridge spanning the River Aherlow and, at Moor Abbey, made the left turn that led to Galbally. He glanced at the monastery only for a brief second. Heading down the final stretch of road, he let out a huge sigh of relief. He felt as though the weight of a thousand worlds had been lifted from his shoulders.

He hadn't had the heart or inclination to tell Spencer that the fifth bottle—the final bottle—had crashed to the ground. When the others had left this morning, Killian had busied himself with odds and ends around the house and had even gone out to the garden to pull a few ripe tomatoes for tonight's dinner. When he was done, he sat down in his favorite chair, just to catch his breath more than anything. Within minutes perhaps, he had fallen into a deep sleep. And the dream came.

When the bottle smashed, there was no blood like before or contents of any kind. Instead, a vision appeared and replaced the shards of broken glass. Spencer was there, at the top of the cliff, screaming and crying as he watched Erica, Buster, and Detective Walsh floating helplessly through the water of the gushing river. As the three met the end of the river and fell into the dark abyss below, Killian woke up.

He checked the time on his watch. He had been asleep for more than an hour. He scrambled to his feet, grabbed his phone, and tried numerous times to call Spencer. When he didn't pick up, Killian tried Erica, and then the phones of both detectives. Though he had no idea at that time, he knew now that the four of them, along with Buster, had likely already been lost in a world that was not theirs.

Then the text from Spencer came. Killian jumped in his car and made it to the roadblock, which was just clearing. Fortunately, one of the power company workers, the one who had been in touch with Detective Walsh, was able to give Killian an indication of where they all might have gone.

He had made it there, of course, to the overlook above the Glen of Aherlow, but not in time. Not that it mattered now, and it may not have mattered even then. Yes, the bottle had smashed. But a couple of dogs, and a determined man, had made certain that not all premonitions went according to plan. Sometimes the human spirit, or even that of a couple of animals, can conquer everything.

Killian was almost home now. When he got there, he would mix a nice strong Scotch and water, maybe even a couple. He was exhausted.

CHAPTER TWENTY-FOUR

"I know I've said it before, but it is so, so good being back here," Spencer said.

He couldn't take his eyes off the enchanting scene in front of them, a scene that he had missed more than he had thought possible. Everything seemed even more beautiful than he remembered, before that dreadful experience in the forest meadow that was a memory only in his mind and that of his dog. Their escape that day and the implausible time-lapse and safe return to the mountain parking area were things that would never be explained.

Buster rubbed up against his leg, and Spencer petted the dog on the top of his head. A saturated tennis ball rested in Buster's mouth.

"I agree, Dad," Erica said. She glanced over from her seat and smiled.

The time was just past three in the afternoon. The two of them were sitting on the patio of the Square One Bed & Breakfast, chairs set next to each other, as they took in the scene of the Galtee Mountains and enjoyed a warm sun on its way to making a descent to the west. The guests would begin arriving in about half an hour. On this Saturday, they were having a small party, a barbecue, to celebrate their return to Ireland and to a life they both cherished. Most importantly, they were celebrating friendships, both old and new.

Spencer looked over as his daughter took another sip from a bottle of beer. She had transitioned from the occasional glass of wine to joining her father each evening for at least one drink, usually two. The habit had been picked up over the last six months as the two of them were biding their time in Colorado, not knowing exactly what they would do or where they would go. Spencer was grateful he no longer had to drink alone, and the time spent together each evening only made their relationship stronger, though it hardly needed assistance these days.

They had made a bit of an early start today; there was to be a party after all.

"Everything ready?" Spencer asked as he stood and made his way over to the barbecue to make certain the gas was ready to fire.

"Yep. The meat is all laid out and seasoned," Erica said. "And the corn is peeled and washed. Elizabeth is bringing the salad, and Danny is picking up dessert somewhere. With all the other things, we'll have more than enough."

Along with Elizabeth and Detective Walsh, Killian would also be here, of course. Detective Dunn was coming as well, and even Colin would be making one of his rare appearances. Spencer could hardly wait to see his young friend. Their last meeting had been so long ago, even before Spencer's extended absence.

Spencer had wanted to invite some of his neighbors and a few other friends from town, but they decided they would keep things intimate this time around. Today, they would not talk of the past and all that had happened prior to their abrupt departure from Ireland. And Spencer determined there was no reason for Colin to be in the know about matters that didn't concern him.

"Maybe someone will get a bouquet of flowers or even a few red roses this afternoon," Spencer said, ribbing his daughter about a relationship that was already in full swing since their return only three short weeks before.

Spencer had already taken a liking to Detective Danny Walsh before he and Erica had left those months earlier. He had really warmed to the man now. The detective had been to the inn multiple times to see Erica, and the two had gone out on a couple of formal dates. To Spencer, Detective Walsh was kind, smart, and sincere. And Spencer could sense that the man's intentions toward Erica were honorable and true. She could do a lot worse.

"Give it a rest, Dad, or maybe I'll have you arrested," Erica said with a straight face. "I have that power now, you know."

Spencer laughed and got up to fetch another beer from inside.

"Need another?" he said, holding up his empty bottle.

"No, I'm good," Erica said.

"You know, Dad, it's weird," Erica continued before Spencer could make his way to the kitchen door, "but these days I almost feel my life just like a river running through."

"What do you mean?" Spencer turned and said, perplexed by the strange statement. His mind flashed to the scene of Erica, and of the detective and Buster, desperately fighting the river's water and slipping over the precipice and into the unknown and ghostly darkness below.

"I don't know really," Erica said. "Perhaps that's a strange metaphor to use, but inside me I feel such calmness and tranquility. It's a serene river, like the Aya, not like the one you described on that day."

"That's wonderful, Erica," Spencer said, understanding her meaning. "This place has a way of making people feel like that, I believe, especially when there aren't ghosts around messing everything up. Anyway, I'm happy to hear how you feel. I'm also beginning to feel the same again.

"And now that you're getting all philosophical on me, I've decided you need another beer."

"Okay, twist my arm, why don't you?" Erica said and turned her attention to Buster.

Spencer looked on as Erica reached down and took the tennis ball from the dog's mouth, hesitating briefly and wiping the saliva on the backside of her pants leg. Her last throw had had him searching the grass for a good five minutes before he had found the yellow sphere. She stood up and tossed the ball again. Buster sprang from the edge of the deck and into the field.

Spencer walked into the kitchen and pulled open the refrigerator door. He removed two cold ones and pried off the tops of both with a bottle opener.

He placed his hands flat on the kitchen counter and stared outside the window, lost in himself and not really seeing anything. Good fortune was his once again, he thought as he reached down, brought the bottle to his lips, and took a sip of his drink.

The episode with the spirit six months before could have and perhaps should have destroyed Spencer mentally. Yet, like before, like before when he should have been warped by all he had been through with the lost dog Shandy, he seemingly had come through things once again relatively fine.

And he did feel fine for the most part, except for the nagging guilt that wouldn't go away. He doubted the feeling would ever disappear completely. A week or so back, he had called Mrs. O'Donnell's son, just to see how the man was doing. He learned that the gate on the road that led to the cemetery was open each Sunday for those who wished to pay their respects. Spencer had gone and spent a bit of time with Mrs. O'Donnell, mostly telling her how sorry he was and asking for her forgiveness. This coming week, or perhaps the week after, he was planning a one-day trip to Galway to visit the graves of Sean and Clare Kelly. He would tell them the same.

Spencer eventually told Erica everything about what had happened that day. When they were in Dublin waiting to depart for the US, he had written down every last detail he could remember, so nothing would be forgotten. Some time later he explained everything to Erica. She had seen enough that she had no real trouble believing him, but her memory was still blank. But she would not doubt her dad again, like she had once before. Over time, bits and pieces began forming in her mind, she told Spencer, but her recollection was never a complete picture or even close. All she knew was that she, and the two detectives, would be dead now if it weren't for her father. And Buster. And perhaps especially a ghost of a dog named Shandy.

As time went by Spencer and Erica together had considered whether Detective Walsh should be told. They determined they would, when they got back to Ireland, if they returned to Ireland. Spencer and Erica had revealed everything to him about a week before today. Like before, the detective struggled to believe, and Spencer had doubts he ever would. He had no recollection at all, not even the short splices of film like those residing in Erica's mind. Perhaps those would come with time. Spencer was quite certain the detective's subconscious was blocking the experience, never again wanting to relive the horror of that terrible day.

They all guessed at whether Detective Dunn remembered anything, but no one would ask him or mention the matter. Sometimes things are better left unsaid, and this was one of those times.

Spencer and Erica had also debated long and hard whether it would be safe to return to this home and to this land. As usual, they relied on Killian's advice to reach an ultimate decision. The risk would likely never disappear completely, they all concurred, but at the end of the day they knew nothing at all.

Spencer had hoped for a sign to tell him everything would be okay. He even had a recurring dream about Shandy in which she shared what he needed to know, but he understood that tales of the night couldn't be trusted, even if they came from her.

Deep down, Spencer knew the spirit was dead. Its time had come and gone. To appease Erica and Killian, packed suitcases were at the ready, and they would leave again at even the slightest hint of something amiss. Tomorrow morning, he had a trail run on his itinerary, to the same trail he and Buster had climbed before descending into the forest of darkness. The reason was twofold. For one, he needed to get back into his exercise routine. And he also wanted to prove to himself there was nothing to fear any longer.

After the run he would be busy again here at the inn. Even though Killian had watched over the place as promised, six months of sitting idly had caused the usual wear and tear that happens when things go unused. Spencer had spent the last couple of weeks getting the place back into shape, and he was finished for the most part. Erica had been busy trying to collect new guests for the upcoming season. Spring was here, with summer just around the corner. Their first visitors would be showing up in a week.

And Erica would be the new head chef when those guests arrived. She questioned herself and told Spencer over and over of her apprehension, but he had every confidence. She had filled in more than admirably after Mrs. O'Donnell's death, and Spencer knew she was ready, and they were ready.

Spencer grabbed a large bag of crushed ice from inside the freezer and carried it outside. He opened a white cooler and filled it half full. He went back inside, picked up and brought out a case of canned ales, and arranged as many as he could within the ice. Erica was out in the field, continuing the game of fetch with Buster. Spencer placed her beer on the small round table next to her chair.

The knocker of the front door banged outside, just loud enough to hear. Spencer had already seen the car coming up the road and knew who was there. He yelled out to Erica. She ran back from the field, her excitement not well hidden. She made Spencer wait as she washed her hands and then joined him as they made their way through the house to the entrance. They let the two detectives in, and Spencer was glad to see them out of their dark suits and in clothing that was more casual and more appropriate for a day like today.

Sure enough, Detective Walsh was carrying a small bouquet of carnations. He said they were for the party. Spencer knew for whom they were truly intended. He chuckled lightly as he turned, amused by Erica's uneasiness.

Ten minutes later came Colin. When he arrived Spencer hugged him to the point of embarrassment for the young man. Spencer didn't care. The two had been through a lot together long ago, and, as with Killian, his friendship with Colin was one that would last a lifetime.

They all sat out on the patio, sipping beer, making new acquaintances, and reacquainting with old ones. Soon Colin was explaining his new life as a fly-fishing guide and sharing the finer points of how to catch a brown trout with this type of fly and in that type of water. Colin had become quite a salesperson as well, and in no time he had a couple of potential new converts in the detectives. Spencer sat back and felt a sense of satisfaction in having converted Colin in the first place. He felt as proud as if Colin had been his own son.

In a short while Killian and Elizabeth showed up. As they walked around the corner of the house and appeared at the patio, Spencer was more than a little surprised to see Killian towing along a young black Labrador puppy, not more than six months old, he guessed.

Even from a distance Buster spotted this potential new friend and scampered up to meet him. Spencer watched as the two dogs danced around each other and performed the obligatory sniff test. Killian unhooked his dog from the lead, and the two animals ran off together to the middle of the field.

"A new dog, huh?" Spencer said. "You didn't mention a thing to me. When did you get him?"

"Oh, just picked him up a couple of days back," Killian said. "I'd been hoping to do so for a while and finally convinced Liz. She had been resisting for quite some time, but once she saw his face, that was that."

"You know, dogs can be wonderful companions if you let them. Even do things we could never imagine," Killian continued, giving Spencer a sly wink.

"So I've heard," Spencer said and laughed. "Got a name for him yet?"

"Yes, his name is Jake," Killian said.

"Jake? Why Jake?"

"Why not?" Killian said, and Spencer laughed again.

"Seriously, why Jake?" Spencer said.

"I had another named Jake long ago," Killian said. "He was a smart dog, that one was. Not as sharp as Buster, mind you, but he could hold his own."

"Anyway, it's great, Killian, and Jake is a fine name," Spencer said as he turned and looked out into the field. "Buster sure is happy about it."

He walked over to the cooler, pulled out an ale, and handed it to Killian.

"I better get busy doing my part now, or I'll be hearing about it soon enough," Spencer said. "Mind getting Elizabeth a drink? There's a whole liquor cabinet inside, as you know."

The evening came to an end just as dusk was slowly letting its presence known. Colin had left early. He was guiding on his own now, no longer an apprentice, and he had an early morning gig set with some novice fishermen from France. He said he wasn't sure of their English ability and that Erica was welcome to join in the fun and act as his interpreter. She couldn't tell whether he was being serious or not. She had politely refused.

Detective Walsh had naturally wanted to stay and enjoy the evening, but they were police officers, and his partner was the designated driver for the day. Detective Dunn had imbibed only one beer this afternoon, and Danny obviously felt guilty making his friend watch as everyone else drank freely.

Spencer peered from the corner of the patio as Detective Walsh and Erica said their goodbyes next to the car as Detective Dunn patiently waited in the driver's seat. Spencer wasn't too crazy about the kiss on the lips at the end, but he realized Erica couldn't remain his baby forever.

Later on, Erica and Elizabeth volunteered for most of the cleanup duty, and the two remaining men gave no argument.

Spencer finished cleaning the grill of the barbecue and then walked over to where Killian was. They cracked a final ale each and sat quietly in chairs on the deck. Spencer leaned back with his legs and feet stretched out far in front of him. This is how life should be, he thought, having a beer with a good friend and watching our two dogs frolic in the beauty of an Irish field.

Spencer and Killian had had many talks over the last six months, including quite a few since the return to Ireland. One topic they came back to time and again regarded a man named Angus. His involvement was a mystery, but it wasn't.

They finally concluded that Angus—certainly not by his choice—and the ghost were one and the same. The ghost had used Angus as a surrogate of sorts, infiltrating his soul and body to do the ghost's bidding when necessary. No evidence existed to prove Angus had committed a murder or any crime for that matter. Spencer and Killian concurred that the ghost had been the only killer in these parts. The official investigations into the deaths of the Kelly couple and Mrs. O'Donnell had both been closed months before.

Since Spencer's departure from Ireland, the Angus routine of visiting the Grafton Pub four or five nights a week had resumed in full force. He was the same old Angus as he had always been. Killian tried his usual methods to pry out any information that would verify their theory, but it proved a useless endeavor. Angus likely had no clue of what truly had happened to him.

As they sat there Spencer thought about Shandy, and he thought about Buster. Yes, as Killian had said, dogs really can do things we could never imagine. Spencer asked himself why he was so blessed. Why was he so blessed to have had two dogs who cared about him so much that they were willing to die for him? He took a sip of beer and smiled. He smiled because he was happy. He smiled to stop the tears that longed to be released.

Buster and Jake had taken a couple of breaks during the festivities, mostly to grab table scraps. As the sun began setting, they were out playing once again. Spencer looked at the dogs and smiled at Killian. They both watched as Buster and Jake moved about the green grass, chasing each other and searching for any oddity that grabbed their attention. Soon they were at the edge of the meadow, next to a thick stand of deciduous trees that ran a considerable distance between Spencer's field and that of his neighbor's.

Spencer leaned forward to see the dogs stop and look into the trees, their ears erect as if they sensed something within. They dashed forward into the woods, and Spencer felt a bit of panic. He stood up, and Killian did the same. In a minute or so Buster and Jake were back out and romping around the edge again. Spencer looked over at Killian, and they both let out a sigh of relief.

The dogs charged into the trees again, and Buster's voice could be heard, but it wasn't one of alarm or anger. Jake soon joined in on the barking. Things went quiet for a minute or two. Spencer continued watching the trees, though he couldn't see what was happening inside them. Worried, he set his beer on the table and began to step off the end of the deck in the direction of the dogs. Killian was right behind. Before Spencer's foot hit the ground below, Buster and Jake came flying out of the woods and resumed their fun.

"She's in there, you know," Killian said as he stood in back of Spencer.

"Yes, I know."

A single tear ran down Spencer's cheek.

Spencer studied for a few moments longer the fringe of trees standing at the edge of the field. He hoped that Shandy would reveal herself again and that he could see her one last time before she went, maybe forever. He knew she wouldn't. *I never knew what you wanted,* he thought. *I guess I never will.*

Spencer yelled out to Buster and Jake, and in no time the two animals were running through the meadow and jumping up onto the deck, both exhausted and happy. Spencer rubbed Buster on the head. He and Killian picked up their half-full ales and made their way into the house. The dogs followed.

THE END

Did you love *Shadows of My Irish Dog*? Then you should read *My Irish Dog*[1] by Douglas Solvie!

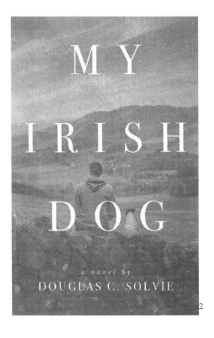[2]

Spencer embarks on a journey to Ireland, desperate that the short vacation will somehow provide the answers to his inner turmoil. Little does he know that a chance encounter with a lost dog named Shandy will set in motion a series of extraordinary events. Spencer is soon propelled into a world where reality becomes distorted, finding himself entangled in a web of enigmatic situations. *My Irish Dog* is a suspenseful and mystical tale that explores the depths of the human psyche and the transformative power of unexpected connections. Journey alongside Spencer as he grapples with his internal struggles, navigates an otherworldly Irish landscape, and unlocks the secrets held within the elusive Shandy. This mesmerizing novel is a tale of

---

1. https://books2read.com/u/4jYV8X

2. https://books2read.com/u/4jYV8X

destiny, redemption, and the remarkable bond between a lost soul and a four-legged guardian.

About the Author

Set in Ireland, Douglas Solvie's first two novels are a series that can be read stand-alone or in sequence. To get a true appreciation of the characters and their full backstories, reading them in order is the preferable option.

My Irish Dog is the debut novel (released in March 2020) and was motivated by a trip taken to Ireland and the chance discovery of a lost dog there. Its sequel, *Shadows of My Irish Dog*, was released in the spring of 2024.

After spending most of his adult life living and working in Japan (and sometimes traveling to Ireland), Douglas now splits his time between Japan and his home in the United States. Taking a break from Irish settings, a third novel is in the works, this time the locale being the beautiful island of Hokkaido in northern Japan.

Made in the USA
Middletown, DE
21 March 2025

73063334R00176